I0566103

AVELER FORM

Qty _____ Date _____

Cut By: _____

Qty _____ Date _____

Scanned By: _____

Scanned By: _____

Praise for the Melanie Hogan Mystery Series

Shear Madness

"Great story – Took a twist at the end that I hadn't anticipated! Rhonda writes in a way that helps the reader visualize the scene – makes it a very fun read and even more suspenseful. I'm ready for the next one in the series!"

Shear Madness

"It was an excellent read, caught your attention at the beginning and held it to the end. Likable characters that are well developed. Rhonda Blackhurst has a way of writing that is very visual."

Shear Madness

"Loved this cozy mystery and can't wait for the next one in the series. Melanie is a charming character, the dialogue is witty and funny, and the mystery has a twist I didn't guess."

Shear Madness

"The author of The Inheritance has a new book out and it's a start to a new series! Shear Madness is an engaging mystery novel ... It reminded me of Scarlett Thomas'

Lily Pascal series which I have also enjoyed. Just like The Inheritance, I have enjoyed the characters and felt I understood them. I liked the suspenseful stalker introduced in the book and enjoyed trying to solve the mystery with Melanie Hogan ... I look forward to the next book in the series."

Shear Deception

"Wonderfully written, kept me in suspense!"

Shear Deception

"Once again Rhonda has written an excellent mystery. Her characters come alive, you feel you know them personally. She gets you interested from the first page and keeps you to the last page. A very good read."

Shear Deception

"Melanie Hogan's story continues in this next book in the series - and Blackhurst does not disappoint. All the lovable characters are back, and one that's not so lovable-a surprising foe to Melanie's sweet character."

Shear Murder

"Very enjoyable cozy mystery. The dialogue draws the reader into the story and helps to develop the characters and story development. I was drawn in from the beginning. The main character attended a reunion gathering of old friends when the unthinkable happens. Great who-done-it with likable characters and a surprising ending. Highly recommended."

Shear Holiday Mayhem

"I love all the Melanie Hogan books and my favorite is always the last one I read - because they keep getting better and better. Take a trip to Minnesota at Christmas to visit Melanie and her friends and you will be able to feel the cold of the snow and taste the holiday cookies. The mystery has surprising twists and the romances are sweet. Best of all are the friendships and Melanie's special relationship with her Nana. If you want to get into the holiday spirit - read this now, though it will be a fun read at any time of the year."

Shear Holiday Mayhem

"Holiday Mayhem indeed. Melanie really didn't have to get involved in this mystery, but of course she does and it's quite an interesting read. I recommend it."

Shear Fear

A Melanie Hogan Mystery
Book 6

Rhonda Blackhurst

Books may be purchased in quantity and/or special sales by contacting the author at www.rhondablackhurst.com or rhondablackhurst@gmail.com.

Published by Lighthouse Press, Colorado
Cover Design by: No Sweat Graphics & Formatting
Edited by Jessica Cornwell Author Services

Library of Congress Control Number: 2021916807
ISBN-13: 978-1-7359393-2-2

First Edition
Printed in the United States of America

Also by Rhonda Blackhurst

➢ The Inheritance

The Melanie Hogan Cozy Mystery Series
➢ Shear Madness
➢ Shear Deception
➢ Shear Malice
➢ Shear Murder
➢ Shear Holiday Mayhem

The Whispering Pines Mysteries
➢ Finding Abby
➢ Abby's Redemption

To Clint, Alex, Ben & Yvette and the littles. You're all my joy. Always and forever my love.

1

Just when I thought life was back to normal after a series of unfortunate events—one of them murder—my gut was now telling me normal wasn't to be. I listened to the faint yet audibly bitter voice on the other end of my phone, the same voice as earlier that day and one that gave me a sinking feeling that all was not well. If I didn't know better, I would characterize the voice as threatening. And here I had been having such a relaxing time hanging out with my two best friends on this Friday evening over adult beverages at Grizzley's Tap House after a long day at work.

"That was weird," I said as I disconnected the call and lay my phone on the table in front of me. Claire and Jack waited for me to go on, concern etched in Claire's enormous brown eyes and Jack from behind the lenses of his black-rimmed glasses. His thick black hair was, as usual, perfectly moussed on top, parted on the side, but with a new skin fade I'd given him a week ago at the salon.

"Are you going to tell us or make us ask?" Jack asked above the din of voices around us.

A sudden eruption of loud laughter from the booth behind us made me jump. I guess I was a little more on edge than I thought. "That was the second call I've had today asking for Daisy. The other was this afternoon. I don't know a Daisy. Never have."

"You sure?" Claire asked, arching a perfectly shaped eyebrow. "Because with the flower-power names in your family, I'd say Daisy fits right in. What makes this even weirder, though, is that someone called the salon phone today asking for Daisy, too."

She made a good point about the flower-power names in my family. My birth mother's name is Violet; my grandmother's name is Rose. Still not sure how I ended up with the name Melanie. Melanie Hogan.

"Hey, Hogan," Jack's voice cut into my traveling thoughts. "I'm pretty sure she was just kidding. Don't look so—"

"I know." I glanced at him and waved a hand in dismissal. "Just thinking. Oddly, the fact that the person called the salon phone makes it less weird. Apparently, the caller is looking for a stylist by the name of Daisy. With the way stylists hop around, it's no wonder this caller can't find her." I thought about how many changes there had been in our salon in the past two years. We lost two, one of whom had ended up dead on my property; but after that we gained Rubie, who seems like she has been with us forever.

Claire and I co-own A Cut Above. Besides the two of us, we now have three people who rent space from us— Rubie, Connie, and Babs. Babs is our one and only nail tech.

After the events of the past couple of years, which included two deaths at the salon, we'd recently completed a major remodel, which was the biggest test thus far of being in business with my best friend. Our tastes are as different as the two of us. While Claire wanted everything as Victorian-looking as possible, I fought for a more rustic, chic look. We ended up with a tasteful combination of both. The best part was I got the gas fireplace I'd wanted for so long tucked in a corner, perfect for those long Minnesota winters.

"Now that you've added two new stations to your salon in the remodel, you can take in another stylist or two," Jack said.

"Yeah, if someone with the name of Daisy rents one of them, she'll already have a following," I said.

The waitress strode up to our corner booth, the one we'd come to think of as ours.

"Another round, ladies and gent?"

The three of us looked at one another in nonverbal agreement. "Thanks, Shannon. That'd be great," I said.

She held up a finger. "The same?"

We all looked at each other again. "Yup," I answered. For us, the usual meant seltzer water with a slice of orange for me, a glass of Chardonnay for Claire, and a lite beer for Jack.

"Ya'll just know what the other is thinking without having to speak," Shannon said and laughed. "Impressive. Where's the fourth musketeer this evening?"

"Rubie went on a cruise with Scott for her birthday," Claire answered. "So we're celebrating her birthday without her."

"Not that Grizzley's Tap House isn't fun," Shannon said with a wink, "but I'm sure the lovebirds are having a better time than the three of you."

"I'd hope they are," Jack said.

"Hey, now!" I scolded, narrowing my eyes. "I take offense to that."

"Simmer down, Hogan," he said with a chuckle. "You're fun and all but, come on, they have twenty-four-hour service, all the food and drink they want, room service, and beaches along the way. We have sub-zero temps and this." He swept his arm, indicating the pub.

"Hey!" Shannon said, scowling. "Now *I* take offense."

"You ladies need to chill," Jack said with another chuckle. Clearly, he was enjoying ruffling our feathers. "I was only joshing. We're good right where we are." He looked at Shannon and held up two fingers, giving her the peace sign.

"You're just trying to be nice so I don't spit in your beer."

Jack grimaced, and we all laughed.

"I have to use the litter box," I said, standing. "I'll be right back."

The pub was hopping tonight, which wasn't surprising since it was a Friday evening and all. Most people probably didn't have to work tomorrow. Not so

4

when you own a beauty salon. Saturdays were our busiest days, and we rarely took one off.

I passed tables and booths, catching snippets of conversation. One of those was so intriguing—albeit a bit inappropriate with what he planned to do with her when they got home—that it prompted me to turn and see who it was having the conversation in public. I was embarrassed to death when the man and woman looked directly at me—at precisely the same time that I had turned to look at them. My cheeks burned when I recognized the man as a client of mine. I'd never be able to look at him in the same way again.

I quickly put my head down as I rounded the corner to the hallway toward the restrooms and nearly knocked over a little girl of about nine or ten. She looked up at me with wide, startled eyes and the cutest little pugged nose.

"Sorry, hun," I said and smiled. "I wasn't paying attention to where I was going."

"It's okay," she said as she slipped past me and out of sight.

After doing my business and reapplying lip gloss, I took a detour through the pub back to my booth, avoiding any chance encounter with the naughty couple. I slid in next to Jack and looked across the table at Claire, leaning forward as I did. "You'll never guess who I saw."

"Probably not," she said, the ever-present look of happiness and contentment on her face.

5

"Mike Benson and his wife," I said, trying to keep my voice down. "At least I hope it's his wife. Especially given what I heard him say."

"Which was?" she asked.

I hesitated, leaned in, and whispered. Jack smirked until he could no longer hold back, and a loud laugh bubbled out.

"Jack!" I said in a harsh whisper, grabbing hold of his arm. "Quiet!"

He rolled his eyes. "Relax. It's a pub, Hogan. People laugh here. They have fun."

I shot him a look. "Yeah, but you never laugh out loud. You're a stick in the mud."

He pursed his lips and straightened his sleeve. "Yes, you never miss a chance to tell me that. And you also always say I need to loosen up, that I'm too uptight. Then, when I do, you scold me." He looked at Claire and shrugged. "I can't win with her."

"It wasn't funny," I said. I touched my hand to my cheek and felt the warmth still there.

"What they said wasn't, no," Jack said. "It was a conversation between a husband and wife — providing that is his wife — that you weren't supposed to be listening in on. What *was* funny was how awkward it was for you to tell us." He struggled to maintain his composure, his frame shaking slightly.

"Because he's one of my clients. And be nice," I sulked, "or I won't invite you out with us anymore." I looked toward Claire, her chestnut-colored skin and eyes fringed with long coal-black lashes. "Kick him under the table with those mile-long legs of yours and make him be nice."

"Not a chance," she said, smiling. "I agree with him. Lighten up. We're in a pub."

I scrunched up my nose and furrowed my brows. "Whatever."

Claire rolled her eyes, tipped her head back, and laughed. "Okay, Sydney."

Sydney is Claire's nine-and-a-half-year-old daughter from the love of her life, Tyler, who died while on military duty when Sydney was just four years old. Claire may have given birth to her, but I'd adopted her as my own. I can't have children, but if I could, Sydney is who I would pick.

"Speaking of the little munchkin," I said, "I bet she's enjoying having your folks here for a few days, huh?"

"Totally. She's got them so wrapped around her finger it's pathetic. In fact," she said, narrowing her eyes, "the same as she does you. You guys are all suckers for her demands."

I grinned. Sydney was demanding, that was for sure, but she was an only child. Kinda goes with the territory. I should know. I'm an only child too, except my childhood was a little more messed up. My birth mother was in prison, and I never knew my birth father. As far as I knew, Violet didn't even know who my father was.

"You're just jealous because she likes me more than you," I said.

"What a grown-up thing to say," Jack said, shaking his head slowly. I looked over at him as he fought off a grin and leaned toward him, knocking my shoulder against his.

"Being that little girl's auntie is the best thing ever." The familiar empty pang made its appearance yet again. I'd come to accept that it would always be lurking beneath the surface. I told my grandmother—the angel who raised me—more than once that maybe it was God's way of telling me I shouldn't be a mother in case I would be too much like my own. And more than once, Nana said that wasn't true, that sometimes things just were, and that God wasn't the cause of the bad things that happened to us.

"I'm relieved Syd got along so well with Jackson since they'll probably be spending time together as they grow up," Claire said.

This time it was sheer fear that sunk its teeth into me. "Yeah."

I felt Jack's eyes burning a hole in me. I squirmed as I focused on the napkin under my almost empty glass.

"What is it, girlfriend?" he asked. "I thought you said they got along great."

Jackson is my boyfriend Levi's ten-year-old son who he shares custody with his ex-wife. When Jackson stayed with Levi for a few days over Christmas break, Levi couldn't get off work on one particular night, so he asked if

I could watch Jackson. To make things less awkward for both of us, especially Jackson, I invited Sydney to spend the night, too.

"Melanie?" Claire said, head tilted slightly.

"It's nothing."

"Bull you-know-what," Jack said. " 'Fess up."

"They got along great. *Too* great," I added and took a deep breath. "We all did."

"Well, then, what's the problem?" Claire asked.

"There isn't one," Jack said. "But Melanie's going to find one." He pressed his lips tightly together.

"Not so," I said.

"So," he countered. "If not, then why are you —"

"What if —"

"The sky came crashing down tonight?" Claire interrupted as she tossed her hands upward. "What *if* the sky comes crashing down tonight, Melanie? What if a star drops to the earth and sets the whole thing ablaze? What if the Stay-Puft Marshmallow Man is real and melts all over Birch Haven, smothering us all? What then?" I snickered. "You know what Rose tells you; 'stop borrowing trouble'," Claire said in a surprisingly good imitation of my grandmother. Jack and I chuckled.

"When it comes to fear of losing your independence," Jack said, "you take two steps forward, three steps back. How about we turn that around, huh? The good detective has proved himself to be tried and true time and time

9

again. Besides, it's a little late to back out now. You've fallen for him hard."

"True story," I muttered, that giddy feeling invading my chest and stomach. "And it's not that I want to back out. On the contrary, I can't imagine my life without him. That's what keeps scaring me to death. In case he would ever leave, I have to be sure I haven't lost *me*."

"Yeah?" Jack said. "Well, you're *going* to lose him if you don't pull it together." He opened his mouth to say more but then shook his head and clamped his lips shut.

"How does he like the night shift?" Claire asked.

I shrugged. "It's okay. But he's glad it's temporary."

"Smart department," Jack said. "They know when they've got a good thing."

"So now he's a thing?" I asked, laughing.

"It's guy-speak."

I laughed harder. "With that, my thing-friends, I'm heading out. I've got some *Mystery Woman* re-runs to watch on the Hallmark Channel."

Claire shook her head slowly. "Gone are the days when my best friend didn't watch TV."

"I'm learning how to solve my next case," I said.

Jack blanched. "Hogan, that's not even funny. You saying something like that is the kiss of death. Quite literally most of the time."

I laughed, leaned in, kissed his cheek, and stood. "My offer still stands for staying at my house if you don't want to drive back tonight."

Jack lives in Minneapolis but spends about as much time at my house as he does at his own. He's a clothing and jewelry designer and owner of Jack's Originals. His displays at my store had spread to more businesses in the area, but he'd promised me that what was at my salon wasn't anywhere else. "I want the *original* part of the title," I'd told him.

"Gotta get home. But thanks," he said.

I leaned over and hugged Claire before wrapping a scarf around my neck. I slipped my black beanie on, tugged on the brim, then shrugged into my down coat. By the time I was done, I felt like the Stay-Puft Marshmallow Man myself. Before I waddled away, I turned toward Claire. "Hey, did you notice the utility light by our salon is out? Was dark as Hades out there when I left."

"Exactly how dark is Hades?" Jack asked.

I squinted at him and scowled. "Pretty darn dark." I looked back at Claire. "We'll have to call the utility company in the morning."

"I'll take care of it," she said.

I put a thumb up and made for the exit.

When I opened the door, the glacial air hit me squarely, causing my eyes to water. My breath came out in puffs of white. This was the coldest February I could ever remember. I'd thought a time or two that this was the part of Minnesota living I could do without. Yet, in the early mornings when I looked at the lake, the snow that blanketed the ice looked like crystals sparkling as the sun rose, lending a peacefulness that was unmatched by anything on this side of Heaven.

As I waited for my car to warm up before leaving the parking lot, I pulled out my phone, warming when I heard Nana's voice.

"Hello, dear. How's my girl?"

"Doing good. Just leaving Grizzley's. How are you doing?"

"Fine as beach sand."

I chuckled. "Anything new?"

"A friend of yours called today."

"Who was it?"

"Didn't leave a name, but it was a woman. First, she asked for Daisy. I told her there isn't a Daisy that lives here. Then she asked for you. Seemed odd, dontcha know."

Odd, indeed. As my mind scrolled back through the day, the same feeling of unease I'd felt earlier that evening seeped its way back in, pushing the rest of my conversation with her to the background.

2

On the drive home, I mulled over my phone call with Nana. Why would someone call her house and ask for me? All my friends know my cell phone number. But the bigger question was, who was this Daisy person the caller was so determined to find? And why would the caller think I knew Daisy?

As I turned into my driveway and saw my little log home, I was finally able to let go of my agitation. The porch light and the glow of the light behind the window partially covered with sunshine-yellow curtains above the kitchen sink were like a friend welcoming me home after a long day. I pulled into my garage and braced myself before getting out of my nice warm car. I pushed the remote to close the garage door behind me and walked across the yard to my front door. The snow crunched beneath my feet, and white puffs of air with each breath disappeared with a slight breeze.

Behind my house, the ice on the lake groaned its knowledge of the cold air. I shuddered. That noise scared me to death the entire first winter I'd lived out here until I learned that lake ice expands and contracts with temperature changes, resulting in cracking that sometimes sounded like thunder. Still now, several years later—and knowing why it did that—the eerie sound sometimes caused me to get gooseflesh. Like tonight.

A loud thunder-like boom, followed by a cracking sound, sent me hurtling toward my front door. I jammed my key in the lock, quickly closed it behind me, and turned the deadbolt, working to still my pounding heart.

I looked across the expanse of darkness between my house and Claire's and saw lights glowing in her windows, including the one in Sydney's bedroom, which faced my house. Claire was a stickler for bedtime, so I hoped for her parents' sake that Syd would be in bed before Claire got home. And then, as I looked toward the road, I sucked in my breath as Claire's car turned in the driveway, her headlights shooting beams of light through the trees that separated our houses. I imagined Sydney dashing for her bedroom, and I laughed as the light in her room went out.

I kicked up the dial on the thermostat, finding comfort in the soft hum of the furnace, then started shedding the layers I'd thrown on before I left Grizzley's. When I slid my beanie off, my hair sparked with static electricity. I caught my reflection in the window, strands standing straight out like I'd stuck my finger in a light socket. I absently smoothed it with my hand.

Snowmobiles roared, cutting through the silence. Two of them zigzagged off the lake and onto my property, one going on either side of my house. From the window, I could see a Yamaha and a Polaris I couldn't recall seeing before. It wasn't unusual for snowmobilers to cut through people's yards, and I typically didn't mind it. Except when it happened in the middle of the night like it did two nights ago.

The snow dust kicked up behind the machines, muting the taillights. I continued watching until they reached the end of my driveway and turned into the ditch. Claire's property didn't reach the lake, so she didn't have to worry about snowmobile motors waking Syd at night. Although as hard as that girl slept when she finally drifted off, I'm not sure anything could wake her.

After trekking upstairs to my loft bedroom and slipping into gray sweatpants and a hoodie, I snagged my book from my nightstand and headed back downstairs. I'd no sooner gotten snuggled under a fleece blanket in the corner of the sofa when my phone rang. Instinctively I smiled, sure it was Levi.

"Hi there. How's work tonight?" Silence. "Hello? Levi?" Still nothing. I pulled the phone from my ear and looked at the number, only to discover it wasn't Levi's number at all. The screen read *Private Caller*. I shrugged, hung up, and opened my book. One paragraph in, and my phone rang again. This time I looked at the incoming number first—*Private Caller*. I clicked the answer button. "Listen," I said, "either you have the wrong number or—"

"I'm pretty sure I have the right number."

Levi. My mood instantly picked up. "Well, hello, handsome."

"That's better." I could hear the smile in his voice.

"Why does your number come across as *Private Caller*?"

"Why did you think I had the wrong number? When you answered, you said I had the wrong number."

"You first," I said.

"I'm calling from a department phone. A landline. Remember those? Businesses still have them." He chuckled. "Sometimes it says *Private Caller*, and sometimes it comes up with some scrambled number. Your turn."

"Thirty seconds before you called, someone else called. When I answered, they didn't say anything."

"Probably a wrong number."

"Smart aleck. Enough about unimportant things." I settled further under the blanket and tucked my knees up to my chest. "How's your evening going so far?"

"Uneventful. Make sure it stays that way, okay?"

"I'll do my best, Mr. Detective." Levi has had to bail my butt out of trouble more times than I ever wanted to admit. Ever since I'd voiced to Claire a few years ago that I wanted some excitement in my world, that I was tired of living a safe, predictable life just so I could prove I wasn't Violet, dead bodies started popping up around me, even in the small town I'd traveled to last summer.

"See that you do," he said gently, his voice low. "What are you up to?"

"Went out for a drink with Jack and Claire earlier. Now living it up with a good book and a cup of hot chocolate."

"Whoa! You're getting a little wild tonight, huh?"

"Just a wee bit," I teased.

"Heard from Rubie?" he asked.

"No, but I wouldn't expect to. Hopefully, she's not even thinking about us back here. For Scott's sake."

Someone said his name in the background. "Hold on a second, babe."

I still got a thrill every time he called me that. Then, finally, he came back on the line.

"I gotta run," he said.

"Crime calling?"

"Yup. A night in the life of a detective."

"Who'd a thunk it. In little old Birch Haven."

"I'll talk to you in the morning."

"See that you do," I said, my heart ready to explode with both contentment and excitement.

"I love you, blondie."

"And I never get tired of hearing that. Just sayin'." I paused for a beat before adding, "Oh! And I love you, too." I grinned.

"You're bad."

"But you love it. Now go. And be safe. Please." My tone switched from playful to worried in a matter of seconds.

"You know I will," he said.

After we hung up, I held the phone in my hand, basking in the warmth that spread throughout my body. I folded the fleece down so it covered my lap only and picked my book back up. Seconds later, my phone rang again.

"Miss me already?" I asked.

"Is Daisy there?" a woman's voice asked.

"Listen, you've been calling this number several times today. I don't know any Daisy, and there isn't a Daisy that works at my salon. Again, you've got the wrong number."

"No, you listen," she said. "Stay away from Daisy. I mean it."

"Is that a threat?" I asked, shaking my head. This woman was a lunatic. "Who is this?"

"Stay away from Daisy. That's all you need to know." And the line went dead.

I held my phone out and stared at it as if I'd be able to identify the caller. What the heck was this woman's deal? Finally, I tossed the phone onto the coffee table in front of me. At this rate, I would never finish this book. I snatched up my phone again, turned off the sound, and lay it face down. Satisfied, I snuggled under the fleece again and got lost in the story.

***

After my alarm went off in the morning, I laid in the dark dozing for a bit, looking through the skylight above my bed at the inky darkness sprinkled with stars. Not only was it still freezing cold for this time of year, but the daylight hours were few. It was getting longer, but not long enough to see a huge difference until spring.

I snagged my thick, fuzzy robe from the foot of my bed and wrapped it around me, flipped up the shawl collar, and tied the belt tight. I turned the furnace down every night, preferring to sleep with lots of blankets. One of these days, I would have to figure out how to set the furnace's timer to begin warming by six. During the summer and fall months, I got up at five-thirty, so I had more time to spend outside on my deck before heading into town.

After tugging the chain on the bedside lamp, I padded into the bathroom then headed to the kitchen for coffee. I snagged my phone from my nightstand before descending the stairs and looked at the screen to be sure I hadn't missed a call from Levi or my grandmother. I'd kept it on silent when I went to bed so as not to be awakened by the annoying person who insisted I knew some woman I didn't know at all. I was relieved when it showed not a single missed call. That meant both Levi and Nana were good and that the mystery woman finally realized she'd been barking up the wrong tree. I pitied her next target she was sure knew Daisy.

After my usual routine of coffee while reading my devotional, checking email, glancing through the news feed, then hopping in the shower, I was ready to head to work at seven forty-five. I pulled my hat down over my forehead and braced for the inevitable cold slap against my skin as I opened the door. One of the perks of working in a salon was the easy access to skin and hair services so I didn't have to worry about messing up makeup or a hairstyle. Although, when it came to skincare, I used the bare essentials. My makeup consisted of a touch of black eyeliner — green if I felt especially crazy — black mascara, a splash of blush on occasion, and tinted lip gloss.

By the time I reached the salon, my Jeep had finally gotten nice and toasty. There wasn't a single car on my end of the parking lot. A few dotted the lot in front of the grocery store at the opposite end of the strip mall. The other businesses in the strip didn't open until ten.

I zipped into my usual parking spot eleven spaces out from my salon. Yes, I'd counted them. My need for consistency bordered on obsessive. This was why when I told Claire some time ago that I wanted some excitement and spontaneity in my life, she was a bit frightened. And given the events that had occurred since I made that statement, she had every right to be.

I hoisted my bag over my shoulder, then grabbed a second bag that contained my high-heeled black boots and other paraphernalia I needed to make myself presentable for the day. When I looked up and toward the salon, I did a doubletake and squinted, as if that would make me see better. Someone was sitting at the little bistro table right outside the door, dressed in nothing but what appeared to be a business suit. A light-colored jacket was draped haphazardly around his shoulders as he sat hunched over the table, arms folded under his head. My breath quickened. How long had he been here? It wouldn't take someone long to freeze to death in these temperatures. The weird phone calls raced through my mind, but I pushed them away. Those calls were from a woman.

My frozen fingers propelled me toward the door and the warmth that lay beyond. I needed to get this guy inside fast. I fumbled with my phone and spoke, "Siri, call Claire Davis."

"Calling Claire Davis," replied the familiar robotic voice just when I reached the man. He appeared to be sleeping. As I waited for Claire to answer, I wondered how to wake him. If he'd passed out or was on something, waking him could startle him, causing an unfortunate reaction. Unfortunate for me. But if I didn't do something fast, it would be unfortunate for him.

"Hi, Mel," Claire said.

I jumped a mile at her voice as I gently poked the man's shoulder. "Claire, are you almost here?"

"Ten minutes out. Why?"

"Cause there's this guy."

"This guy?" she said. "Where are you?"

"At the salon. Hold on."

"Mel—"

"Hold on. Stay on the phone with me, okay?" I touched the man's shoulder again. "Sir, wake up. It's freezing out here." I shook him a bit, but his body was stiff as could be. I shrank back and gasped. "Oh no! Claire, he's dead!"

3

"Who's dead?" Claire's voice screeched across the line.

"This man outside the salon. I have to go." My mind was screaming at me louder than Claire's voice a second ago—*Not again*!

"Melanie—"

"Please hurry." I hung up from Claire and dialed 911. The dispatcher took all the pertinent information, keeping me on the phone until I heard sirens approaching. I cringed. The police have become all too familiar with me the past two and a half years. But on a positive note, that's how I met Levi. Speaking of Levi, I needed to call him before he heard about this fiasco from someone else. Or over the police radio.

I pressed the speed dial button for his number and turned to face the parking lot, immediately ending the call. Too late. His car zipped up next to the salon, his door opened before the engine stopped. Officers Johnson and Miller—with whom I'd become too acquainted lately—strode up behind him. And behind them, an ambulance raced in with lights and sirens, parking behind Levi's car.

"Might want to tell them it's too late," I said, my voice muffled against Levi's chest as he pulled me toward him.

"You okay?" he asked.

"Yeah. Just a little shaken."

"Do you know who it is?"

"I don't know." I pulled back and glanced at the man. "I mean, I didn't see his face. I just knew he was dead by how he felt. I didn't want to move him."

"That's good."

"Isn't that like tampering with evidence or something?" I said, shivering. Reducing a human body to evidence saddened me.

"Let's get you inside," he said, taking my keys from my shaking fingers. They were so cold by now they burned like the dickens.

"Melanie!" Claire's voice called. I turned to see her running toward me. "What happened?"

"Let's take this inside where it's warmer, ladies." Levi opened the door and ushered Claire and me past him.

"What happened?" Claire asked again. "Who is it?"

"I don't know," I said, blowing into my hands. "I didn't see his face."

"What's he doing here?" she asked.

"I'd say homeless, but he's not dressed like someone who's homeless," I said. The words tumbled, slurring, my lips too cold to form them properly.

"We need to get you warm," Levi said, taking off his police coat and wrapping it around my shoulders. He rubbed my arms vigorously over the coat.

"Were you still at work?" I asked him.

"On my way home. Heard it on my radio. Tell me what happened."

"Nothing happened," I said. "I pulled in and saw him sitting there. I tried to wake him up when I realized he was dead. As cold as it got last night, I'm assuming he froze to death."

"At first glance, that would be my guess," he said. "It's also my guess that you have the worst luck with bodies turning up wherever you are."

"Maybe you should turn and run like the wind before it's you, Detective," I said, giving him a sorry excuse of a half-smile.

"Not a chance. You're stuck with me."

I leaned into him, straightening when Officer Johnson came through the door. "Detective, I need to talk with Ms. Hogan." He looked at Claire.

"Uh." Claire shifted. "I can go in the office."

"No, we can go talk in the office," I said, touching Claire's arm. "Officer," I said, "I'd say follow me, but unfortunately, you know the way all too well." I shook my head slowly and walked back toward the office, Levi right behind me, Officer Johnson behind him.

"Detective Wescott," Johnson said once we got into the office, "it might be a good idea for you not to be in here when I'm talking with Melanie. I'd say go speak with Ms. Davis but that would be a conflict as well."

"Listen here, Johnson—"

"With all due respect, sir, a body has just turned up outside your girlfriend's business." He looked at me, shook his head slightly, and said, "Again."

"Don't worry, Johnson, I'm not going to get in your way."

"It's okay, Levi," I said. "I'll be fine."

"I'm sure you will," he said, sitting down on the chair opposite mine at the desk. "But I'll feel much better if I'm here to make sure of that."

I scowled and felt something constrict in my chest. I knew he meant well, and I knew he worried about me, as I did about him when he was at a scene, but it threatened my independence. And the way he said it caused me to think he didn't believe I could take care of myself. These very things were what scared the living daylights out of me about getting involved more than we already were. My whole life, I'd depended on myself—my strength, my determination, my will—and my grandmother. She's the only other person on whom I've allowed myself to depend entirely.

"Levi," I said, "I'm fine. I'm a big girl." The words were sharper than I had intended. I looked at my feet for a moment, then back at him.

He met my gaze and held it for a little too long. I shifted in my chair and looked at Officer Johnson before leaning over to remove my boots and replace them with the ones from my bag. Levi was retreating from the office when I sat back up, his back stiff, his bald head still covered by his black beanie with the thin blue stripe that circled it. I had some explaining to do when I finished talking with Officer Johnson.

"Officer," I said, "how long do you anticipate your men being here? It's bad for business."

"That I'm sure is true," he said, watching me remove my hat and smooth my hair with a hand. "After the last year or so, I'm just happy you're still *in* business."

I tilted my head to the side and shot him a visual arrow. "Really? That's what you're going to say right now?" I shook my head and sighed. "Is the coroner here yet?"

"On their way."

"Can you tell how long the man has been sitting there?" I asked. "Though I'm sure it wouldn't take long to freeze in this weather. Does he have identification on him so you can notify his family? What do you suppose he was doing sitting there?" Questions tumbled out like marbles from a tipped jar.

"That's what I'd like to ask you. What time did you get here?"

"Just a few minutes ago. As soon as I got out of my car and saw the man, I had an odd feeling. We don't open until nine unless we have a special request from a client. We make accommodations accordingly. No one was scheduled this morning."

"Do you always come in this early?"

"Always. Sometimes earlier. Why?" I frowned. Where was he going with this?

"How late were you here last evening?" I paused to try clear the confusion, and he continued. "I'm just trying to form a timeline of what happened when."

I relaxed a bit. "Six. We left right at six."

"We?"

"Me, Claire, and Jack. Jack is mine and Claire's best friend," I added.

"We'll talk with Claire this morning. Do you have a number for Jack?" His pen sat poised, ready to jot down the number.

"I do. But why do you need it? He left to go back home last night as soon as we left Grizzley's," I said.

"We probably won't need to talk with him, but I'm just getting every piece of information I can right now."

I gave him Jack's number as Levi and Claire's voices traveled through the door from the salon into the office. Claire said at a dangerous decibel, "What do you mean *killed*?"

My back stiffened, and I leveled my gaze on Officer Johnson. "Something you want to tell me?"

He exhaled slowly and rubbed the back of his neck. "Sounds like you already know."

"You could have just told me instead of trying to trick information out of me."

"I have to follow policy, Melanie. You know that. *Especially* when it comes to you."

At least he sounded sincere.

There was a knock on the door a half-second before it opened. Levi stood there, his hand still on the doorknob. His beanie was off and in his other hand.

"Johnson," he said, "what have you got for me?"

I looked at Levi, startled, the sting of betrayal bubbling beneath the surface. "You knew?"

"I just found out now. What have you got for me, Johnson?" he repeated.

Johnson's jaw slackened. "Isn't that a conflict of interest, sir? For you to be investigating this?"

Levi's eyes shot darts at the young officer. "You questioning my judgment and integrity, Johnson?"

His cheeks flushed. "No, sir."

"I didn't think so," Levi said, his tone rigid. His eyes looked tired, the edges rimmed in red.

"But Chief might."

I caught my lower lip between my teeth at Johnson's sudden boldness.

Levi sat back down in the chair. "Well, until Chief takes me off the case, I'm doing my job. And just for the record," he added, giving Johnson a dark look, "I don't let anything or anyone interfere with an investigation."

I shook my head and said to Johnson, "No, he sure doesn't." Levi tried to suppress a tired grin, and I shrugged. As long as we've known each other, I've heard that very statement far too many times, *Don't interfere with my investigation, Melanie.* Most of the time, I tried hard not to, but sometimes I had to look out for my friends' best interests.

"Melanie is not a suspect here," Levi said.

"But the body was found by her at her salon," Johnson countered.

"We'll treat it as a conflict if, and only if, Chief has a problem with it." His gruffness deterred Johnson from protesting further. "You can either go help out there," Levi jerked his thumb toward the salon, "or stay in here to keep me honest."

I watched the exchange between them with interest. What was it with men and their power struggles, their show of dominance? "How about the two of you sit here and decide how to best handle this, and I'll go check in with Claire." I pushed my chair back to stand.

"Claire is fine," Levi said. "Another detective is talking with her now. And Cole showed up. He's out there with her."

Did I detect a hint of resentment in that last statement, or was it my imagination? I sat back down and mumbled, "Alrighty then."

"Okay, sir, as long as you don't need me in here," Johnson said, heading for the door, "think I'll go check the scene."

"Leave the door open behind you," Levi instructed.

"Yes, sir."

As soon as Johnson was gone, Levi said, "We'll have to speak with everyone who was here between last night and the early morning hours."

"That's only me, Claire, and Jack. The others left before us, and no one else would be here after business hours."

"That you know of."

I blinked. "What are you saying?"

"That anyone could have come by here, and you wouldn't have any idea. That camera out there looks broken. How long's it been like that?"

My eyes popped open wide. "Oh my gosh! The broken utility light outside wasn't the result of local kids, was it?"

"We can't know that for sure, but since the camera appears broken as well, that's a little suspect."

"Especially with a body showing up the next morning. The light was working the night before that."

"And the camera?" he asked.

I shook my head slowly and sighed. "I don't know. I haven't looked at it in a while."

"We can look at the footage to see what's been happening out here when it *was* working."

"I need to—"

"You need to not get involved," he said.

"I'm already involved. It happened at my salon."

Levi groaned, tipped his head back, and closed his eyes briefly. Then he leaned forward and covered my hand with his, locking his gaze on mine. "Listen, green eyes, you know I'll do whatever I can to be sure the truth comes out and we find the killer. Trust me," he said.

I tilted my head slightly. "You know I do. That's not in question here."

"Isn't it?"

I tried to read his eyes, what he wasn't saying. "Levi—"

He stood. "Can we talk about this later? Right now, I need my head in the game. A dead man showed up outside your business. Your safety may be compromised."

I leaned back in my chair and bit my lower lip again. I knew what this was about, and I felt terrible. I did. This was about the rejection he must have felt when I asked him to leave the room. But I desperately felt the need to protect my independence. Because in the end, I may need to depend on it again. "Ironic," I whispered to myself, shaking my head slowly. My fear of him someday leaving me may be by my own hand.

"What?" he asked.

"Nothing."

"Melanie, please understand. I need to figure out who planted this guy outside your salon and why."

I sat forward, my attention on high alert. "What do you mean by planted?"

"It doesn't sound like he died out there. Sounds like the crime scene was somewhere else."

"How can you be sure?"

"Because it looks like he may have died from blunt force trauma. There's very little blood here. The face and head bleed a lot. But, of course, we won't know COD for sure until the medical examiner concludes the autopsy."

Unfortunately, I'd become too familiar with police acronyms, and COD stood for *cause of death*. "Of course," I mumbled, my memory trying to recall anything that might have identified the man. Anything that looked familiar. But I came up with nothing. Without moving him, it was impossible to see his face. "Why would they have moved him here? Why the salon? Unless they wanted Claire or me to find him. Or one of the other ladies. But why?"

"Don't jump to conclusions. It might have nothing to do with any of you. It could have just been a convenient location for a body dump."

I thought about it a moment, putting together the minimal pieces of the puzzle I had so far. "It wasn't just a dump, and you know it. Body dumps don't usually include posing the body as if the person were sleeping. And someone wouldn't go through all that trouble without a good reason—the broken light and camera," I said.

He nodded. "I hate to say I agree, but I do. Back to the facts—as soon as we get an ID on the guy, I'll let you know, and we can go from there. See if you recognize him. Might be a client of the salon." His tone was all business which I found oddly attractive, helping me forget the present circumstances for a split second.

As if on cue, Officer Johnson poked his head around the corner. "Detective, we have an ID on our John Doe. Found a wallet in his pocket. They took everything out of it except his driver's license."

Levi frowned, stood, and faced him. "Guess we should tell the killer thank you for making identification easier. Who is it?"

Johnson looked at his notepad. "Name's Lenny. Lenny Martin."

4

I stood abruptly, sending my chair hurtling against a metal filing cabinet. The room spun, and I sat back down and hunched over, sure I was going to be sick. Sounds around me seemed to fade in and out.

Levi's presence as he knelt beside me, hand resting on my back, was comforting, and I was finally able to sit up safely. He propped my feet on a chair, and a paramedic took his place at my side.

"I'm fine," I said as the paramedic wrapped a blood pressure cuff around my arm. "How did you get here so fast, anyway?"

"I was already here tending the man outside."

"A little late for that."

"She's going to be okay," Levi told the paramedic. "She's back to normal, sarcasm and all." He winked at me.

I got to my feet, and the paramedic placed his hand on my arm. "Sit tight for a bit, Ms. Hogan."

I looked at Levi, recalling the shocking blow. "Did I hear right? The dead guy is Lenny? I need to go see him to be sure," I said, struggling to get back on my feet.

"The coroner is already here," the paramedic said.

"I know." I pushed past him, holding onto Levi's hand as he followed me. As I reached the window, they were zipping up the body bag. I looked to where Lenny had been sitting at the table and shuddered. Levi's arm circled my shoulders.

"I called the first appointments of the day and rescheduled," Claire said. "There were three of them. I also called Connie and Babs so they didn't walk into all this police presence unknowingly."

I looked out the window and groaned at the growing group of people gathered in the parking lot in front of the grocery store, gawking toward the salon. *Great.*

The other detective at the scene, who I'd too recently been introduced to, Detective Walker, called Levi off to the side. I watched them, trying to read their lips. Levi looked grim but then nodded, patted Walker's shoulder, and came back toward me.

"What was that about?" I asked, looking into those gray-blue eyes of his. Sometimes they appeared more gray-green, depending on what he was wearing. And his mood. Today he could have been wearing kelly green and his eyes still would have looked blue.

"He's taking over the case."

"Why? Because the body was at my salon?"

"That's partially it, yes. But—well, it's become a conflict of interest. Officially," he said as he looked away.

"Levi?" I stepped in front of him and looked up.

He took a deep breath. "Because of your relationship to Lenny, you've made the person-of-interest list." I opened my mouth to speak but he held up a hand. "I know what you're going to say, that a person-of-interest is the same as a suspect. While ordinarily I wouldn't dismiss that as unfounded, that isn't the case here. You're simply a person of interest because of what I already said—your relationship to the deceased. They're interested in what you have to say and what you can tell them. That still makes it a conflict of interest for me to be on the case."

Only somewhat mollified, I narrowed an eye. "How did they find out about my relationship to Lenny? And don't call it a relationship. That's gross." I shuddered.

"Okay, your connection to Lenny."

"Still gross. And you didn't tell me how anyone even knows about that."

"Oh, let's see," he mused, stroking his chin with his thumb and forefinger. "Maybe because he's been a problem in one of your, uh, shall we say *incidents*, in the past? Despite what you read in books, police can put together the pieces. They aren't stupid."

"Well, I hate to break it to you, but some of them are. And that's all the more reason for you to stay on this case."

"We both know Walker isn't one of them," he reasoned.

My mouth suddenly felt dry. "If I did it, how stupid would I be to bring his body back to my salon? You know I didn't do this."

"I know you didn't. But not investigating the case won't be all bad. I'll be able to be there for you as your boyfriend. For support."

"I'll be fine."

"And there it is," he grumbled, exhaled, and turned from me.

"There what is?"

"The I-don't-need-anyone attitude." He sighed and shook his head ever so slightly. "I'll talk to you later," he said as he leaned over and briefly brushed his lips against mine.

An uncomfortable sinking feeling in the pit of my stomach refused to go away. What was the matter with me? We had some issues to untangle if this thing was going to work. More like *I* had some issues to untangle if this was going to work. I wrapped my arms around my middle. Had Jack been right about me? And who could blame the man if he decided it was too much work to be in my life?

I took a deep breath and watched as the coroner wheeled Lenny away on a stretcher and loaded him into the van. Nothing but cargo. Evidence.

"What happened to you, Lenny Martin?" I whispered to myself. "And who did this to you?"

"There's the million-dollar question," Cole said, now standing beside me, Claire on the other side.

I looked at Cole in his uniform. "You're on duty?"

"No, I dress like this every day."

"Cole Mahoney!" Claire scolded. Well, she didn't really scold, because Claire doesn't scold anyone. Cole is Claire's boyfriend and Levi's coworker and best bud. "You sound like you've been hanging around Melanie too long."

She turned to me. "Has Lenny tried to contact you lately, Mel?"

I felt like a child standing between them. I was only five foot two, and Claire had me by six inches, Cole more than that. When I had my heels on—which was nearly every day—it narrowed the margin to three. "Not since last summer. And then I didn't actually talk with him. Not really. He just made his presence known to me."

"I remember," Cole said. "He definitely had it in for you."

"All because of Violet." Lenny had been Violet's bookie forever. I never knew that information until a few years ago during an unfortunate event at my house when Violet came to stay with me, supposedly to celebrate my birthday. I found out afterward that when she left me with Nana and Granddad to raise me when I was four, she not only left to make it as a big star in Hollywood, but that Lenny was her motivation. He'd promised her stardom, but, instead, she got a loser boyfriend and a dead-end career. And yet she stayed in L.A. while me, her flesh and blood, dealt with the debilitating pain of a mother's rejection. In the end, Violet had turned on Lenny, too, which is why he had it in for me. I was a means at getting back at Violet. "Lenny called me later in the summer," I told Cole. "Something about making amends. I hung up on him."

"Amends?" Cole asked, clearly taken aback. "After all the despicable things he did to you in the past, I think he owed you more than an amends."

"I didn't want anything from him. Not even the so-called amends he offered."

"For what it's worth," Cole said, "looks like he paid for it with his life."

I shrugged. "What I want to know is who hated Lenny so much? Besides me. And why did they want me to find him?"

"Good Lord, Melanie, don't say that out loud," Cole said with a groan. He shook his head.

I shrugged. "I can't pretend to like the guy just because he's dead."

"Just watch what you say, then," he said.

"We'll find out what happened to him and why it happened at our salon," Claire said. "Won't we, babe?" she said to Cole.

"*We* won't find anything out," he said, looking from her to me then back to her. "Not we as in we standing here in this circle. We, as in the police, will figure this out." He looked directly at me. "Please don't go getting Claire involved in this."

I made a face at him. "I'm insulted. I would never put her in danger."

"Not intentionally, no. But you have, Melanie. You have. Admit it."

"Cole," Claire said quietly, "now's not the time."

40

We stood in silence until it got too heavy, and I had to have some breathing room. "Excuse me." Escaping back to the office, I closed the door, leaned against the desk, my rear end resting on the edge. An inevitable headache was quickly approaching. I rubbed my temples with my fore and middle fingers, then rotated my neck slowly, my eyes closed. A quiet creak made me aware someone entered the small room. I opened my eyes, and Levi's frame filled the doorway.

"You okay?"

"As okay as I can be right now."

"We'll get through this, Melanie. Can you take the day off work? I can stay if you want." His voice was soft and so genuine it hurt.

"What I need is to stay here at work and go about my life as usual. But thanks for the offer."

"I expected that." I heard the shift in his voice.

I went to stand by him, circled my arms around his waist, and looked up at him. "I'm not trying to push you away. It's just that I need some space to try to figure things out."

"Figure what out? Help me understand."

"To work through things the only way I know how."

"By yourself? Where does that leave the people who love you?"

"In my corner, knowing what I need to do." I looked deep into his eyes and said quietly, "Please, Levi."

He leaned over and kissed my forehead, his lips lingering there. "You know where I am," he whispered.

"I do."

"I mean in your corner."

"I know," I said, "and I appreciate it more than you know."

***

By the time Connie and Babs came in, Lenny's body was gone, as well as most of the police presence. And only Detective Walker was still there by the time the first appointments arrived. With no time to do anything with my hair, I whipped it up into a ponytail. It was getting long enough to center it high and still have the pony hang down beneath the collar of my black sweater. I'd thought about cutting it a time or two but decided to let it grow a bit.

With the hum of blow dryers and salon gossip flowing freely, the smells of hair color and acrylic nails thick in the air, it didn't take long to get out of my funk. Until those moments when the door opened and I saw the bistro table outside, the vision of Lenny coming back for all of a few minutes before I forced it out of my mind again. I was the master of pushing out of my head the things I didn't want to think about or deal with. Claire called it avoidance; I called it survival.

At one o'clock, I had a free minute to run to the grocery store to grab some lunch. My next appointment was due in fifteen minutes. On Saturdays, the salon is always humming along, and for the next eight days we had planned to work in Rubie's regular clients wherever we could. The air was warming up nicely today, expecting to hit a high of twenty degrees. A regular heatwave. Not quite there yet, though. But it was still an improvement over yesterday evening and the early morning hours today.

I strode back toward the salon, clutching the bag that held my turkey sandwich, and glanced at the parking lot when I was almost at the door. Even though some businesses between the salon and the grocery store were closed on weekends, cars packed the lot. A woman standing by an old beat-up white Chevy Cobalt, dirty from the sand and salt poured on icy Minnesota roads, caught my attention. She was looking directly at me, watching. Her hair, a color we in the beauty industry called dirty or dishwater blond, hung beneath a knit hat. But she was standing far enough away that it could have been shadows that cast dark on blond hair. Given the car's condition and the dirty oversized man's coat she wore, I doubted it. Could she be looking for the man at the table this morning—Lenny? Was she connected to him somehow?

I glanced at my watch. My client was probably already in the salon waiting for me. But I couldn't let this woman get away if she held the key to some answers. I paused for just a second before turning toward her. I held up a hand, indicating I was coming her way. But as soon as she saw me walking toward her, she jumped in her car, revved the sick-sounding engine, and hightailed it out of the parking lot, spinning tires on a patch of ice. That hesitation, while the car's tires spun, was long enough for me to see her vanity license plate—*DAISY*.

5

The license plate added another layer of confusion to the mysterious phone calls. Why would someone call me looking for Daisy? I'd never even had a client by that name. Why did the caller think I did? The woman by the Cobalt at my salon was a complete stranger unless she was somehow related to Lenny. His latest girlfriend? I shuddered. And then an unexpected wave of emotion struck me. Lenny had attempted to make amends, and now he was dead. I realized I didn't owe him forgiveness after everything he'd put me through. Heck, I didn't owe him anything at all. But I couldn't shake the doubt that if I'd forgiven him, would he still be alive? Was I to blame in some way? But as quickly as the thought surfaced, I pushed it aside. Why did I care? *Because despite being a jerk, he was still a human being.* I had an angel on one shoulder, the devil on the other, both vying for my attention.

"Melanie," Claire's voice called out, interrupting my self-absorbed thoughts. "Your client is waiting. How long are you going to be? And get in here, girl. You're going to freeze." She folded her arms around herself and rubbed her biceps vigorously.

After a second longer of looking where Daisy's car had been just moments before, I turned toward Claire. "Coming right now."

"You okay?"

"Yeah. I think so," I added. "Remember the person who kept calling for Daisy?"

"Uh-huh. What about her?"

"Daisy was just here."

"Here?" Her smile dimmed. "What do you mean she was *here*? And who *is* she, this mystery woman?"

I met up with her at the door, and we both stepped inside. I waved to my client, who was in the waiting area. "I'll be right there, Millie," I called to her above the din of voices and blow dryers."

"Take your time, honey," she said, waving a hand. "Feels good to get out of the house and around people. I'm getting cabin fever with this cold snap."

I chuckled. "Don't I know it, Millie. I'm ready for June." I looked at Claire. "Where's your appointment?"

"Under the dryer. Her hair processes for such a short time that I didn't dare schedule anything else until she's done."

"Come 'ere for a second," I said, pulling her with me toward the office. "I have no idea who this woman is, but she was standing by an old beat-up car and staring at me. I started walking toward her to see if she was here because of Lenny. She looked worse for wear and down on her luck, and I felt sorry for her. When she saw me coming toward her, though, she got in her car and sped off. She had a vanity plate that read *DAISY*. But Claire, I've never seen her before. I hope she wasn't another victim of

Lenny's. How ironic," I scoffed, "that Lenny is the quote"—I made air quotes with two fingers on each hand—"victim."

"Well, I have to admit the timing is a little suspicious," Claire said, a rare wrinkle in her forehead.

"I'll have to watch for her to show up again to find out what the deal is. If she is with Lenny, she might not even know yet that he's dead."

"Or she could be the one who killed him."

"Yeah, there's that," I mused.

"Do you think Violet knows?"

"About what?" I asked.

"Lenny," Claire said.

I jerked my head back, chin down. "How would I know?"

"You wouldn't. It was kind of a rhetorical question."

"Pshaw. She's probably the one who put the hit out on him," I said. "I left Jack a voice mail when I walked to the store and asked him to call me. I can't imagine he's going to be too pleased that I've gotten into yet another fiasco."

"This time, it's not your fault. You can't control the fact that someone killed a man and left him on your doorstep."

I took a deep breath, exhaling slowly. "You know, in the feline world, it's considered a gift when they leave a dead body on your doorstep. Except the body is a mouse."

Claire gagged. "That's gross. But I'm serious, Lenny's death is not your fault, and Jack will know that. Come on," she said, spinning me toward the salon area where my customer still waited. "You're going to drive yourself crazy over this. Do what you do best; lose yourself in your work."

"Good plan." I took one last cleansing breath and followed her into the salon.

But as good of a plan as it was, I couldn't get Lenny's body and the sight of Daisy out of my mind. We closed the salon doors at six, and Jack still hadn't called. I wanted to fill him in before anyone from the police department called him.

"Mel," Babs said, "when's the last time we stayed here after work for our own little happy hour?" I looked at her, our nail tech, highly decorated with piercings and tattoos.

"Geez," I exclaimed. "I can't even remember the last time."

"Exactly my point. After the day you've had, and it being Saturday night, happy hour is calling, my friend."

"I'm sure Connie has plans—"

"Yes, I do," Connie said, putting an arm around my shoulders and squeezing me into her ample figure. "I plan to have happy hour here with you ladies."

I pulled back a smidge and stared at her. "Who are you, and what have you done with Connie?" Of all of us, Connie led the quietest life by far.

"I come out once in a while," she said with a chuckle.

"I ran out and got a bottle of wine this afternoon," Babs said. "You were so preoccupied you didn't even notice I left, did you?"

I scrunched my nose. *Busted*! "Sorry, Babs, I didn't."

"I'll forgive you. But only this one time," she said, pulling out a bottle of wine.

"Hey, did you get a new tattoo?" I said, studying her arm. As tattooed as her arms were, it was no wonder I didn't notice it until now.

"Yes, ma'am, I did," she said, showcasing it for the group. "It's an addiction I'm sure you didn't know I had."

"Not a clue," I said, chuckling. "Girl, what are you going to look like when you're old? All that ink will fade and droop. It'll look like you're melting."

She waved her hand and snickered. "You're just jealous. Someday, woman, I'm going to get you to go with me. We'll get the name of that man of yours tattooed on your—"

"No, we won't." I laughed. "Not a chance."

"The tat or the name?" she asked. Her sultry voice never ceased to amaze me. It was a contradiction to her body image.

"Neither."

We each plunked down in the comfortable chairs in the waiting area, each of us kicking off our shoes. Connie poured the wine in little plastic Dixie cups.

"I went all out on the wine glasses," she said.

"I see that," I said, holding it up in mock admiration.

We talked about everything except the elephant in the room — Lenny — everyone careful to keep my mind off it.

"My cousin, Andie, moved here last month," Babs said. "She's an addiction counselor but also got a part-time temp job at the coroner's office."

"Annnnd there it is," Connie said, rolling her eyes. "Good going, Babs. You just had to drop that bomb, didn't you?"

"What?" she asked, hands out, palms facing upward.

"We're trying to keep Melanie's mind off of dead people."

"Listen, folks," I said, taking a sip of the delicious red wine, "I appreciate what you're doing, but it's reality. Avoiding it is not going to make it go away."

"I'll have to ask Andie if she has access to the autopsy records," Babs said.

We were half done with the bottle when someone knocked on the door, and all four of us screamed. "Jumpy much?" I asked as soon as I caught my breath, hand to my chest.

Claire leaned over in her chair, then stood and crept around the wall far enough to see the door. "A guy is standing out there," she whispered and zipped back into her chair, hiding.

I set my wine glass down and got up.

"Where are you going?" Claire said, still whispering.

"To see what he wants," I said. "And you don't have to whisper. He can't hear you."

"Are you crazy?" she asked, eyes wide. "It's dark out there, and we have no idea who he is."

"There's four of us; what can happen?"

"With your luck? Just about anything," she said.

"Tell you what," I said, "I'll ask him without opening the door. I'll yell through the glass."

When I got within feet of the door, I saw a little girl of maybe ten standing hidden partially behind him. When she saw me, she came into full view. "There's a little girl with him," I told the others. I stood in front of the door, contemplating what to do. It was cold out there. Finally, I unlocked the door and cracked it open a couple of inches. "We're closed," I said. "Can you come back tomorrow?" He had coal-black hair and familiar green eyes; stubble lined his jaw. The little girl was cute as could be with a blond pixie haircut and the cutest pugged nose. It seemed I'd seen her before but couldn't remember where.

"We're not here for a haircut," the man said. "We're looking for Melanie Hogan."

"I'm Melanie," I said. "If you're not looking for a haircut, what—"

"I'm Max and this," he lay his hand on the little girl's head, "this is my daughter, Daisy. I'm your half-brother, and this here is your niece."

6

I stared at the little girl. *This* was Daisy? The image of the license plate popped into my head. I was someone who liked order in my life. Heck, not only liked it, I *needed* order. If my world could have gotten any more unstable, I didn't know how. Starting with the calls for Daisy yesterday, then Lenny's death, and now this. I didn't believe in coincidences.

I closed my eyes and shook my head, trying to rid myself of the nightmare. I felt Claire's presence on one side, Babs and Connie on the other.

"Mind if we come in?" the man asked. "It's cold out here."

"Why should we trust you?" Babs asked. "Melanie doesn't have any family, and now you come busting in here out of the blue to say that she does?"

"She doesn't have any money if that's what you're hoping to get," Claire said, her tone quiet and gentle. Claire will find the best in anyone and give everyone the benefit of the doubt. But this even shook the ground *she* stood on.

"If you let me come in, I can explain," he said.

I looked at Claire, to Babs, then Connie, and back to Claire. I couldn't just let this little girl stand out in the cold, but I also couldn't allow a strange man in here unless they all agreed to it. For all we knew, he could have been a murderer, Lenny's murderer, using the little girl as a ruse. I glanced at the girl again. She looked happy enough, although shivering.

"Mel, you got your gun here, right?" Babs's voice cut into my wavering thoughts.

"Huh?" My head swiveled toward her.

"Silly question. You always have it," she said, exhaling dramatically.

It took a moment to absorb what she was doing. "It's behind the desk here." I stepped back to allow them room to get past us, leaving the door unlocked if any of us should have to make a fast exit. I stopped him from moving past the desk. "That's far enough. It's just as warm here as it is anywhere else in the salon." I looked at Daisy. "Are you warming up—Daisy? I can make you a cup of hot chocolate if you'd like. It's from a Keurig, but at least it's hot."

"I'll get it," Claire offered before Daisy could answer.

The girl smiled, revealing teeth still developing. The gaps in between them made her smile as awkward as a deer's legs as they learn to walk. But, boy, if she wasn't the cutest little thing. Besides Sydney, that is. No one is cuter than my Sydney.

"Thank you," she said shyly as she clutched her father's hand. She looked up at him with clear admiration, then back to me. She appeared to be about Syd's age.

"How old are you, Daisy?" I asked.

"Nine. My dad is — "

"Old enough," he interrupted, gently tugging her hand. He offered her a bemused smile. "Honey, she doesn't care how old I am."

"Let the girl talk," I said, smiling at her then leveling my gaze on him. "So how old are you — what's your name again?"

"Max. My name's Max."

"Connie," I said, still looking at Max, "can you take Daisy over to Claire? Her hot chocolate should be just about ready."

Connie reached her hand out to the girl. "Certainly. Come on, Daisy. Let's go check on your hot chocolate, shall we?"

Daisy looked up at her father, uncertainty in her eyes — eyes a few shades lighter than her father's. His were the same bright green as my own. Many people assumed I wore colored contacts. I'd never met anyone else with eyes the same color. Until now. And it was eerie.

"Daddy?" she asked.

"Go ahead, honey," he said gently, nodding toward Connie. "I'll be right here."

She gave him a delighted smile, eyes sparkling. I watched as her skinny nine-year-old legs followed Connie. When I was sure she couldn't hear, I looked back toward Max. "How about we start with you telling me what this is all about. I don't have any money, and I don't have any family except my grandmother. I'm an only child of a woman who is an only child. What's the scam? And using your daughter?" I gave him a disgusted look, felt my eyebrows pinch together.

"I would never use my daughter," he said as he slowly shook his head and rubbed his thumb and forefinger over his dark eyebrows before looking back at me. "That's insulting. She's my whole world."

"And I'm supposed to just take your word for that? *That's* insulting—that you would think I'm that gullible. What do you want from me, Max? If that's even your real name. What's *really* up here? And how did you happen to come by the salon? It's after hours. Our lights are off except for the one in the waiting area." His tone had sounded genuine, but sociopaths had that gift, didn't they?

"I did my homework." I wasn't sure if I should feel impressed by that or creeped out. "Given the fact you run a salon, I didn't think showing up during the daytime would be good for business. And when I came by just after closing and saw you all, I thought it would be best to wait a bit."

Babs cleared her throat, and her arms remained crossed. "Ever heard of a phone?"

He glanced at her briefly, then back to me. "This isn't exactly something you drop on someone over the phone." His voice was quiet, his tone even.

"Or at all," Babs said.

Max rubbed the stubble on his chin then the back of his neck as he exhaled. "Look, Melanie, I know this sounds a little crazy, and —"

"A *little*?" I said, hardly recognizing my own shrill voice.

"I thought it would be best —" His phone rang, and he fished it out of his pocket. "Hello?" As he listened to the person on the other end, the color in his cheeks paled. "Uh-huh. No. Okay. We'll be right there." He hung up. "Pumpkin," he called to Daisy, "we gotta go, honey. Come on."

"We're done here then, I assume?" I asked. "Or should I expect another visit during off-hours?" I watched as he appeared torn between staying and leaving, ultimately deciding that leaving was the better choice.

Daisy tucked her small hand into her father's large one. "What's wrong, Daddy?"

"Your mom's friend called. She needs me to stop by." His mind appeared to be miles away already.

"I get to see Mom?" Daisy asked, her eyes brightening.

Her behavior, the hope in her eyes, tore in my chest. "Is she okay?" I looked at Max, this stranger claiming to be family I don't have. And yet, there was some sort of pull, some familiarity I couldn't put my finger on.

"I hope so," he said. "Come on, Daisy." He pulled her behind him as he headed out the door. He turned before the door closed, catching it with his hand. "I'll come back tomorrow."

"During business hours, please." I didn't know what kind of game he was playing, but it wasn't going to happen after dark in an empty salon. This kind of thing was exactly why we had the rule that no one stayed alone after dark.

I locked the door behind them, and all of us watched as he jogged to the car, pulling Daisy behind him. The light in her eyes at the hope of seeing her mother burned into my mind.

"What do you suppose that was about?" Connie asked.

"I have absolutely no idea," I said absently. "He's obviously got me mixed up with someone else." But even as I said the words, I wasn't sure I believed them. His eyes haunted me.

"You have to admit it's weird," Claire said. "First, someone is calling you asking for Daisy. Then, you see a woman in the parking lot watching you, a vanity plate on her car with the name Daisy on it. And now this stranger shows up out of nowhere claiming to be your half-brother and has a little girl named Daisy. That's not a common name."

"All things I'm well aware of," I murmured as I watched them drive out of the parking lot in a dark-colored Volvo SUV.

"Come on," Babs said, "let's get your mind off all this."

"As much as I would love to hang out some more with you ladies," I said, "I think I need to just get out of here." I picked up my shoes from the floor and headed toward the office to get my snow boots on. "Think I'll spend the night at my grandmother's since we're closed tomorrow."

"I need to get going too," Claire said. "My folks are at my house."

"Yeah, but they're there to see Syd, not you," I teased.

"True that," Claire said, laughing. "Come on, ladies. Let's do this again soon."

***

When I walked outside, I glanced at the bistro table and shuddered. It was hard to believe it was just hours ago that Lenny's body was there. For the life of me, I couldn't figure out what he was doing at my salon. Why would someone purposely place him for me to find? My mind felt like it had run a marathon today. Some good, light TV watching with Nana was precisely what I needed. And I didn't want to be alone tonight. Which in itself was odd. Usually, I do alone exceptionally well.

Claire, Connie, and Babs sent me on my way and said they would pick up before leaving. While my car warmed up, I rehearsed the events of the day trying to purge them from my mind so I could concentrate on the icy roads.

Finally, I looked in my rearview as I pulled away and saw the headlights go on from a dark sedan parked beneath the still-broken security camera. I shivered and kept looking in my rearview mirror all the way to my grandmother's house, calming down when I hadn't noticed it again the entire way there. My nerves were apparently on overdrive.

When I pulled into her driveway, the living room light glowed warmly. I couldn't wait to get inside and snuggle under a blanket on the couch and Nana in her recliner chair from which she loved to watch TV. I'd called her on my way over so I didn't startle her. It was only seven-thirty, but it had been dark by five, making it feel much later. It makes one understand why bears hibernate. The dark and the cold can be downright exhausting.

I let myself in. "Nana, I'm here," I called to her. Before I could say anything else, she met me in the kitchen and pulled me into a tight hug.

"I was so happy when I got your call, dontcha know," she said, her cornflower blue eyes twinkling with merriment. I never tired of seeing this woman and spending time in her presence. "And you're staying overnight!" I laughed at her excitement. "Are you hungry, dear?"

"A little. But don't you fuss; I can help myself."

"It's no fuss," she insisted, heading for the refrigerator.

I inhaled slow and deeply. I loved my grandmother's kitchen more than just about anywhere. This kitchen, these walls, held so many secrets, late-night conversations, and shared meals. She's made it her mission to teach me to cook. At first, I was terrible at it because I didn't care and had no interest. I only did it to appease her. But, when I discovered it was fun, I'd also realized there was a lot more to it than just throwing things together. And one of her very favorite things to do was teach me. Spending time together in this kitchen, whether we were talking about something important, not so much, or not talking at all, was one of the things we did best.

She pulled out a light green Tupperware container and a white one, followed by a loaf of homemade sourdough bread from the breadbox. My mouth watered. I was hungrier than I'd thought. Nana always had homemade bread, and it beat, hands down, any other bread I'd ever tasted. I watched her scoop some wild rice hotdish onto a plate, followed by some glazed carrots. She covered the plate with a sheet of plastic wrap and slid it into the microwave. I pulled the honey from the shelf in the cupboard beside the stove.

"How was your day?" I asked her. "You didn't go outside, did you?"

"Just to get the mail. Spent the rest of the day crocheting some afghans for the homeless shelter." She beamed when she talked about her volunteer work. "Working on a couple of pink ones so the men won't take them all." She winked at me. Nana always looked out for the underdog and aimed to build them up. I'd always believed that's what made her a better nurse than any others she worked with before she retired. Or any others in the state as far as I was concerned.

"When are you dropping them off? Can I go with you?"

"You betcha. I'd love for you to come with me. Probably won't be until tomorrow evening, though."

"All the more reason for me to go with. You shouldn't be out alone after dark. I know Birch Haven isn't a huge city, but it's still home to some unsavory characters."

"It's safer with that man of yours at the police department."

"Speaking of..." I picked up my fork and toyed with it, then looked at Nana. Her eyes narrowed.

"Melanie Hogan, what have you gone and gotten yourself into this time?"

"I swear I didn't do anything. It's just that..."

"Out with it, child. You're worrying this old woman."

"You're not old, so don't say that."

"Denying it doesn't make it not true," she said. "Now out with it." She came and sat down on the chair next to me at the table, her hand warm over mine.

"Before I do, realize I didn't tell you sooner because this isn't something I could tell you over the phone."

"Out with it already." She pressed my hand.

"There was a body outside of my salon this morning."

She gasped. "A body?"

I explained how I came to find him. "I thought he froze to death, but the police said it looks like it was blunt force trauma and that he was moved there after he was already dead."

She frowned, and her blue eyes dimmed with confusion and worry. "Well, now, why would someone place him there? Did you know this man?"

I hesitated and swallowed. "Not really. Well, kind of..."

She sighed. "Oh, for goodness sakes. Either you did, or you didn't, Melanie."

The urgency in her voice broke my heart at what the name would mean to her. It would mean her only daughter, who was already in prison, could be in danger. The only thing I could do was what she'd always preached — tell the truth. "It was Lenny."

7

"Lenny?" she asked, appearing not to grasp the meaning.

"Yes, Lenny. As in Violet's bookie and significant other." I shuddered at the thought that she would give me, her daughter, up for that slime ball.

"Oh my," she said, her eyes wide and her hand alongside her cheek. "Do the police have any leads?"

"Not really," I fibbed.

"Well, at least the suspects aren't anyone you know this time, then. It was probably one of Lenny's goons."

I set my fork down, my stomach suddenly upset.

"Oh, dear Lord." She groaned, tipped her head back, and briefly closed her eyes. "One of you is a suspect, aren't you?" She leveled her gaze on me with fearful hope. "Please tell me it's not you." When I didn't say anything, she said, "Melanie Hogan, why does this keep happening to you? You're a magnet."

I sighed and exhaled long. "Yup."

"Well, do fill me in, dear." She slowly shook her head.

I swallowed hard. "Because Lenny was from California, his body was found clear out here at my salon, and because of our so-called *history*. I guess that plops me in the so-called suspect pool. Like I would be so stupid as to land him at my salon." I pushed my plate away, my appetite completely gone. "Levi says I'm not a suspect, only a person of interest who they hope can give them some information."

"Well, I have full confidence in that man of yours. He'll prove who it was."

"He can't be on the case. It's a conflict of interest." New concern cast a dark shadow over her face. Her long, silver braid lay over her shoulder, and I gently pushed it back. I held her hands in my own. "Now, Nana, listen to me. Levi will do everything he possibly can to clear me. You don't have to worry." *Yeah, Melanie, no need to worry. Right.* A wave a nausea came over me.

"But I thought you said he couldn't be on the case."

I cocked my head to the side and said, "Well, *technically*, he can't. But that doesn't mean he won't do anything at all." That seemed to mollify her a bit.

I debated whether to tell her about Max and Daisy and decided against it. Max was obviously some lunatic who had me pegged as the wrong person. And Daisy, well, as weird as that whole thing was, it was just that. Weird. And nothing more.

"Does Jack know any of this?" she asked.

"We've been playing phone tag since this morning." My thoughts traveled back through the day. "Hard to believe this all happened less than thirteen hours ago. It seems like it's been at least a week and yet feels all too recent." I shivered as I remembered Lenny's body. "I just wish I knew who benefits from me finding the body. It would have to be somebody who knows our history."

She gasped, and her hand flew to her chest. "Oh, dear, you're right! You might be in danger."

My heart was heavy as I watched what this was doing to her. My life these past couple of years has caused her more stress than the rest of my decades combined. "Now, Nana, I don't want you to go worrying. I'll be fine. You know I'll be careful."

"I don't want you only to be careful, dear; I want you to stay the heck out of it, dontcha know."

"I won't go getting into trouble, and I won't get in the way of the investigation. All I'm going to do is find proof that I didn't kill him. Though I've thought about it a time or two," I said under my breath. But quiet enough.

"Melanie Hogan! Don't you even let words like that come from your lips. With your luck, the wrong person will hear."

We talked for a few minutes longer before my phone rang. I looked at the display. "It's Jack. I'm gonna take this in my bedroom, okay?"

"Sure, dear," she said, patting my hand. "Give him my best."

I answered the phone right before it went to voice mail. "Hang on, Jack," I said. I leaned over and pecked Nana's cheek before going to the bedroom and closing the door. "Hey, buddy, I'd ask what's new, but I can't imagine you haven't heard by now."

"You could say that. What in Sam Hill is going on, Hogan? I swear trouble follows you more than anyone I've ever known."

"Right? I don't even know what to say. Who told you about it?"

"Levi called just to give me a heads up before someone called me out of the blue. Threatened he'd have my head if I mentioned it to anyone."

"Ooh, and you just did," I said, trying to ease the seriousness, if even by a fraction.

"Detective Walker called to get my statement of that evening not five minutes after I hung up from Levi." He half-exhaled, half-groaned.

"It's not like you have anything to worry about. They're talking to everyone who was there that night. You've got nothing to hide, Jack. You went straight home as soon as you left Grizzley's." When he didn't say anything, I said, "You did go straight home, right Jack?"

"What do you think? Yes!" he grumped.

"Well, maybe find an alibi anyway. Just in case."

"I've got a receipt from when I stopped at Miller's Pond for gas and coffee. Only thing is, I tossed the garbage from my car in the trash."

"You'll have to dig it out."

"Oh, joy," he grumbled.

I could almost see him grimacing. "Hey, guess what happened at the salon tonight?"

"What, finding a corpse this morning wasn't enough? How are you doing, by the way?"

"As well as can be expected," I said, lying back down on the bed. I had one leg bent at the knee, my foot on the bed, the other leg crossed over that knee. "Do you think I should tell Violet?"

Jack whistled. "That's a tough one."

"If I tell her, I wouldn't do it over the phone. I'd make a trip down there to see her."

"Do you think that's a good idea?"

"I need to see her reaction."

"Oh, crap," Jack said and groaned. "You think she had something to do with it, don't you?"

"I don't know. That's what I need to find out. I'm not about to let her make me take the fall for something she might have done. Not again."

Jack exhaled loudly. "Hogan, you've given me gray hair these past couple of years."

I knew that was a lie—his hair was coal-black, and Claire and I are the only ones he allowed to touch it. "Would it make you feel better if I take someone with me?"

"I'll go."

"Seriously?" I said, wondering if I had heard correctly. "You're gonna go? Why?"

"Because I would just love to see Violet," he said with dry sarcasm. "I haven't seen her since the year she came for your birthday. And because I don't want you dragging Claire into this."

"Ugh. That's something I'd like to forget," I grumbled. "That particular birthday visit, not Claire."

"Obviously. Let's go tomorrow. Your salon is closed anyway. Besides, if she did have anything to do with it—Violet, not Claire—she's setting you up again. Witnessing her behavior when you tell her about Lenny will be intriguing."

"Intriguing?" I repeated. "Really?" Silence fell over the line. "Fine. It'd be great to have you with to referee. Nana said to tell you hi, and she loves you. I'm staying over at her house tonight."

"That should make Levi happy so he doesn't have to worry about you."

"I didn't tell him."

"Why not?" he asked.

"Haven't talked to him. We've both been busy."

He paused a moment as if studying my words. "You sure that's all it is?" he asked.

"Yeah. What else would it be?" I strove for a light tone. "I'll pick you up about eleven, okay?"

"Is that your way of saying 'Mind your own business, Jack?'"

"Pretty much. So is eleven okay?"

"I'll be ready."

"I'm sure you will, Mr. Punctuality. See you tomorrow. And dig out that gas receipt."

"Dumpster diving. Yay, me," he said dryly.

I laughed. "I'll help when I get there tomorrow. Night, Jack."

After we hung up, I laid there for a moment. I hadn't seen Violet since she went to prison. Would she even agree to see me? A myriad of feelings overwhelmed me, including just a teensy bit of anticipation. I was going to see my biological mother. But I certainly wasn't as happy about it as Daisy had been.

The hum of the furnace soothed me, preventing a spiral into full-blown panic mode. I spun so I lay on my back crosswise on the bed, letting my head hang over the edge. I used to lay this way a lot when I was in my early teens due to the old wives' tale that it would cause the blood to nourish the hair, making it grow faster. I also religiously practiced the trick from Judy Blume's book, *Are You There God? It's Me, Margaret*, to increase bust size too. That didn't work either.

A tiny spider inched its way across the ceiling and proceeded down the wall. As if noticing my presence, it stopped its descent, playing dead if I didn't know better. I didn't think they were that smart. I would have killed it, but I didn't want to be involved in yet another death. After a few minutes, as if sensing impending doom, the spider began to climb back up the wall and onto the ceiling.

There was a soft knock on the door, and I righted myself, swung my legs around, and sat up. "Come on in, Nana."

"You okay, dear?" she asked, leaning against the door frame, hand on the doorknob.

"Jack and I are going to see Violet tomorrow. I'm picking him up at eleven, so I'll have to leave here about nine."

Concern etched her face. "Mind if I come with you?"

"To see her or because of me?"

"Both, perhaps."

"Afraid I might kill her and find myself a prisoner in her cell?"

"Don't say such things."

"I could tell you not to worry about me, but I know that would be wasting my breath." She opened her mouth to speak, but I put up a hand. "I get it. I do. I feel the same way about you. I want to protect you from everything bad in the world."

"Well, that's not very realistic, dontcha know. I know I can't protect you from everything, but that doesn't mean I can't be there to help you through it." She sat beside me and put an arm around my shoulders, pulling me toward her, our shoulders touching.

I smiled. "I would love for you to come with us. What about dropping off the afghans at the shelter, though? Can we do it when we get back?"

"You betcha. Monday is okay, too. The shelter is always open, thank goodness. Those poor folks depend on it so desperately."

My phone rang, and I picked it up. "Hey, Jack. You backing out on me?"

"It's not Jack. It's the other lucky man in your life. And what is Jack backing out on?"

I grinned and looked at Nana, mouthing, "It's Levi." With a pat on my leg, she pushed herself upright and closed the door behind her. "Nothing. Whatcha up to? Heading into work early?"

"I've got some time, so I thought I'd stop by and see you for a bit first. Are you home?"

"I'll save you some time. I'm in town at my grandmother's. I've decided to spend the night here."

"Even better. I haven't seen Rose for a while."

"She'd love to see you too," I said, knowing I wasn't saying anything that wasn't true. She loved Levi. Her only complaint about him was that he hadn't asked me to marry him yet. Even though she knew I'd say no if he did. Much to her dismay, I wasn't ready for marriage yet. What I haven't told her is I might never be ready. I had too much baggage to drop on someone else. It wasn't fair to Levi. Not to mention my mean independent streak.

"See you in ten?"

"Can't wait."

"Me either. You have no idea," he said.

I chuckled. "Oh, yeah, I think I do."

We'd no sooner hung up when my phone rang again; the ID showed *Private Caller*. I left my phone on the bed and went to join Nana. The last thing I wanted to deal with right now was another call asking for Daisy or some other unforeseen surprise. I'd had all I could handle for one day.

8

Nana was delighted that Levi was on his way over. "That man," she said with a wink, "is quite a catch, Melanie Hogan. Don't you let him get away."

I chuckled and shook my head. "I know that. And no one is getting away. But there's something to be said for taking time to get to know each other. I'm sure you don't want us rushing into anything."

She cast me a sidelong glance. "No one is rushing here. If you move any slower, you'll be my age and alone. He's not going to wait forever."

I laughed. "You never give up, do you? Trust me, okay? And trust us. We're fine." The area around my eyes seemed to constrict. *We were fine, weren't we?*

"You know, your granddad asked me to marry him six months after we met. And we lived a good, long life together. I want you to have as much time together as you two can. Please don't waste it. You're not kids anymore."

"Well, gee, thanks for that reminder. And just because we're not jumping into marriage doesn't mean we're wasting time, Nana. For now, we're happy with the way things are."

The doorbell rang. I pumped a fist in the air. "Saved!" I laughed and went for the door. Levi stood there in his black leather coat and leather gloves, holding a bouquet of beautiful white lilies. I stepped back to let him in then stood on my tiptoes to kiss him before reaching for the flowers. He pulled them out of reach and behind his back. "These," he said, smiling, "are for Rose."

"Trying to buy her affection, are you?" I teased.

"If it'll work, yes." His eyes twinkled.

"Don't bother. She's already more in love with you than I am."

"Melanie Hogan!" she scolded from behind me. I jumped.

"Well, it's true, isn't it?"

She swatted me on my rear end and accepted the flowers from Levi. "Let me go get these in some water before I retire for the evening so you two can have some time to yourselves. With your jobs and your schedules, I'm sure you don't have much time."

"For goodness sakes, you don't have to go, Nana. We want you to stay out here with us, right Levi?" I looked at him, unintentionally putting him on the spot. Or *was* it unintentional? As much as I loved spending time with him, I feared he would want to talk about our earlier conflict if we were alone. I wasn't ready to talk about that. Not yet. I just wanted to enjoy our time together.

"I have this last afghan to finish," she said. "I must if we're going to bring them to the shelter this weekend. And we'll be gone all day tomorrow."

"And where are you ladies off to tomorrow?" Levi asked.

"You wouldn't believe it if I told you," I said.

"Try me." He slipped off his beanie, followed by his gloves, and ran a hand over his beard stubble.

"We're going to the prison to visit Violet," I said, taking his coat and laying it over the back of a chair.

He froze momentarily. "What brought this on?" he asked, his eyes carefully searching me out.

"I'll fill you in later." I took his hand and led him toward the living room. "Come on, Nana."

"I told you I'm going to my room to work on the last afghan and watch a little TV while I do, dontcha know." She still clutched the flowers. "Now scoot. And maybe you could put these in water for me." She handed me the lilies.

"Of course," I said.

Levi reached a vase for me from the cupboard's top shelf while I took the wrapping off the flowers. We worked in tandem, placing the flowers in the center of the kitchen island. The fragrance followed us into the living room. I sat on the sofa, folding one leg underneath me, pulling the other one up on the couch, knee to my chest, foot on the edge of the sofa cushion. Levi sat next to me and lifted my chin with his finger, planting a gentle kiss on the tip of my nose.

"Let's talk," he said quietly.

"And here I thought things were going so well," I said, trying to make light of it, as I typically did when things got uncomfortable. Consistency was what I was best at.

"What's going on in that head of yours?" he asked, turning sideways on the couch, facing me. He rested his elbow on the back of the sofa, his head resting on his hand. I watched as he traced circles with his other hand on the back of one of mine. "You can start talking any time," he teased gently. I swallowed and breathed in deep, exhaling slowly. "Talking to me isn't that hard, is it?"

I looked into his eyes, finding myself comforted there. "Levi," I began, "I know you want to take care of me. I get that. And as nice as it is, not only do I not need to be taken care of, it's not a luxury I want to afford myself."

"I'm not Cain. Don't lump me into the same category."

"This isn't about Cain."

"Isn't it?"

Cain was my less-than-faithful ex-husband who'd gotten someone else pregnant when we were still married. He'd been engaged to her before the ink was even dry on our divorce papers. The fact that I can't have children made the sting of betrayal that much greater. "I never said you were him. Or anything like him."

"I think if you get honest with yourself, you'll find you're afraid I'll do the same thing to you that he did. The man's a fool, Melanie." I looked away, but he gently turned my face back toward him again. "I know how much your independence means to you, and I'm not out to take that away. Hell, that's one of the things that I find so sexy about you."

"*One* of the things?" I asked, raising an eyebrow. "Should I ask what the other things are?"

"Not right now you shouldn't, no," he said, winking. "But letting me be there for you, in good times and bad, is that so wrong?"

In good times and in bad. Fear rippled through me at the sound of those words. The last time I'd said them landed me a lot of pain. I pushed it aside as best I could. "No, it's not wrong. Just give me time to find my way in this, okay? I've worked hard to get to where I am. I'm chartering all new territory here."

"Every time I think we've had a breakthrough, you revert to pushing away."

"That's pretty much what Jack alluded to as well."

He rubbed his finger lightly against my arm. "You can push all you want, Melanie; I'm not going anywhere." He raised an eyebrow and took a deep breath. "I'm not saying I won't get frustrated. But I'm here to stay."

"You might want to tell my grandmother that." He raised an eyebrow, and I shook my head. "It's nothing."

"What's with going to see Violet tomorrow? Want me to go with you?"

"Nah. Nana and Jack are going. I'll be fine." He was silent for a moment, and I read the uncertainty in his eyes. "I'm not shutting you out," I assured him. "I swear I'm not. But the three of us will be good. I'll fill you in on everything. I promise."

"Did she call and ask you to come see her? If she did, be careful. I don't trust her."

I shook my head. "Like I do? No. My grandmother just wants to see her daughter, I think. It's gotta be so hard for her; I can't even imagine. And Jack and I want to see her reaction when I tell her Lenny is dead. I need to see for myself whether she had anything to do with it. I don't trust that she wouldn't set me up again. You and I both know it wouldn't be the first time."

He pulled me into a hug and held me, neither of us saying a word. No words were needed, just the beating of our hearts, the warmth between us. "Thanks for always being there for me," I said against his chest. The smell of his aftershave stirred me. "I mean it. I know I may not show it, but I appreciate it."

"I know," he said, his voice husky. "Call me after you've left the prison?"

"Yes. I promise."

"I'm gonna hold you to that."

I remembered the visitor at the salon and jumped back. "Get this! Some guy came to the salon this evening after we closed, claiming to be my half-brother. The whack job had his nine-year-old daughter with him."

He pulled back and looked at me, forehead creased. "What kind of sick joke is that?"

"Right? Babs was pretty rough on him; she made sure to tell him I didn't have any family or money." I chuckled at the all-too-recent memory. Babs to the rescue. "Maybe I should ask Violet about that too. Maybe this guy isn't crazy for all I know, and she gave birth to another child. Poor guy if that's the case."

"Did he offer up any proof?"

"No. Got a call from his wife and had to run." I told him about Daisy's joy at being able to see her mother. "It broke my heart to see that, Levi. There must be a history there, and not a good one."

"Did you get a name?"

"Just Max. Max and Daisy. I didn't get the last name. He said he'd be back to talk."

"I'm going to relay this info to Detective Walker. He'll want to speak with him. I find it unsettling that he showed up at the same time someone killed Lenny. Tell me you won't let him into the salon again after hours. And don't walk out to your car alone after work."

"You sound just like this bossy Detective Wescott I know." I leaned into him, my muscles fully relaxed. Nana's cat, Callie, jumped up on my lap and curled into a ball.

"I hear he has an incredibly stubborn girlfriend."

I chuckled, and he kissed the top of my head. I was so contented and relaxed I darn near started purring along with Callie.

We sat in silence for a few minutes until he finally stirred. I turned my face up to look at him, and his lips met mine.

"I hate to, but I gotta run." He looked at his watch. "Roll call in twenty minutes."

I stood, draped the blanket around my shoulders, and walked him to the door. After one more kiss, he said, "I hate that I have to leave. But—"

"Duty calls, I know," I said, smiling at him. "The fine citizens of Birch Haven need you to keep them safe."

"Especially one. There's a killer out there intent on making you the center of his business. I'm glad you're staying here tonight. I'm going to get a patrol car to swing by throughout the night."

My heart hit the floor at the realization of his statement. "Is my grandmother in danger by me staying here?"

"Both of you stay in the house."

"Well, yeah," I said, frowning. "It's too cold to go outside, and it's nighttime. What would we do, have a middle-of-the-night bonfire and roast weenies?"

"I mean it, Melanie. We don't know who we're dealing with. What we do know is he's capable of murder."

I put my hand on his chest. "I promise we'll stay in the house. Now go."

As soon as he closed his car door, I closed the front door, locked it, and watched him through the window. A minute later, his taillights disappeared around a corner. And right after that, a vehicle pulled out from a side road and slowly rolled by my grandmother's house. I watched until its taillights were out of view, shivered, and pinched the curtains tightly together.

SHEAR FEAR

9

Sunday morning brought with it a fresh dusting of snow that had fallen throughout the night. The aroma of freshly brewed coffee wafted through my bedroom door. I wrapped myself in an old, thick, fuzzy robe. It used to be black but faded to a dark gray over time and after countless washings, but I loved it too much to part with it. I slid into my slippers and padded out to the kitchen. Nana was nowhere to be seen. I put my ear up to her bedroom door and heard her quiet voice talking to God. I tiptoed away and back to the kitchen, snagged a coffee mug, and filled it to the brim before heading to shower. Nana kicked on the furnace earlier and closed the bathroom door, keeping the heat in so it was toasty warm.

After ten minutes of the steaming hot water relaxing every muscle, I nabbed a towel and began drying off my hair before wrapping it around my body, tucking the end to hold it up. I snatched my phone from the vanity to be sure I hadn't missed a call from Levi. He hadn't called, but I did have a text from an unknown number.

I don't know if you remember me but this is Max.

I froze for a moment, a bit freaked out about how he got my number. And what did he mean 'if you remember me'? How couldn't I? It's not like that was something one could easily forget. His claim, 'I'm your half-brother', came back to haunt me.

I looked away from my phone and into the mirror, clearing the steam from the shower with my hand. Could Violet have had another child? Was it possible this guy was telling the truth? If so, did I even want a half-brother? I'd been so accustomed to it just being Nana and me; I wasn't sure I wanted anyone else to break into that bond. But if what he said was true, I didn't exactly have that choice. It wouldn't be fair to my grandmother to keep it a secret if she had another grandchild out there. And Daisy would be her great-grandchild.

My heart began racing with the possibilities of what this could mean. That is until I forced it to a halt. "For God's sake, Melanie," I grumbled, "for all you know, this guy is some crazy person, and there's no foundation whatsoever to his statement." I looked back at my phone then into the mirror at the emerald eyes that matched his.

How'd you get this number? I tapped.

Too easily. You should think about beefing up your security. I shuddered. I'd have to think about doing just that. *Do you have time to meet today and talk? I think you'll want to hear what I have to say.*

"Or not," I said into the mirror. I briefly thought about what to text back and set my phone down instead. This required some serious thought before I said anything at all to this man. If I agreed to meet and he didn't have solid proof, all it would do is encourage his misdirected behavior. But if he did provide proof, well, I feared that even more. What if — those two words held enough weight to sink a ship.

I began tapping keys. *Can't today. Tomorrow?*

I picked up the blow dryer, disappointed in myself that I watched the screen of my phone to see if it would light up. What exactly was I hoping for? My life was perfect with the people that filled it now. I didn't want any more. *Did I?* I tried to recall Max's face, to remember if there was any resemblance to Violet. She didn't have our eyes. Hers were almost — well, almost *violet.*

I'd just finished applying mascara when I caught the light from my phone out the corner of my eye. I took a breath and looked down at it.

Monday it is. Eleven work? And where?

The coffeeshop off Oak and fourth. Bring proof to back up your story or it will be a short meeting. I held my breath and watched my phone.

Got it. See you then.

Got it? Got what? The proof or the fact that it was going to be a short meeting if he didn't? I opened the door to go to my room. I had to get a move on, or I'd drive myself crazy with questions.

***

We picked up Jack right at eleven. We both got out of the car to let him know we'd arrived, but I should have known he'd be not only watching but letting me know if I was a minute late. He met us before we were halfway up the walk. He hugged Nana, then me.

"Do I need to go through your trash first for your receipt?" I asked, wrinkling my nose.

"Already done. Took a pic and forwarded it to Detective Walker."

"Good. Because I was afraid of what I might find in there."

"Whatever." He scowled and shook his head. "Let's roll," he said. "Want me to drive?"

"You kidding?" I scoffed. "Get in."

"I'm a good driver, I'll have you know." He looked at my grandmother and pointed at me. "She has control issues," he said.

Nana laughed. "Yes, she does."

"Hey now!" I protested. "Stop talking about me like I'm not here. Now get in," I said again.

He opened the door for my grandmother like the perfect gentleman, waited for her to get in, then climbed into the back seat. "Let me tell you what a treat it is to ride in your car instead of Claire's."

I laughed. "Why's that?" Rhetorical question, that one.

"You know why. There's room to sit in your car. And it's as clean as it was the day you bought it. It even still smells new."

"In her defense," I said, smiling at him in the rearview mirror, "she has a child."

"In *my* defense, not much of that stuff in her car is Syd's. I think she keeps half her wardrobe in there."

Just yet another way she and I were complete opposites. But we balanced each other perfectly.

With all the talking and laughter while driving to the prison, I'd nearly forgotten the events of the past forty-eight hours. Or where we were going, for that matter. Until I saw the sign that directed us toward our destination — *Women's Correctional Facility 5 miles.* Seeing the words felt like a punch in my gut, and I had to catch my breath. I glanced at Nana, who had suddenly grown quiet. The skin at the corners of her eyes, usually crinkled from smiling, was drawn. I reached over and covered one of her hands with mine. I saw Jack's hand resting on her shoulder.

"You okay?" I asked. "Me and Jack will both be right there with you."

She squeezed my hand and patted Jack's hand with her other one. "I know. You kids are such dears."

"You are not the reason Violet is in here, Nana," I said, reading her mind. "If that were the case, I'd be in here, too. I am who I am today because of you and only you. Well," I added, "and Granddad."

"At least I know where she is these days and know that she's safe," she said. "Before this, I never knew from day to day."

"I can't even imagine," I said, thinking of Syd.

The Women's Correctional Facility housed hundreds of women. I had never been to see Violet a single time since they transferred her there. Nana had tried but was denied by Violet each time she did. Violet sent me a few letters, but I hadn't opened a single one. I hadn't tossed them either, however. I wasn't sure why I hung onto them. Hope perhaps? Hope for what might be in those letters and saving myself the disappointment if what I hoped for wasn't there. Nana received a few letters as well, Violet letting her know she was sorry, and she denied the visits because she was ashamed. I, however, didn't buy it. She'd burned her bridge with me, and I wasn't willing to rebuild it.

"Hey, guys?" I said, suddenly remembering a critical piece. "I don't think we can just show up and see her. I'm pretty sure we have to fill out an application."

"An application?" Jack said as if I'd just said I'm running for president.

"You're right," my grandmother said and sighed. "I assumed you did."

"How did you know that?" Jack asked me. I didn't say anything. "You've thought about going to see her," he said, digesting the revelation. "Wow."

"Wow?" I asked, looking at him through the rearview mirror again.

"I'm not disappointed," he said quickly, "just surprised."

"Then you're not surprised that I never followed through with it."

"Well, since we're this far," Jack said, "I say we stop and see if they'll let us in. What have we got to lose?"

"Maybe since both you and I have completed an application in the past," I said to my grandmother, "just maybe they'll accept us if we register in plenty of time before visiting hours are over."

Jack's brows raised. "You even went so far as to fill out the application?"

"They should have our background check on file," I said, ignoring his question.

"Well, that counts you out," Jack said dryly. "Rose and I should be good to go, though."

I made a face at him in the mirror. "Very funny. Since you think you're so smart, use your phone to look up the visiting hours."

Following orders, he began typing into his phone. "Eight to two-forty-five on Sundays," he said.

"Well, as least we're within the range," I said. My grandmother stayed silent. "A dollar for your thoughts," I said quietly.

She looked over at me and raised an eyebrow. "A dollar?"

I shrugged. "Inflation."

"Does that go for me, too?" Jack asked. "I could tell you everything and make enough to quit my job."

"Yeah," I said, looking at him, "I don't want to know yours." He pushed his glasses up with one finger. I snickered. "Ouch!"

"I'm so close to her right now. What if she doesn't want to see me?" Nana asked, ignoring Jack and me.

"Well, we'll see if we're even able to," I said gently. "They might tell us to fly a kite when they find out we haven't submitted an application recently. I don't know if we have to submit something every time we come here or if it's a one-time thing and then just register during visiting hours. Not that there will be another time," I muttered.

"Let's give it a shot," Jack said as we pulled into the parking lot. "There's nothing to lose by trying."

After we parked, we sat in the car in silence for a couple of moments. We looked at the enormous brick structure with bars on windows high up on the walls and an exceptionally tall black iron gate surrounding the entire thing, barbed wire running along the top—Violet's home. I swear my heart was beating a thousand times per minute. Thank goodness it appeared my grandmother was handling this better than I was.

Nana and I followed Jack when he made the first move to get out, leading us into the building. Not knowing whether we were going to see Violet or not had my stomach tied up in knots. The not knowing part of something went against my very nature of control.

We finally aimed for the front entrance, Jack opening the door for Nana and me. We strode up to the front desk,

Jack stepping aside, allowing me front and center stage. A large woman slouched in her chair behind the desk as she stared blankly at a computer screen. It was apparent she'd rather be anywhere else but here.

"We're hoping to visit an inmate," I said, a slight tremor in my voice.

"Have you completed an application?" she asked without so much as a glance.

If she were any more disinterested, she wouldn't be here at all. "My grandmother and I completed one a while back. I assumed we didn't need to fill out another?" I crossed my fingers. "It's important."

That garnered an annoyed look, but at least she looked up. "They all are, honey. Names?"

"Rose Donnelly and Melanie Hogan."

"Got a driver's license?"

Nana and I fished through our purses, each producing ours.

"Who's that?" she asked, looking at Jack over the top of her readers.

"Jack Dancy," he said. "I've never completed an application."

"Afraid you'll have to stay out here in the lobby. Can't be havin' just anybody back there." She coughed a sound that left me wondering if I should duck. I wanted hand sanitizer at the very least. "Who you here to see?"

"My daughter, Violet," Nana spoke up. "Violet Donnelly."

The woman studied her computer monitor—if one could call it studying. Absently gazing is more accurate. "Don't see her." My heart fell. "Oh, wait." She shook her head slowly. "No can do. Says no visitors here."

"May I ask why?" I asked. "We've come all the way from Birch Haven." I crossed the fingers on my other hand now as well.

She looked up at me and rolled her eyes. "Honey, Birch Haven isn't far. Besides, you shoulda called first."

"I realize that," I said, scrambling to think of something to sway her. Jack came to my rescue.

"Ma'am, Ms. Donnelly here doesn't have much longer left," Jack said as he draped an arm around my grandmother's shoulders and patted lightly. "Please don't deny her the chance to see her only daughter."

My head spun, and I glared at Jack. Until the woman looked at Nana with the first sign of interest and said, "I'm so sorry, Miss Donnelly. Let me see what I can do." She picked up the phone and punched in a number.

"She doesn't have much longer left?" I said in a harsh whisper. "Don't even say a thing like that!"

"He meant well, dear," Nana said, holding onto Jack's arm.

"See?" he said to me. "Besides, I didn't say not long left for *what*. She doesn't have long left *here* if we don't get to see Violet."

I couldn't help but chuckle. "You're impossible. Good, but impossible."

"Just remember the *good* part," he said.

The woman hung up the phone. "You'll have to stay out here," she said to Jack, pointing to a row of black metal chairs.

I leaned toward Jack's ear and whispered, "I guess you don't get to be *intrigued* today." This resulted in an elbow to my ribs.

"Violet has denied all visitors, but the sergeant will go check if she'll make an exception given the circumstances."

My grandmother looked at me, horrified. "She's going to think I'm dying," she mouthed.

"It's good for her," I said, grabbing her hand and squeezing lightly. "Serves her right."

"Melanie Hogan!" she scolded loud enough for the woman behind the desk to look at us over the top of her brown-framed glasses.

"Problem, ladies?" the woman asked.

"My granddaughter here just needs to be reminded of manners sometimes," Nana said.

It was a rare thing for her to scold me in front of people, even as a child. "Sorry," I murmured, feeling all of twelve years old.

"You should be," the woman said, clearly disgusted. "Treating your dying grandmother that way."

Jack pinched my arm. Not enough to bruise, but it sure got my attention. "Don't say it, Mel," he whispered in my ear.

I inhaled slowly, counting to five. We were all a bundle of nerves here, and they were all getting tied in knots.

The woman's phone rang, and she listened to the caller without speaking, hanging up a second later. "Violet will see you ladies. Have a seat until someone comes for you."

I swear she glared at me again. But then maybe she was mirroring the look on my face.

10

Twenty minutes later, a guard fetched Nana and me.

She said, "Anyone who comes from a hundred or more miles away'll get three hours."

I almost choked. We definitely wouldn't be here for three hours. "We're from Birch Haven," I said. "I don't think that's quite a hundred miles away."

"Close enough," she said. At least she sounded a little more interested in being here than the woman behind the desk in the front. "Cell phones, cameras, recording or music devices, or any type of electronics are not permitted. You'll be placing them in here." She turned a corner leading us into a room with several lockers. While we unloaded all our unauthorized items, the guard continued speaking. "The only contact during your visit can be a brief kiss on her cheek upon arriving and again when you leave."

No worries there.

"You may not leave your seat once you're inside the room," she continued. "Not even to use the restroom. If you do, that terminates your visit." She looked us both up and down. "Looks like both of you ladies dressed appropriately so no problem there. But your coats need to stay in a locker even though we've searched them already."

Criminy, this was worse than going to the airport. Not only did they make sure trouble didn't escape outside the prison walls, but they made sure trouble didn't find its way in either. She droned on, and as much as I knew I should pay attention, my mind wouldn't cooperate. All I could think about was that I was going to be face to face with my birth mother in a few minutes.

Finally, she led us to a room with several tables, two chairs on either side of each table. "Violet is a good lady," the guard said, looking across the room at the woman sitting by herself in the far corner, shoulders slightly hunched. "Just got herself in some trouble, is all."

My face burned. *Some* trouble? Try murder! And *good lady*? Clearly, she didn't know Violet. Then, as if she sensed me staring, Violet turned toward me, and our eyes met. Nana followed the guard, but I stood frozen in place, unable to move. I couldn't even breathe. More than anything, I wanted to turn back and wait in the lobby with Jack. Or call Levi and disappear in his voice. But suddenly, my feet began moving without my doing, a strong force propelling me forward. It felt almost supernatural.

Before I knew it, I was standing in front of her, looking at the shell of the woman she used to be. She'd lost several pounds. Her hair, swept up in a hair tie, appeared thinner than before. Her eyes were hollow and her skin sallow. I wondered if she was sick. I struggled not to feel sorry for her, but I couldn't help it. I glanced at Nana, her beautiful eyes sad, glossy with pain.

"Hi, my darling," she said to Violet, a tremor in her voice. "It's nice to see you."

"What do you have?" Violet asked.

Were those tears in her eyes? I blinked rapidly, clearing the disbelief.

"She's not dying," I said. "Jack came with. He said that so we could get in here to see you."

She rubbed her palms over her eyes and across her cheeks before folding them in her lap. She looked at Nana. "So you're okay then?"

"Yes. I'm sorry if we caused you alarm," my grandmother said.

Violet glanced around, then at me. "Where's Jack?"

Her voice was quiet and sad, and I couldn't determine if it was genuine or not. She was an actress, after all. "In the lobby," I finally answered.

"How are you doing?" she asked me.

"Couldn't be better. And you?" I had a nasty tone, and I didn't like myself for it right now. All that has happened was water under the bridge. And yet—well, seeing her brought it all to the surface again, and it felt like I had to fight to stay afloat.

She looked over the room, seeming to disappear far, far away, and then she returned. "As well as can be expected. I have no one to blame but myself."

Her answer threw me for a loop. Did she just take responsibility? Will wonders never cease? "That's true," I said.

"Are you eating?" my grandmother said. "You've lost weight." When Violet didn't answer, she asked, "You're not ill, are you?"

Violet shrugged. "No, I'm fine. Mom—" she stopped and looked away, her eyes misting over. She swallowed and looked at my grandmother again. "I'm so sorry. For everything I've put you through, I'm sorry." Tears ran unchecked down her cheeks. She took a moment to get herself together then looked at me. "And you. Look how beautiful you are. My little girl."

"No, actually, I'm not. Your little girl. She grew up after you chose to leave her." I wanted to kick myself. What was with this hostility I displayed? I took a deep breath, looked down then back at her. "Sorry."

"It's me that's sorry, Melanie. I've done horrible things." She looked away and sniffed, then back to me. "Such horrible things. I'll never be able to make them up to you, I know. But maybe, just maybe, you'll be able to forgive me someday."

The problem is I thought I had until now. "I hope so," I whispered, tears on the heels of the words. I quickly looked away, taking in the surroundings until I was sure I could look at her and not cry. A man and woman sat across from one another at a corner table on the far side of the room. She reached out to slap him, and a guard was at the table in a second flat. I tensed, and Nana's hand rested on my thigh, giving me strength. I rested my hand on hers, and she squeezed, a nonverbal agreement that we'd always been there for each other, and we were now. "I wanted to come and tell you about Lenny," I said.

Her eyes glistened with fear. Or was it interest? Her chalk-colored cheeks shaded ever so slightly. "Did something happen?"

I narrowed my eyes, trying to read her. Did she know? Had she arranged it? "He's dead."

She made a sorrowful sound, like a wounded animal. Nana reached out for her hand, and a guard was there in a split second.

"No touching," the guard said.

"How?" Violet asked.

"You don't know?" I said, studying her every breath.

"If you're asking me if I had something to do with it, I wouldn't blame you. But no, I didn't. I—Lenny—it's complicated," she said through tears. "I hated him, and I was scared of him, but he could be a good man. And I loved what he gave me."

"Which was what?" I asked. "What could he possibly have given you that was more important than your child? I hated him for taking you away from me, you know that? I hated him, and I still hate him."

"If only you knew the Lenny I knew." She wiped her nose on her sleeve.

"Which one, the one you hated or the one you feared? No, thank you," I said.

"Melanie—"

"No," I said, standing up. "No. I can't do this." The guard was at my side. "I'm ready to go," I told her. I turned to Violet. "Just one more thing—did you have any more children?"

She looked at me, confusion cutting into the raw emotion that had been there a moment ago. "No. Why?"

"Just wondering if I have any brothers or sisters out there somewhere." I searched her eyes for answers but didn't pick up anything. Was Max the one not telling the truth?

"Ready to go?" the guard asked me.

I looked at Nana. I'd been so caught up in emotion I'd completely forgotten about her for a moment. She appeared so small and helpless sitting there. The strongest woman I knew was facing one of the most challenging trials of her life. There was no way I could leave her alone. "Sorry about that," I said to the guard. "A few minutes more, please." I sat back down and held Nana's hand.

We made small talk for a while before my grandmother asked Violet, "Why have you denied my visits? I've been worried sick, dontcha know. You said you felt guilty, but how does denying your mother a visit make that better?"

Violet sighed. "Chicken," she whispered as she looked away then back at Nana. "Mom," she said, pain that still looked shockingly genuine plastered on her face, "I'm not proud of what I've done. I've messed up every life I've touched. It's painful to see how much I've hurt the people I love."

Anger resurfaced. "*Love*? Do they have a therapist in here you can see?" I asked. "Maybe that would help. Because I gotta be honest, Violet, cutting yourself off from us may make you feel better, but it only hurts us more. Once again, putting yourself first."

"Melanie, stop," Nana said in a pained voice. She patted my thigh.

I took a breath and exhaled, closing my eyes briefly.

"In answer to your question," Violet said, "yes, I am seeing a therapist. It might not seem like it, but I think it's helping."

I opened my mouth but clamped my lips shut before spewing another retort that would serve no purpose and would only hurt my grandmother.

The next fifteen minutes went surprisingly fast, much of it spent in silence. Yet, I didn't have the heart to pull my grandmother away before she was ready, and I couldn't leave her here alone. When I saw her getting tired, I said, "Nana, we should get you home."

"Maybe just a bit longer, dear."

I looked at Violet, hoping she'd see that grandmother was tired. She gave me a sad semblance of a half-smile. "You go ahead and go home, Mom. I'll be fine, I promise. And the next time you want to come, I won't deny your visit." My grandmother hesitated. "I promise." She lifted her hand on top of the table and made like she was going to reach for Nana's hand, then drew hers back. Out of shame or knowing she wasn't supposed to touch anyone, I wasn't sure—either one would have surprised me since that would mean she had a conscience.

Hesitantly, my grandmother stood up, looked at the guard, and reached over to kiss Violet on the cheek. I could tell she wanted to hug her, and it pained me to see her denied that. I blinked away tears.

Nana walked ahead of me, and I stopped before following and turned toward Violet for a moment, another guard watching me closely. I had to ask. "Violet?"

"Yes?" she looked at me, a small ray of hope shining in her dimmed eyes.

"What did Lenny give you that I, your flesh and blood, your child, couldn't? What did he give you that was so important?"

She studied me carefully, then said, "You. He gave me you, Melanie. But he never knew it."

My knees buckled, and I grabbed the edge of a table to stay on my feet as I listened to her, in a detached tone, reveal a past that made my worst nightmare pale in comparison. The room seemed to sway around me until I felt a firm grip on my elbow. I focused on the dark hand that kept me from crashing to the floor. The news had shaken my foundation so severely that for a moment, I was disoriented and thought it was Claire who'd taken hold of my elbow. When I finally pulled it together, I searched around me. Violet had escaped the effect of the blow she'd dealt me. But more than that, and more importantly, I was grateful my grandmother had as well.

11

Before we left the prison to go home, I went to the restroom, and Nana followed. I lingered in the stall until she left to wait with Jack. I slowly opened the door and peeked out to be sure no one else was in there. Finding it empty, I walked on heavy legs and leaned my weight against the counter with the sinks, the palms of my hands rested on the top, my fingers curled underneath, clutching tightly.

I stared at my reflection in the mirror, my eyes even brighter against my now pale complexion. Nana and Jack knew me well enough that they'd be able to see right through any facade I tried to portray. I just hoped they would give me the space to sort through everything without having to regurgitate the garbage Violet fed me.

Thank goodness Nana was lost in her thoughts on the entire ride home, and Jack gave me the space he knew I needed. When I dropped him off, I stepped out of the car to hug him, promising to call him when I was capable of talking through everything.

You. He gave me you. Violet's words haunted me. Lenny was my father? The thought was so ludicrous I almost wanted to laugh. Or throw up. My range of emotions covered every dot of the spectrum. I'd always wondered who my father was. I hoped, I dreamed, I imagined. Growing up, I'd see a man about my mother's age and wonder if that could be my father. I looked at every man as a possibility, wishing some were and praying to God some weren't. Lenny was one I would have prayed to God wasn't. But he was. This had to be some cruel joke. But by who—Violet or God? In my heart of hearts, I knew it wasn't God.

The news weighed heavy—a dead weight, pardon the pun. Would I have wanted to know Lenny had I known before that he was my father? And more importantly, would I have forgiven him when he asked? And had he known I was his daughter? Violet said she never told him, but can I trust anything she said? I remembered the green eyes I'd seen in pictures, and they haunted me now nearly as much as Violet's confession. No one else in my family had such unique green eyes—only me. And now Max.

Suddenly a tornado of thoughts stormed through my head, and I was on the verge of a panic attack when we finally pulled back into Birch Haven. However, as soon as we crossed the town line, my anxiety quieted to a dull roar. I was back home in familiar territory—my turf. I finally felt some semblance of control again.

When I dropped off my grandmother, I walked her in and stayed with her until she let me know it was okay for me to leave because she planned to lie down for a nap. The fact that she wanted a nap at four o'clock in the afternoon spoke volumes and made me a bit suspect. She rarely napped at all. I made her a cup of herbal tea, set it by her side, covered her with a green fleece blanket, and locked the door behind me.

I fished my phone out of my pocket and texted Levi: *Just dropped my grandmother off. Running one more errand and then going home. Probably spending the night in town again tonight. Talk later?* I wanted to talk to him, or better yet, see him, but there was one more thing I needed to do first. Someone else I needed to see, and it couldn't wait until tomorrow.

Levi shot a text back within seconds, which meant he was up and getting things done before going to work for the night. *You okay?*

Been a long day, I tapped back. *Tell ya later.*

I took tonight off. Come by?

Your house or my grandmother's? I really should stay with her tonight.

Understand. Okay if I come by there? He sent back to me.

Hoping you would. Looking forward to seeing you. I watched the three tiny dancing dots on the bottom of the screen, waiting for another response. When the dots disappeared and another message never came, I dropped my phone into the center console. I needed to regroup before I made the next call. Home was the best place to do that.

When I walked through the door, I half expected it to look different. My entire life had been upended today; everything I knew to be true had changed. Instead, everything was the same, and it was like a warm embrace from an old friend. I shed my coat and boots, grabbed a bottle of orange seltzer water from my fridge, turned, and put it back, opting for hot cocoa instead.

After sticking a left-over candy cane from Christmas in the hot mug of chocolate, I walked over to the sofa and sank deep into the cushions. I tucked my legs underneath me and rested my head against the back of the couch, staring at the ceiling. A silvery cobweb waved its appearance. I looked away from the reminder that it was time for a good deep cleaning. The thought exhausted me. At this point, each breath was exhausting. I replayed the day's events over and over until I thought my head would explode.

I picked up my phone then set it back down on the cushion beside me. It would be nice to spend time alone here with Levi tonight, but I had to get back to my grandmother. At least for this one more night. She'd looked so frail. And his presence at her house two evenings in a row would make her happy. She loved the man almost more than I did. Almost.

I picked up my phone again. Delaying the inevitable was only drawing it out. Pulling up the list of previous contacts, I scrolled to the one I needed. I paused for a minute, took a deep breath, and tapped in the words, *Max, this is Melanie. We need to talk. It can't wait until tomorrow. Five-thirty at the same coffee shop as initially planned for tomorrow?*

I watched the screen for what seemed like hours but was only minutes. I drained the last of my hot cocoa, licked the candy cane, savoring the sweet peppermint, before going upstairs to my loft bedroom to change and grab a change of clothes for tomorrow. The one set of clothes I kept at my grandmother's I wore today. I threw a few more items into a duffel bag and went back downstairs. Just as I reached the bottom, my phone chimed with an incoming text. I sucked in my breath and stood rooted in place before finally getting the nerve to look at the screen.

Need to drop Daisy off with my mom first. Can we make it six?

That works, I typed back.

I thought about calling Nana to let her know I'd be there about seven but didn't want to wake her if she was still sleeping. After another moment, I picked up my phone and called anyway. I had a heaping suspicion that she may have wanted some time alone and hadn't planned to nap at all. She answered on the second ring and sounded a bit more refreshed. And just as I'd suspected, she hadn't slept. Instead, she finished crocheting the last afghan. And also, just as I'd suspected, she was thrilled that Levi was stopping by again.

"You don't have to babysit this old woman," she'd said when I told her I was spending the night again. But I knew she was secretly happy about it when she didn't object further.

I slipped into a pair of tennis shoes instead of my boots—a rare occasion for sure—a black leather coat and wrapped a black and white plaid scarf around my neck. I opened the door to my Jeep and slid onto the still-warm seat. Seat warmers were a must when I looked for this car, and they were so worth it in a state where I swear the temperatures were sometimes too cold for polar bears to survive.

The ride back to town went too fast; my mind flooded with today's revelation and the endless possibilities the direction of the upcoming conversation could go. My mother hadn't had another child, but Lenny possibly did. And were there any more of us out there?

Before I knew it, I was pulling into the parking lot of Stomping Grounds Coffee Shop. I took a deep breath before opening my car door. My legs shook and felt a bit unstable, but they managed to carry me to the entrance without incident. I looked around the room then glanced at my watch. Five-fifty. I walked up to the counter and ordered my drink—decaf dark roast, no room for cream. Caffeine was the last thing I needed. My heart already felt like it was going to jump right out of my chest. When I reached to grab my cup, my hand visibly shook. "Can I get a lid, please?" I asked the barista.

She smiled and slid one across the counter. "Here ya go," she chirped, revealing pink and green rubber bands on braces.

I captured a corner table next to a window, away from the hub of activity, and watched the door. At six-oh-five, Max ambled in. Instead of waving at him, I watched as he scanned the group of people in the front then the rest of the room, finally seeing me. He put up a hand in acknowledgment then stepped up to the counter. I studied him, his movements and his features, as he waited. I tried to remember what Lenny looked like, but I hadn't seen him but a couple of times in a photo or two. Other than his eyes, I couldn't remember anything other than the image of his dead body.

Next, I found myself looking for similarities to Violet—anything at all—just in case my less-than-honest mother had lied again. The mother Max spoke of might have adopted him. But there were no similarities that I could see. I was relieved but had no idea why, other than it would be less messy if he were Lenny's child and not Violet's. I already had a bazillion questions. He had short, dark-brown hair, longer on top with loose curls. A strand curled down onto his forehead. He had deep dimples in a face that looked like he hadn't shaved in a few days. His tall, thin, yet strong frame looked like he was perhaps a runner. Or perhaps a swimmer. I remembered his oh-so-serious eyes from when he'd come to the salon. And the familiar striking green. Mine were proving to be more common than I'd ever thought.

He turned toward me, drink in hand, and I quickly looked away, embarrassed that he caught me staring at him. He set his cup on the table, slid out of his pea coat, and hung it on the back of his chair. He left his black scarf draped around his neck.

We both sat looking at one another in awkward silence until he spoke up.

"So I'll get right to it. What did you hear that required meeting this evening instead of tomorrow as planned?" His voice was soft, from lips that resembled a perpetual pout. There was a sadness in his eyes that belied his tone.

"And I'll get right to it too," I said, observing him. "Is Lenny your father, or is Violet your mother? I'm assuming it's one or the other." I had a strong suspicion which it was but needed to hear it anyway.

He took a drink of his tea, the string of the teabag hanging alongside his cup. Black Chai. He set his cup back down. "Lenny is — was my father."

My breath caught. "Was? That means you know — you heard —"

"That he's dead? Yes, I heard." Emotion I couldn't place flickered in his eyes.

"How?"

"He was murdered. But you already knew —"

"I mean, how did you hear about it?"

He frowned. "Why wouldn't I? He was my father."

"Did you do it?"

"No."

"Appears a bit suspect that you show up in Birch Haven at the same time I found Lenny's body." I narrowed my eyes at him. "The police will want to question you, ya know."

"I'm aware. They can question away. I've got nothing to hide."

I relaxed a tiny bit. "You can understand why I'm having a difficult time believing all of this. For all my life, I've been an only child. Or so I'd thought." I carefully studied him, his expressions—of which were few and subtle—and his moves—again, which were few and subtle. "And you can certainly understand why I have so many questions. Instead of scattering bits of information like feed to chickens, maybe you could start at the beginning. Spare us both the time and frustration."

He sat back, coffee cup in hand, and crossed his legs, an ankle resting on the knee of the opposite leg. He wore brown leather zipper slip-on loafers.

"You said Daisy is with your mom. Who's your mom? What's her name? And does she live here in Birch Haven?" I mentally ran through all my clients, those about the age his mother would be.

"I thought you wanted me to start at the beginning."

"I do. But I have questions. Who is your mom?"

"She lives in Phoenix, Arizona. That's where I grew up."

"You said Daisy is with her now?"

"Yes, but here in Birch Haven. When my mother dropped all of this on me a couple of months ago, I told her I planned to find you. Which wasn't difficult, by the way. You ought to be more careful."

I narrowed my eyes. "Meaning?"

"Meaning it's no wonder Lenny's goons found you. You're a sitting duck with having your own business and all. Advertising, phone book—let's just say it took minimal research to find you."

"Goody." I rolled my eyes. "In my defense, who'd a thought thugs from California would be looking for me in the first place? Or some man who claims to be a half-brother? You do have proof, I assume?" He twisted and fiddled with the white gold band on his left ring finger. "You're married?"

"Yes."

"Yes, you're married, or yes, you have proof?"

"Both." He slid a piece of paper my way—his birth certificate.

"This only shows Lenny is *your* father. I don't know for sure that he's mine. The information didn't exactly come from a reputable source." I looked at the paper again and tapped my finger on it. "Are you telling me you've never seen your birth certificate before now? I find that hard to believe." His credibility dipped about even with Violet's.

"It used to be just my mother's name on it. But we went through the court process and got an order to add Lenny's name. A relatively short, uncomplicated process."

My mouth dropped open, and I squinted. "Why would you want to do that?"

"In case I need to prove something to anyone. But mostly because it's every child's dream to have two parents. At least it was mine. And when I learned I'd been living a lie forever, I wanted something real and true. Something solid."

"Ha!" I scoffed. "I'd call Lenny a lot of things, but solid would not be one of them."

He didn't react but stayed rather stoic. "My mother is here as proof as well. It's one of the reasons she came here with me. To help with Daisy and to be the proof if you shouldn't believe me."

"And why would I believe her if I don't believe you?"

"Because she has details that would put to rest any doubt you might have."

"Why not bring her to begin with? Are you so certain I'm that gullible to believe anything a strange man has to say?"

"Thought I'd give it a shot first. I'm not exactly happy with my mother at the moment, and spending time with her isn't my favorite thing to do these days."

"We do have that in common," I said, shook my head slowly, then took a sip of my coffee.

"You too?"

117

"You could say that. At least your mother isn't in prison."

He took a deep breath. "Yeah, I heard about that. I'm sorry."

"Don't be. She earned her place there." An awkward silence followed. Max shifted in his chair, uncrossing his legs, and recrossing them the other way. "How did you come to find all this out? Did guilt get the best of your mom, and she just blurted out one day, 'Hey Max, by the way, your real father is a criminal bookie who is also a murderer'?"

He sighed and sat back in his chair. "Let me start at the beginning as you originally proposed I do."

12

Max toyed with his cup for a moment before looking into my eyes. I shivered. It was like looking into a mirror.

He said, "Up until the time she told me about Lenny, I thought my stepfather, George, was my real father. It wasn't until after my father died—George, not Lenny—and my mother found out Lenny was ill and dying that she decided to tell me the truth. She had no way of knowing that Lenny would die so soon or in the manner he did."

"Are you sure about that?" His cheek twitched. I'd touched a nerve, and oddly, I regretted it. This man, whether I liked him or not, had been nothing but honest so far as I could tell. Yet, I had to know. And I couldn't unless I asked the hard questions.

"What are you getting at?"

"Someone killed him, Max. How much did your mother hate him?"

"I could ask you the same thing." His voice was tight.

He may be upset with his mother for keeping this news from him, but he sure didn't take kindly to someone accusing her of murder. "Mine's already in prison for murder. Unless she sneaked out at night, killed him, and sneaked back into her cell, which we both know isn't possible—"

"Did she know someone on the outside to do the job for her?" he asked.

I shook my head. "Sadly, I already thought of that. No. When I told her about his passing this afternoon, she seemed genuinely surprised. And sad." Those words coming from my lips surprised the heck out of me. The fact that I believed her said I had made enormous progress over the past year or so. "Besides, Lenny would have had his goons go after *her*, if anything. Prison is probably the safest place for her. You don't roll over on a criminal and get away without any consequences."

I'd been the recipient of those consequences last summer, but I wasn't telling Max about that yet. Someday maybe. Depending on how this whole thing played out. I was used to — and liked — my grandmother and I, alone, just the two of us. There was a real threat of that bond getting disrupted by another party. I could stop this right now if I wanted to, and part of me did want that. But a larger part of me wanted to know if I truly did have a brother. I realized I'd been staring at him and quickly looked away, my face burning with embarrassment.

"Except your eyes, I don't see any physical characteristics of Lenny in you either, if that's what you were looking for," he said.

"It wasn't. How old are you?" He looked taken aback, but only slightly. This man didn't show enough emotion for me to read him at all, and it was unnerving. "Just wondering which of us was first. *If* what you claim is true."

"I'm older."

"How can you be sure? I never told you my age."

"You didn't have to. You look like you're about thirty. Even if I'm off by a few years, you're still younger than me."

"Flattery," I said flatly.

"Forty-five."

With the lack of energy behind the age confession, he may as well have said ninety-five. "How did your mom and Lenny meet?"

"At a bar."

I chuckled. "How unique."

"Nothing good happens when you meet someone in a bar. Not in my experience, anyway."

There was a small flicker of something in his eyes, but I couldn't tell what it was. "And?" I pressed. "What happened?"

"According to my mom, they had a volatile relationship. Lenny didn't want anything to do with the child—that'd be me—and ordered her to have an abortion. Instead, she left the city and had me without telling him and married my dad—George—when I was about ten months old."

"That's why you thought he was your real dad. You were too young to know anything different."

He nodded. "Right. And George feared that if Lenny found out my mom had the baby, that he would someday take me away from him. So he and my mom moved to Phoenix and agreed to keep it quiet. Said nothing good would come from me having any contact with Lenny. I can see why they would have made that decision when I was young. But when I was older, they had no right to keep it from me. I had a right to know who my biological father was."

I took a drink of coffee and shook my head. "Why? What good would it have done? Would you have been okay knowing you had a criminal for a father? How would that have made you feel better?"

"It was my right to determine whether I wanted him in my life or not."

"Knowing who he was, would you have made that choice? Think about it, Max."

He looked away, then back at me, and grumbled, "You already sound like an annoying little sister. Don't make me regret finding you."

"Don't get ahead of yourself. I haven't decided whether I'm your sister yet or not."

"It's not a choice you get to make. Lenny made that choice for you. We can do a DNA test if that'll make you feel better."

"Might," I said. "How did your mom know about me?"

"She looked Lenny up years later. He was her first love, and she just couldn't let him go. A secret she'd kept from my dad." His voice quivered slightly. "He died, never knowing his wife always loved another man." He looked away from me again, then focused on his cup. "I think that's the part that makes me the most ticked off. That so many lives were built on lies. My whole family structure."

I shuddered. What a horrible thought. Mine was based on the truth—that my mother just didn't want me. Ugly, but still true. "Well, either Lenny was a whole lot different back then, or your mother had meager standards."

"A life of crime'll take its toll on you. Besides, love is love, I guess." He exhaled and shook his head slowly. "We often don't choose it; it chooses us."

I wrinkled my nose. "That sounds like a very bad poem."

"The one I feel bad for is my dad. He was an exceptional father and role model. He got cheated by his wife and raised a son that he knew wasn't his."

"Wait," I said, holding up a finger when I remembered an earlier statement. "Weren't you the least bit suspicious that George's name wasn't on your birth certificate?"

"Not really. I knew they hadn't married until after I was born so I just assumed that's why they got married."

"You just assumed and never asked?" I said, incredulously.

He shrugged. "Guess it wasn't important to me. Those things happen all the time. That and I'm obviously not as nosey as you."

Touché. "Did she love him? George?"

"I think so. She just couldn't get over Lenny. My dad got second best. He deserved so much more than that."

"Why are you upset with your mother for not telling you about Lenny but not your father? Seems they're both equally at fault."

He shrugged again, his eyes looking far away. "Guess it's easier to be mad at the living than the dead."

A bitter laugh escaped my lips. "That works in Lenny's favor then, doesn't it?" I took a moment to regroup. "Did he ever know about you?"

Now it was his turn to laugh bitterly. "My mother told him about me two years ago. He said he'd like to meet me. Said he was thinking of getting out of," he raised two fingers on each hand, curling them into quotations, "the business." He dropped his hands again. "My first reaction when I heard he was dead was to assume they— whoever *they* are—killed him when he tried to get out. They don't let you out once you're in."

I squinted at him. "What the heck? Are you saying he was in the mafia?"

"May as well have been," he said.

"But I thought he was the one who called all the shots," I said.

"There's always someone else bigger and higher up."

"Unless you're the top."

"Even if that were the case, it wouldn't be a stretch to imagine someone lower on the pole killing him so they can be the top. Have you noticed anyone odd following you lately?"

I shrugged. "Just you."

He remained stoic. "Anyone else?"

I thought about it then shook my head. "Not that I could prove. You watch too many crime shows. *The Godfather* is probably your all-time favorite movie."

He reared back as if I'd slapped him and said, "It's a classic."

That was agreement enough for me. I shook my head. "No, I think it's more personal than that. If one of his goons wanted him dead, why wouldn't they have killed him in California?"

"Maybe they did."

I chortled. "What, they just transported a dead body on an airplane without anyone noticing?"

"It's called car transportation," he said dryly.

"Fair enough. But the fact that he was killed—" I tossed my hand up— "God only knows where—and placed in front of my salon, someone purposely wanted me to find him. Why?"

"I told him I was coming here to find you. Maybe he did the same."

"Unfortunate for him," I quipped.

125

"It wouldn't be out of the question to assume he told someone from his payroll—obviously the wrong person—that he was coming here and that you're his daughter."

I shivered and gagged as if I'd just eaten a slimy oyster. "Eww. Saying that out loud makes it too real. I'm not ready for that. Besides, I haven't decided if it's real yet."

"Again, it's not up to you to decide if it's real. It's only up to you whether you're going to accept it or not."

I screwed up my mouth and said, "I'm leaning more toward *not*."

"Denial won't change the facts," he said.

I marveled at how he could be so matter-of-fact about the whole ordeal. Although, he'd had more time to process this thing than just a matter of hours as I had. But even still, how could he be so kind to me instead of resenting the heck out of me? More time to process it only gave him more time to develop a bigger resentment. And yet, it didn't appear that way. "Denial is sometimes an easier land to live in than the alternative."

"Only prolongs accepting the inevitable."

"Or not," I countered.

"Or not," he repeated and half-heartedly shrugged.

"You never told me how your mother found out about me."

"She looked Lenny up a few years after marrying my dad—George—and saw him linked to your mother. When she arranged to run into him to see for herself how serious it was, she immediately knew that they weren't just friends. Seeing him with your mother was what it took. She closed that chapter of her life for good. Years later, curiosity got the best of her again, and she looked up your mother and did her homework. All the while, my stepdad was in the dark. If he did know, he never let on. She found out Violet had a daughter, put the timing together when she saw her with Lenny. She contacted your mother, they talked, and commiserated with one another. Over him."

A spark of anger in his eyes was the first sign of something other than complete composure I'd seen since we'd begun talking. But just as quickly, it was gone again. "Violet told your mother about me? That Lenny was supposedly my father?"

He nodded. "Yes. My mother said she and your mother—"

I put my hand up, palm facing him. "Wait—you keep saying 'your mother'. It's Violet. I call her Violet."

He nodded and said, "Noted. My mother and *Violet* said they felt a connection with one another, knowing their children were siblings."

"And they chose to keep that from us?" Anger toyed with me at that revelation.

"Your moth—Violet swore my mother to secrecy. And she held onto that secret until late last summer, early fall, when Lenny called to tell her he was dying. Cancer. He said he was leaving everything he had to me as his only heir."

I narrowed my eyes. "Then why did you find me? Why risk having to share the inheritance, however meager it might be."

He chuckled, the first sign of happiness I'd seen. "Oh, it's not meager. To say his empire was substantial is an understatement. There's more than enough for the two of us."

"You realize this is even more reason for the police to like you for the murder. Not that I'm complaining because it takes the heat off me."

"Thanks," he grumbled.

"Well, I don't want his money. It's dirty," I said with indignant determination.

"All money is. The root of all evil and all that jazz," he said, his tone flat again.

"It's crime money, Max. Could you, in good conscience, accept it?"

He shrugged. "If we don't, it'll go somewhere. And what good would that do? The state will determine how best to distribute his assets."

"Which means the government will get it," I said more to myself than to him. I looked at him and smirked. "Huh. You have to appreciate the irony in that."

His eyes sparkled. Just a little, but they did. "Yes, I do appreciate the irony in that. When my mother found out Lenny was dying, she broke her promise to your mother and told him about you. She wanted him to have the chance to get to know his daughter. But obviously, he didn't reach out to you. But like I said, it's probably why he was here to begin with."

So Violet had been wrong. He did find out about me. She just didn't know it. Or did she? I thought about the phone call last fall. "He called me and asked for my forgiveness. I couldn't, and I didn't."

He nodded. I expected judgment, but nothing came. "If you knew then what you know now, would you have forgiven him?"

"That's a tough question to answer. Eventually, maybe. But not so we could have a relationship. He burned that bridge long ago."

"I don't blame you."

"You don't?" I gave him a sidelong look.

"No. He told me what he did."

His statement shook me off my center for the ten millionth time. In a matter of two days, it seemed like everything I knew to be true wasn't, and everything I didn't know was, in fact, true. "Why would he do that?"

"Was trying to make last-minute amends, he said. Guess death makes a person do that."

"Daisy," I said, desperately needing a change of verbal scenery. "Tell me about her."

He relaxed and sat back in his chair, smiling a natural, genuine smile. His eyes brightened, appearing almost electric. "As you already know, she's nine going on eighteen. And a spitfire at that."

I grinned at the image. "Sounds like my best friend Claire's daughter, Sydney."

He shook his head slowly. "Daisy's the reason I get up every day. The reason I do life."

I told him about my mysterious phone calls and, after I finished, asked, "Why do you think someone would have been calling me asking for Daisy? Who knows about our — well, our *possible* connection?" At this point, I knew in my heart it was greater than just a mere possibility but wasn't quite ready to make it official by admitting it.

"My guess is it was Pam, Daisy's mother. She hasn't been in the picture for the past year except for when she needs something."

"Like the other night at the salon."

"Yeah, about that." He shook his head slowly. "Her supposed friend that called didn't know anything about the phone call. When I got to the address the caller gave me, the woman was completely confused, said she doesn't even know a Pam."

The image of the car beneath the broken security camera popped into my head. I told Max about it and he frowned. "Now I wonder if it was one of Lenny's men — or women, in this case since it was a woman who called — trying to steer you away."

"Someone was," he agreed. "I think you'd better watch yourself closely."

"You too. For all we know, whoever killed Lenny could make one of us his next target." I shivered as I glanced around the coffee shop. "What's the deal with Pam?"

He took a deep breath, exhaling slowly. "Long story for another time. I think we've both had as much conversation as we can handle for one sitting. I don't know about you, but I'm exhausted."

"You're an introvert," I said. "Me too."

"A what?"

I half-smiled. "That's for another time, as well. But yes, I'm spent and need some space." I pushed my chair back, the legs scraping on the floor. As I stood, a loud crash beside me hurtled me back down into my chair. I screamed and ducked when shattered glass from the window beside me rained over the table and landed on me, causing painful pinching on my hand. A commotion ensued as other customers rushed over.

"Gunshot!" someone yelled, and more screams followed.

It was as if everything was happening in slow motion. I put my arm up, shielding my face from the unknown, and saw a brick balancing on the edge of our table. I looked at the window then toward Max. He reached for the brick, but I put my hand on his. "Don't touch it," I said. "Not unless you want your fingerprints on it."

He frowned. "They'll know it wasn't me. I'm sitting right here with you."

"You could compromise any fingerprints that *are* on it."

He studied me through narrowed eyes. "Have experience in this sort of thing, huh?" He looked back at the near murder weapon. "Looks like there's a message written on it."

I looked closely without moving it. *Drop dead Melanie.* My blood turned cold. Had I not pushed my chair back and stood just before the brick came through the window, I would have done just that. Die. "Oh, there's a message on it, all right," I said.

13

The red, white, and blue lights of Birch Haven's finest lit up the sky above the Stomping Grounds Coffee Shop's parking lot. Levi wasn't far behind.

"I was at Rose's having a nice conversation while we waited for you when Cole called me," he said, folding me into a hug. "You're trembling."

"At least I'm alive to tremble. Please tell me you didn't say anything to my grandmother," I said, pulling back and looking deep into his eyes. "She's had enough stress for one day."

He shook his head. "No, I didn't. I just told her I had a call that needed my attention. It wasn't a lie." He pulled me close again before I felt the muscles in his back stiffen. He stepped back and nodded toward Max, who stood silently at my side. "Who's this?"

I imagined how it must have looked. Levi waiting for me at my grandmother's while I was having coffee with another man. "You wouldn't believe it if I told you," I blurted before Max could say a word.

"Try me." He sized up Max and looked at me, waiting for an answer.

"This," I said, jerking my thumb toward Max, "might be my half-brother—Max."

Levi appeared to search for words, but nothing came. He shook his head. "You didn't think to tell me you were meeting him here?" His eyes never wavered from Max as he talked to me.

"I know how it looks. And, yes, I should have mentioned it."

"That would have been nice. And much safer."

"I'm no threat," Max said, putting his hands up, palms facing Levi.

"No offense, but I have every intention of making sure of that," Levi said before breaking his stare and looking at me.

"I have so much to tell you," I said as I closed my eyes, tipped my head back, and rubbed the back of my neck.

"Melanie," Levi said, shaking his head slowly, "I just spoke with you this morning. How much can happen in one day?"

I laughed bitterly. "Oh, you have no idea. I'll tell you everything, but not here." I looked at Max and back at Levi. "I still need to stay with my grandmother tonight, though."

"I'll follow you there," he said.

"It'll be late by the time we're done here, won't it?"

"Shouldn't be. The guys'll be here a while, but there's no reason you need to be. For once, you won't be considered a suspect."

Max's eyebrows shot up. "Maybe I should have asked *you* a few more questions," he said.

"If you knew, you'd just be one more in a line of people who suspect me," I said.

Levi took his coat off and wrapped it around my shoulders. I pulled it tightly around me as I shivered against the frigid air and adrenaline still racing through me.

"You're bleeding," he said.

I glanced at my hand he held in his as he inspected it. "It's fine."

He pulled out a tissue and blotted at the blood. "I'll see about someone getting your statement done so I can get you out of here." He was back within moments with a cop following him. "Officer Winn said he can take your statement now and Max's right after that."

It didn't take long to give my statement because I didn't have much to tell. I was dumbfounded as to who it might have been. When I finished, we went to where Max patiently waited.

Levi looked at Max. "Talk tomorrow?"

"Sure."

As we left him with Officer Winn, Max gave Levi a two-finger salute.

***

My thoughts tumbled and tripped over one another on the drive back to my grandmother's house. I had called her while I was still at the coffee shop, letting her know I was having coffee with a friend but that I'd be at her house right afterward. *Friend* was pushing it, but what else could I say? I'm having coffee with my half-brother? Not without a bit of warning for her first. And I couldn't give her that explanation over the phone. This news required a face-to-face chat.

When I pulled into her yard, a dim light glowed through the kitchen curtain, and I could see a sliver of light between the drawn living room drapes. Either she was still up, or she left the lights on for me. I partly wished it was later so she would be in bed; that way, I wouldn't have to worry about telling her anything tonight. However, this way, I could tell both she and Levi at the same time and only explain once between the two of them. There would be a second time for Claire, but not until tomorrow. It occurred to me that before Levi and I got involved, Claire was the first one I talked to about everything. And vice versa before she and Cole. A pang of emptiness gnawed at me, but I chalked it up to processing how closely I'd come to death tonight.

Levi pulled his car up behind mine and followed me into the house. Nana met us at the door and pulled me into a hug.

"Come in out of the cold, you two. What are the odds that both of you got back at the same time?" She narrowed her eyes and answered her own question. "Not very good." She looked at Levi. "Your call had to do with my granddaughter, didn't it?"

He nodded. "Yes, ma'am, it did. I can't lie to you."

Nana's gaze settled on me. "I think you have some explaining to do, Melanie."

I looked up at Levi, who shrugged and smirked. "What? You heard the lady."

I took a deep breath. "Okay, you two, let's go in here," I said as I led them into the living room. "You'll both need to sit down for this. Nana, how are you doing? It was a tough day for you." She settled in her rocker, and Levi and I sat on the couch.

"I'm stronger than you think, dontcha know," she said. "I keep telling you I'm not some frail old woman. Old, yes. Frail, no. Now on with it." Her long, silver braid hung over her shoulder.

I chuckled. "Yes, ma'am."

"I already told Levi about the visit to the jail today," she said. "I hope you don't mind. But you weren't here, and he wanted to know."

I smiled at her. "Why would I mind? I expected you would." I took another deep breath, then started in, first by telling her about Max and Daisy coming to the salon when the ladies and I attempted to have some overdue R&R together after hours. I studied her for a moment as she sat perched in her recliner, then I moved to the edge of the couch, holding Levi's hand.

"Nana, there's one part of what happened at the prison with Violet that you don't know about yet. I wasn't keeping it from you, I promise. I just needed time to process it first."

"When we left?" she asked. I nodded. "I turned around once the guard led me out, and you weren't there. I assumed you had something you had to say to her. I sat with Jacky until you came out."

"Violet dropped quite the bomb on me," I said. I looked from my grandmother to Levi and back again. A lump formed in my throat. "She told me who my biological father is."

"Who?" They both asked at the same time.

My grip tightened on Levi's hand in anticipation of his reaction, but I focused on my grandmother. In addition to the lump in my throat came a knot in the pit of my stomach. "Lenny." Saying it out loud had a similar effect as if I'd just swallowed a giant gulp of sour milk.

"Lenny?" They both echoed one another again. Nana's eyes grew wide, and her mouth fell open. Levi's fingers clasped mine a bit tighter.

I nodded. I was so dizzy from the events of the day I thought I might be sick. "Can I ask you to get me a glass of water?" I asked Levi.

"Dear Lord, the lady really has had a difficult day," he said, eyes wide. "Not only is she *letting* me do something for her, she *asked* me."

I rested my hand on his leg. "You're just a laugh a minute. And don't get used to it."

"I knew it was too good to be true," he said, shaking his head, a small smile playing on his lips. "I'll get you water, but I need something stronger after that bombshell," he said as he rose from the couch. "Rose, can I get you a cup of tea?" he called from the kitchen doorway.

"I'm good, dear," she said. "But thank you."

I waited for him to get back before I continued. My grandmother had rare worry lines creasing between her eyebrows.

As soon as he sat down, she said, "Okay, go on. What did your mother tell you?"

I absently studied the water in the glass for a moment, then took a drink before starting. Levi traced comforting circles on the back of my hand with his thumb. "Violet met Lenny on her first trip out to California. He swept her off her feet, promised her the moon. Instead, she ended up pregnant and alone. That's why she came back here."

"Did she tell him she was pregnant?" my grandmother asked, sitting forward, elbows on her knees, hands clasped.

I shook my head. "No. She said she knew he didn't want children and that, to be honest, she didn't want children either but didn't know what to do. She thought leaving me with you and Granddad was the best thing for all of us."

"Well, I know it was the best thing for your granddad and me," Nana said, her voice filled with emotion. My grandmother was the strongest woman I knew, but even a sturdy oak can break if the wind is strong enough. And the winds these days seemed to be of hurricane force.

"She said when she went back out there, they tried to make it work, but it wasn't good for either one of them. Instead, they maintained their business relationship and kept it at that."

"Exactly what kind of business?" Levi asked. "I mean, I know it's betting, gambling, the likes, but did she give any more specifics?"

"No. And I didn't ask. I was doing my best just listening without throwing up," I said. "I can't believe she kept this from me all these years. Until after that man was dead." I stood up and paced from one side of the room to the other. "I mean, why tell me at all?" Another wave of nausea hit, and I folded my arms in front of my stomach. "For so many years, Nana, every man I saw that was about Violet's age—heck, even men much older—I would look at them and wonder if they were missing a daughter." I sat back down beside Levi, and he lightly rubbed circles on my back, the warmth of his hand medicine for my soul. "After I dropped you off at home, Nana, I went to my house and processed all that I'd heard. It was then I knew I had to contact Max." I looked at Levi. "That's why I hadn't told you yet. I was trying to figure out the bag of crap dropped on my doorstep." I shook my head, clearing away the potential consequences of the news. "I believed what Violet said about not having any other children but knew it wasn't a stretch that Lenny might have.

"I texted Max, and after he dropped off Daisy with his mother, he met me at the Stomping Grounds Coffee Shop." I continued to fill them in on our conversation and all that I'd learned. "As we were leaving, I stood up, and a brick came flying through the window. Someone yelled, 'Gunshot!' Then there was a moment of panic that spread throughout the room. Had I not slid my chair back, stood, and taken a step back when I did, that brick would have hit my head. And it had a message for me."

"How do you know it was for you?" Nana asked. I hesitated. "You must tell me, dear."

"Because it said *Drop dead Melanie* on the brick. In red."

She gasped, her blue eyes enormous in her frail, tired face. "Levi, is my granddaughter in danger? You must protect her."

"You know I'll do everything in my power to be sure she's safe," he assured her.

"Can you stay at the house with her?"

"Nana, you know he can't stay indefinitely," I said quickly. "He has a house. And we don't know how long it will take to catch this guy. Besides, Levi works nights which is when I'm home. And Claire is right across the field from me. I'll be fine." I could tell I hadn't convinced her. "I promise if there's anything that's out of the ordinary, I'll come into town, okay? I'm staying here tonight, aren't I?"

"Yes, but that's because you think you need to keep an eye on me."

I chuckled. "The apple doesn't fall far from the tree, as the old saying goes."

"I want to check out Max's story," Levi said. "I know he sounds legitimate, showed you his birth certificate—which, honestly, proves nothing—and the things his mother told him are pretty convincing that he's telling the truth, but one can never be too careful. Especially after what happened tonight."

"Not to mention his eyes," I said. "They're like looking into a mirror. No one else has green eyes quite like ours." Levi nodded slightly. "You know, I don't even know what he does for work," I said. "Or anything about him, personally, at all. He may be my half-brother, but he's a complete stranger." Silence fell over the room, then I said, "Know what the most frightening thing is? That the thing—the *one* thing—he and I share is Lenny's DNA," I said without waiting for either of them to respond.

"Like I said," Levi said, "I want to have this guy looked into a little further."

"You don't believe him?" I asked. "And I thought I was the skeptical one."

"Oh, you are," Levi quickly assured me. "You definitely are."

I knocked his shoulder with mine. More like his arm since he sat a whole foot taller than me. "There's just too many dots that connect."

"What are the chances that he killed Lenny for the money?" my grandmother asked.

Levi and I shared a quick glance, eyebrows raised, that those words came from such a sweet woman.

"To be honest, I wondered about that too," I said. "But I don't think so. First of all, he wouldn't risk losing Daisy. Second of all, if it's the money he's after, he wouldn't be so willing to share it with me."

"There is that," Levi said. "That being said, the detective part of me just jumped Max to the top of the list and bumped you to the bottom."

I gasped. "You mean I wasn't at the bottom of your list to begin with? How rude!"

He half-smiled. "You've always been at the top of my list, darlin', but at the bottom of the suspect list."

"Good recovery," I said.

"I'm going to relay this information you've given me to Detective Walker—again."

"Tell him he owes me a thank you for solving his case for him," I teased.

"I want to do my own research on this guy too. I want to know his history and what ghosts he's hiding in his closet."

"Being related to Lenny is demon enough," I said.

"How are you doing with this, babe? Truth," he said, watching me closely.

"It's all just been so much to take in. I need some time to process." I thought of Daisy and the similarities we have with absentee screwed-up mothers. "If there's an upside to this whole thing, it's that I've gained a niece. And a cute one at that. About the same age as Syd. And Jackson," I added, looking at Levi.

"What does Max make of someone calling you yesterday asking for Daisy?" Levi asked. "Did you mention it?"

"Yeah. Said it's probably her mother. She's not allowed contact with Daisy right now. I don't know the whole story. We hadn't gotten to that yet."

"Well," my grandmother said, "if this boy is right, and you are half-siblings, it sounds like you have a lot of catching up to do."

"Just do me a favor and don't meet with him anywhere other than a public place for a while," Levi said.

"He was with me when the brick came through the window. He couldn't have thrown it at me."

"Promise me, Melanie," he said, his voice stern.

"You have such little trust in me," I said, giving him a half-smile.

"And she wonders why," he said, getting the first chuckle of the day out of Nana.

14

I lingered in bed Monday morning, burrowed under the weight and warmth of the blankets, and stared out the window. The view from Nana's ranch-style house was at ground level as opposed to the sky through the skylight of my loft bedroom. Ironically, it even made me feel a bit more grounded this morning. The sun was just barely beginning to rise. Ice crystals formed on the window, looking like tiny, jeweled snowflakes. White frost lined each of the tree limbs, looking like a picture-perfect postcard.

I ran yesterday's events through my mind, up to last night when Levi left at twelve-thirty. He asked me to promise him not to meet Max in a nonpublic place, but I didn't promise. Instead, I skirted around it. I couldn't back myself into a corner when there were still so many unknowns. I didn't yet know what was required to get more answers to find out who Lenny's killer was. Finding out he was my biological father put a whole new spin on things. I needed to discover now, more than ever, who killed him and why. They'd made an effort to let me know they were aware of the connection between Lenny and me. Was I next? I shivered at the thought.

Never in a million years would I have ever dreamed I'd hear the news that Lenny was my father. I felt an odd sense of closure and nausea at the same time. For Violet and Max's mother to fall so madly in love with this guy made me wonder who he really was. Did he have a good side, or was he simply that good at manipulating women? Now that he was dead, I'd never get to find out. Had he known I was his daughter last summer, would he have pulled the same shenanigans that he did? *Shenanigans* was too light of a word. He had toyed with my life by making me feel as though I was losing my mind and setting me up for murder.

Nana's puttering in the kitchen broke into my thoughts. I heard the water running and a pan or two clanging followed by a soft, "Oh, shoot!"

I broke into a grin, slipped out from under the blankets and into my robe and slippers. I pulled my hair back into a haphazard ponytail, sneaked into the kitchen behind her, and hugged her.

"Morning, Nana. What are you doing up so early?" Her silver hair was hanging loose down her back, free of its typical braid.

She turned, kissed my cheek, and continued with the pans. "Did I wake you? I tried to be quiet, but these pans had other plans."

"I was just lying in bed. It's time to get up anyway." I took one of the pans from her. "Let me make breakfast for you this morning."

"But I'm out of cereal." Her eyes sparkled with amusement.

"Very funny," I said, making a face at her. "Seriously, what do you want?"

"Let's make omelets together," she said. "I'll dice the ham and shred the cheese. You get the eggs out and prepare those."

I paused, bit my lower lip, looked at the refrigerator, then at her. "What do you mean prepare the eggs? I usually chop the ham and grate the cheese. What do you do to *prepare* the eggs? Eggs are just eggs."

Nana laughed softly. If nothing else, it sure was good to see her happy again from yesterday's fiascoes. "You take care of the ham and cheese, dear. I'll get the eggs."

I did as instructed while watching her from the corner of my eye as she flawlessly cracked the eggs into a bowl, added some water, salt, pepper, garlic, a dash of melted butter, and whipped them. "Ouch!" I exclaimed, examining my knuckle. "I shredded my knuckle along with the cheese."

"Get a bandage. Blood isn't an ingredient in my omelets," she said and winked at me.

I rummaged around in the bathroom until I found a flex bandage. By the time I got back to the kitchen, she had both of our assignments done. She folded the filling inside the egg mixture.

"What time do you want to run the afghans to the homeless shelter?" I asked her as I filled her cup with coffee and poured one for me.

"As soon as we finish with breakfast?"

"Works for me," I said, taking a sip from my *Back the Blue Birch Haven Police Department* mug, compliments of Levi. "Levi said he'd come take down the outside Christmas lights today." Last year we didn't get them down until March, so we were doing a little better this year.

"He's such a nice man. Men like that don't come along but once in a lifetime, dontcha know," she said, giving me that look. The one that lets me know I'm doing something wrong.

"I know that, Nana. I don't know what else you want me to say about it. We've had this talk numerous times."

She frowned at me. "I don't know whatever you're talking about. All I said is he's a nice man."

I chuckled and shook my head. "If we go to the shelter right after breakfast, we'll be home easily by noon. I'll call him in a bit and let him know."

"Don't you need to shower?" she asked.

"Why, what are you trying to tell me?" I teased. "I've got a baseball cap in my car. I'll throw that on. Doesn't make sense to shower before packing up your Christmas lights. When we finish with those, I'm just going home anyway."

She dished the omelets, complete with chopped green pepper and shredded cheese garnish on top, while I poured us each a glass of orange juice.

"You forgetting something?" she asked as I took a bite and groaned my delight.

I stopped chewing and looked at her, waiting—until I remembered I'd broken the most important house rule—not a bite before praying over the food. It was a rule that had been drilled into me since as far back as I could remember. Apparently, I was more than a little preoccupied. I quickly set my fork back down, swallowed my food, and took her hand in mine as she said grace. When she finished, I waited for her to take a bite before I continued with mine.

"What have you decided about Max's offer to split the inheritance with you?" she asked.

"I haven't given it any thought. As in none at all." I looked at her. "Weird, huh?"

"Give it some time before you make any decisions," she said. "Until someone reads the will, there might be nothing at all. The man might have been up to his eyeballs in debt, and everything will have to go toward paying it off."

"I honestly wouldn't care if that was the case. I think—well, I think what I'm more worked up about than anything is the fact that I supposedly have a half-brother and a niece." I set my fork down, looked deep into her eyes, and said quietly, "I'm not sure I even want that. I'm used to being alone—just you and me. I don't want anything changing that dynamic. I'll take the niece, but the brother?" I hung my head. "Selfish, isn't it?"

"There's already more to our family than just you and me, dear. Don't discount family we've chosen—Claire,

Jack, Rubie, Sydney, and now Levi and Jackson. We're building quite a tribe, dontcha know." She smiled and gave me a moment to process that truth. Our circle was, indeed, growing. "But don't put the cart in front of the horse, Melanie. Though, the bottom line is if he is your brother and that little girl is your niece, you don't have a choice whether you have other family or not. It is what it is. It's only your choice whether you choose to accept it."

"If I didn't know better, I'd think you were the one who talked with Max," I said. "He said those exact words."

"It's all too new to make any rash decisions right now. You might find out there was nothing to worry about in the first place. Might be that there's some confusion, and it's not true at all."

I studied her closely, what her eyes were telling me and what my heart knew. "You and I both know that's not the case. That he is telling the truth. He has too many details as proof." Then, without any notice at all, tears sprang from my eyes and down my cheeks.

"Oh, my goodness," my grandmother said, turning her chair toward me and pulling me toward her. "Come here." She folded me in her arms, the comfort only making me cry harder.

After a minute, I pulled back, ran my palms over my face, and wiped at the tears. "Nothing like a middle-aged woman acting like a baby." I laughed a short, bitter sound.

"Melanie Hogan," she scolded, "you've had an emotionally charged three days. Crying is completely normal." She snickered and scoffed, "Middle-aged. You're just a hoot."

"Not for me, it's not. Normal to cry, I mean."

"Under these circumstances, it would be normal for anyone. Even you."

"Well, I don't like it," I said defiantly, wiping my face with my hands again.

"Give yourself time to adjust. Whether it's a day, weeks, or even longer, allow yourself that time."

"I would enjoy seeing Daisy, but I'm not ready to see Max again. Not yet."

"Then don't. There will be plenty of time, dontcha know. Doesn't sound like he's going anywhere right now."

I heaved a breath and sat back in my chair before standing up. "I think I'll take a shower after all."

"You've hardly touched your food. Another five bites?" She smiled coyly.

I laughed through new tears, remembering how many times she'd played that game with me as I was growing up. "I'm not hungry." I sat back down. "But I'll sit with you until you're finished. I want to call Claire before we go, too."

"Tell you what. You call Claire, then take a shower. I'll finish up here and get dressed. Goodness gracious! If you wait for me to finish eating before doing your thing," she flung her hand in the air, "we won't get to the shelter before five."

I laughed again. "Drama is Syd's forte."

"Go," she ordered.

***

Two hours later, we were on the road with all of Nana's afghans in the back seat of my Jeep. I looked in my rearview mirror at the rainbow of colors piled there. It was so cold out today that I wanted to wrap one around my grandmother and me, but when the seat warmers kicked in, the thought melted away.

"Good thing you plugged in your Jeep last night," she said. "We could have taken my car since it was in the garage."

"We could have. But this baby started right up." I patted the dash with my gloved hand. If Minnesotans must leave their cars outside in the winters, they depend on block heaters like ice depends on freezing temps.

"How's Claire this morning? Her folks still there?" she asked.

"Yup. I think she's going a little crazy. They've been there for a few days and staying for another two."

"Bet Syd loves it, though."

"Everyone in the house doting on her, are you crazy? I bet she hates it." We both laughed.

"How'd she take your news?"

"I thought she passed out until she finally started talking again. You know how she does that high-pitched squeal when she hears something she didn't expect?" I glanced over at my grandmother. "She didn't even do that. I told her the minimum and will fill her in more when I see her later today. She's dying to get out of the house for a little, so she's stopping by this evening."

"That will be good for you girls. It makes my heart happy when the two of you make time for each other. Both your lives are so busy."

I glanced over and saw wrinkles form between her brows. "What's going on? I don't think this is about Claire and me."

"Just a culmination of events, I suppose."

"Well, I can tell you this, these past few days have been way too heavy. Neither of us is used to this crap." I reached over and touched her arm. "We'll get through this. We always do."

"Turn here," she said, pointing to the right. "We can go in the back door."

I made a sharp turn as we darn near passed the street, and my grandmother grabbed the dash with one hand and the door handle with the other.

"Uffda!" she exclaimed.

"Oops," I said, grinning. "Sorry about that. But without notice, what's a girl to do?"

There were only a handful of cars parked in the back of the building. I zipped in between two of them. Two desperate smokers, a man and a woman, hovered near the door. Huddled as they were, it was difficult to tell how much smoke was from the cigarettes and how much from exhaling into the frigid air. The man reached to pull open the door for us.

"Careful so you don't start your glove on fire there," my grandmother said to the woman holding the cigarette.

"That would be the luck, wouldn't it?" the woman said. "The way it's been lately, I wouldn't be at all surprised if I went up in flames."

The orange glow of her cigarette almost touched the worn, dirty pink knit fabric of her glove. A small, dark stain that resembled old blood made me wonder what happened. I could only imagine what these people had to live with out there on the streets. While they had places like this to take shelter, especially on bitterly cold days and nights, I knew most of them spent the majority of their time outside in the elements, whether those elements be inclement weather, wild animals, or other people. The world could be a cruel place. Her long blond hair hung beneath a pink hat, touching her shoulders, and my heart went out to her. She looked familiar, but I couldn't remember from where. It was like the past few days jumbled my brain cells.

We walked in further, both my grandmother and I carrying afghans and some gloves and hats Nana had picked up on sale. Tables were scattered throughout the large room on tile that might have been white at one time. It was hard to tell. Folks played card and dice games, some eating as if they hadn't had a meal in weeks, and a couple of folks had their heads down on the tables, napping.

Along the edge by the wall, a few people lay curled up and sleeping. They probably hadn't slept well in days, if not weeks. I noticed a woman in the corner by herself. Another went over and sat down by her, words I couldn't hear spoken between the two. The one that had been sitting there first stood, said something in haste, and stalked away.

I turned to see where Nana was and found her in the kitchen talking with some staff members. I strolled over to her.

"Your grandma is the best volunteer we have," said the man. "Everybody just loves her here."

I smiled and looked at her warmly. "Yeah, I kind of love her too. I'm a pretty lucky lady."

"Well, she sure speaks highly of you," said a woman wearing a red and white apron splattered with brown. I could only hope it was gravy.

"I pay her to," I teased and looked around me. "How many people on average do you have here in a day?"

"Twenty-five, give or take," said the man. "The majority are men, but as time goes on, we see more and more women."

"Isn't there a women's shelter here in town? I would think it'd be safer for them there."

"Most of them are domestic violence victims. Homelessness doesn't mean they're DV victims. Many are homeless because of poverty and lack of resources, addictions, mental illness, what have you."

I visually swept the room again. The man and woman from outside were now at one of the tables with a plate of food. One of the women in the earlier argument laid down and balled her coat up for a pillow, jamming her fist into it, making it just so.

After talking for a bit more, my grandmother nodded toward the front door. "Looks like we have another volunteer. A bit overdressed, I'd say."

I glanced behind me to where Nana was focused and frowned. "That's not a volunteer. That's Max."

15

Max scanned the room, his gaze resting on the four of us standing in the kitchen. He paused as if deciding whether to acknowledge us or pretend he didn't see us. Ultimately, he decided to come over to our little group.

"What brings you here?" I asked him. "A text would have been sufficient if you wanted to talk some more. But I, for one, hoped to give it a rest for the day."

He shuffled his feet then glanced around him again. A look of recognition crossed his face on one table in particular. "I'm not here to see you," he said to me.

My cheeks grew hot. *How presumptuous was I?* I turned to look at who he spotted. It was the woman in the pink gloves that had been smoking by the door. "Friend?"

"Melanie, perhaps you would like to introduce us," my grandmother said.

"Sure," I said, keeping my eyes on Max for a moment longer before performing introductions all the way around. "This is Max," I said, gesturing toward him with my hand. "Max, this is my grandmother —"

"Nice to meet you," he said with a hint of a smile before he glanced briefly at the table in the corner. He extended his hand toward my grandmother. His tone was subdued and a bit preoccupied.

"Likewise," Nana said. "And this is Alice and Henry." She nodded toward them.

"Max is from out of state," I said. "I'm assuming you'll be going back as soon as everything is over?"

He looked toward the table across the room again and cleared his throat. "Uh...well...that's uncertain at this time."

"Why?" I asked, my pulse picking up. "Why would you stay?" My heart was confusing me. What was that I felt—a sprig of hope? And why hadn't he mentioned this last evening?

"Would you excuse me for a moment, please?" he asked. As he walked past me, he touched my arm lightly. I flinched. The woman, the smoker from outside, met him halfway across the room, and they began talking.

"Melanie," Nana whispered to me, "trying to listen to someone else's conversation isn't polite."

"I've never been the polite type, Nana," I said, struggling to hear what Max and the woman were saying.

"Never asked you—" the woman said in a harsh whisper, the rest fading away into the background.

"No? How could—someone—not—Daisy—" said Max.

After some heated words from the woman and Max's shoulders slumping slightly, he finally turned and walked toward me. "Rose," he said, "it was nice to meet you." He looked toward Henry and Alice. "Henry, Alice, the pleasure is mine." He shook hands with them and turned toward me.

"I'll walk you to your car," I said. He nodded and started for the door. I turned to my grandmother. "I'll be right back."

"Should I come with you, dear?"

"No, I'll be fine. Stay here where it's warm." She held my gaze, so I leaned in and whispered, "I promise, I'll be fine."

She sighed, giving Max one more glance. "Okay, then, dontcha know. If it's all the same to you, I will stay here and help Henry and Alice for a bit. Would it be too much for me to ask you to come back and pick me up in a while?"

"Certainly. About an hour? Two?"

"You betcha."

I chuckled. "One or two?"

"However long it takes you." She put her hand on my elbow and walked with me to the door, then leaned in toward my ear. "Stay in a public place until Levi has had a chance to look into him a bit more. Seems like a nice young man, but let's be sure, shall we?"

Nana thought everyone was a nice young person. "Know what for sure, that he's not a mass murderer? Or just a murderer. Chip off the old block."

"He might be as different from his father as you are. And as different as you are from your mother. Don't paint them both with the same brush. We just want to be sure before putting yourself in jeopardy."

I tilted my head, digesting her words. Geez, I wasn't only presumptuous, I was quick to judge. This whole revelation had turned me into someone I didn't like so well.

"Why the scowl?" she asked.

"No reason." I kissed her cheek. "I'll call Levi and let him know we won't be back to your house until later this afternoon."

"Sounds good, dear."

I turned to see Max standing in the foyer between the two doors. I followed him outside. "It's freezing out here," he said, "so I'll make it quick."

"That would be nice," I said, shivering and rubbing my hands together before tucking them into the pocket of my black leather coat. "Or we could go somewhere warmer if you're up for it."

"I thought you wanted it to be quick. Not to mention you said you were hoping to give it a rest for the day," he said, cocking his head to the side.

"Changed my mind."

"Naturally," he said. He tilted his head back, exhaled slowly, then looked at me. "Is this what I have to look forward to in having a sister?"

My stomach fluttered at the sound of the word. *Sister.* I'd never been anyone's sister. I didn't know how. And someone's aunt? Oh boy! "You're an only child?" I asked.

"Yes. Or at least I thought I was until a little more than a month ago. I just might decide to travel back in time," he said.

"What was that about back in there?" I asked, jerking my thumb toward the shelter.

"I thought we were going somewhere warmer." He cupped his hands together and blew into them.

"People from warm climates don't know how to dress for the weather here. If you dress appropriately, you wouldn't be so cold right now."

"Says the one shivering," he said, leveling his gaze on me.

I tilted my head then nodded slowly. "Yeah, there's a good chance we might be related." He stared at me through white clouds of fog with each breath. Or *condensation*, as my grandmother taught me when I was about five and obsessed with it. "The little cafe just around the corner?" I asked him. "That way, I'm close to come back and pick up my grandmother. It's walking distance."

He looked at me as if I was a one-eyed cyclops. "For you, maybe."

"Come on," I said, beginning the short half-block trek. "Stop being such a girl."

His long legs carried him at twice the pace, and by the time I'd reached the cafe, he was already inside and waiting. We'd just sat down at a corner table in front of a window when the ring tone on my phone played. I looked at the screen and held a finger up to Max, indicating I'd be just a minute.

"Hey, Claire," I said. "Can I call you back in a bit?"

"Yeah, that's fine," she said. "But just real quick before you go making other plans—Cole and Levi want to go out for dinner tonight."

"The Fishing Hole or Grizzley's Tap House?"

"Does it matter to you?" she asked. "I'm sure they don't care which."

"I don't care which either. We haven't been to The Fishing Hole for a while. That might be fun."

"Perfect. It's closer for you and me too."

"It'll probably be just as close for Cole and Levi," I said, expressing hidden hope. It'd been a while since Levi and I had time alone at my house in front of the fireplace.

"Maybe for Levi," she said, "but not so for Cole."

"That's right," I said. "Your parents are still here."

She groaned. "I love them to pieces, Mel, but I'm ready to have my house back again. They spoil Syd rotten, and she acts like it. It takes weeks to get the little monster back to normal."

"It's only one more night," I said, trying to be positive. "Hey, I gotta go. Max and I are at the Oak Street Cafe."

"Again? I thought you needed a break from all that today. That's what this dinner tonight was supposed to be for, to take your mind off it. But you just go jumping right in the middle every time you turn around."

"It kind of fell in my lap this time," I said, looking at Max, who was playing on his phone. "Levi's coming over to my grandmother's this afternoon to help take down some Christmas decorations, so I'll get the final details from him then, okay? I don't even know if he has to work tonight. Never even thought to ask," I added, feeling like the world's worst girlfriend. If he didn't dump me sooner or later, it'd be a miracle. As soon as we hung up, I said to Max, "Just one more call. I promise it will be quick. Can you order me a cappuccino?" I began to walk away, then turned and took a step backward, adding, "If they make them. If not, a hot chocolate. Thanks."

Not five minutes later, I was back at the table, a cup of hot chocolate topped with whipped cream and a cherry waiting for me on the table. I wrapped my hands around the white well-used ceramic coffee mug, soaking in the warmth.

"Had to check in with the mister?" he asked.

"I don't *check in* with anyone," I said. "We had plans about noon, so I called him to set the time back a bit due to an unexpected run-in with you." I smiled. Kind of. I didn't want to be a complete jerk. I was still feeling the sting from my arrogance, assuming he was at the shelter looking for me. "What's with the woman at the shelter? She didn't look too happy with you. What'd you do?"

He stirred some creamer into his coffee. A delay tactic if I ever saw one since I noticed yesterday that he drinks his coffee black. "It's not what I did. It's what I won't do."

"Which is?"

"You ask a lot of questions," he said. A slight trace of a smile belied the complaint.

"So I've been told." He didn't say anything. "Well?" I pushed.

"I won't take her back. Not yet."

I frowned. "Take her back where?"

He shook his head slowly and took a drink, grimaced, then looked out the window at the empty alley. "She's my wife."

My eyes popped open. "Your what?"

"We're in the process of a divorce. I've filed the papers, anyway."

"She's homeless?" Max just bottomed out in the respect department. Anger percolated beneath the surface. "How could you let that happen? She's Daisy's mother?"

"Yes."

"That's wrong, Max. How could you let that happen?" I repeated.

"I didn't let anything happen. She did."

"She's the mother of your child. How horrible for Daisy to see her mother in that place."

"Pam doesn't get to see Daisy, supervised or other." Our eyes met. "I know what you're thinking, and you're way off. It's court-ordered. Until the Court decides otherwise, it is what it is. I try to keep Pam in the loop as much as possible."

"I'm listening." And I was. Even if I'd already had myself partially convinced that Max wasn't far off from Lenny.

"Not that it's any of your business, but—"

"But I might be your half-sister, so it *is* my business." I shrugged and raised my eyebrows in a come-on, out-with-it look.

"You're pretty demanding."

I nodded. "Yeah. So? Are you going to tell me?"

He took a breath and rubbed his forehead. "I'm a pharmacist. Pam used to be a drug rep, and one of the pills she sold was a prescription pain med. Highly addictive. When we were skiing out in Colorado, she fell and broke her pelvis, was in a lot of pain, and, well, you can kind of figure it out from there.

"When she couldn't get prescriptions anymore, she turned to cocaine." Raw pain shown in his eyes. "She almost lost everything we had, including our house. She wasn't paying bills. When I took them over, she was beyond mad and threw huge tantrums. She began to disappear for days at a time, and when she came home, she wasn't the same woman I'd known. She'd hit Daisy, locked her out of the house, left her alone for twenty-four hours while I was at a conference, you name it. Daisy was six when that happened. The neighbors called Social Services. Pam claimed she didn't do it. I finally had to give her an ultimatum—either she goes in for treatment, or she had to leave. She insisted she didn't have a problem but that I was the problem, turning Daisy against her. It got pretty ugly."

I felt sick. Because of the story he just spewed and because of my quick judgment. Again. "How did she end up out here in Minnesota?"

"I told her I was coming here." Seeing my bewilderment, he said, "She might not have visitation, but she's still Daisy's mother."

I put up both hands, palms facing him. "Hey! No judgement here."

"Right." He rolled his eyes. "When people say 'no judgement', they're judging."

I shrugged. "Fair enough. She followed you here?"

He nodded.

"What exactly did you tell her?"

"Just where I was going. She asked why, and I told her it was personal."

"Does she know about Lenny?"

"You'd have to ask her."

"No, thank you."

"She's extremely intelligent and, shall we say, resourceful. I'm sure she could have figured it out if she wanted to."

"If she was sober, maybe," I said. "What was the purpose in following you here?"

"She said she was hoping to get me to come to my senses. And maybe a little curiosity." He shrugged. "I don't know, honestly. I've stopped trying to figure her out."

I tipped my head slightly, processing the answer. Then, finally, I said, "She's living in a homeless shelter because of her drug use, and she's hoping *you* come to *your* senses?"

"It's not easy. Leaving her there. That's not who she always was. And she wouldn't be now if it weren't for the drugs. Drugs took my wife away from me. Kind of ironic that I'm a pharmacist, and I hate drugs."

I touched his hand with my own, a gesture that surprised both of us. "I'm so sorry, Max."

"The one I feel sorry for is Daisy," he said, an unmistakable quiver in his typically controlled voice.

"What are your plans now? Back at the shelter, you said you might stay."

He shook his head, then took a drink of his coffee, screwing up his face. "This stuff is terrible with creamer in it."

I chuckled. "I wondered what you were doing doctoring it up but decided to leave it alone."

"Of course you did," he said. He signaled the waitress over and ordered fresh, black coffee. "My mother has been looking for a new start. In the short time we've been in Birch Haven, she's become quite fond of it. And now that I've found I have family here, I've decided to look for employment. I want Daisy to be around family."

"Birch Haven isn't exactly a good market for pharmacists. There's only one pharmacy in town."

"I know. Harvey's. I'm planning to use some of the money from Lenny to buy it."

"Harvey's?" I asked, surprised. My hand, holding my cup, froze halfway to my lips before I set it down on the table again. "I hadn't realized it was for sale."

"It wasn't on the market yet. I spoke with him about possibly becoming a partner. He said he's retiring and wants to sell; we talked numbers and reached an agreement."

I frowned and took a sip of my hot chocolate. "Man! He's had that thing for a hundred years. Or so it seems. At least fifty years from what I've been told."

"That's what he said."

"You have to promise me that you're going to keep the drink counter. He serves cherry Cokes by pouring Coke into a cone-shaped cup and adding cherry syrup. The stuff will give you a sugar high; it's the best."

He chuckled. "I promise."

"I bet Daisy would love them."

"If there's sugar involved, there's no doubt she would. I try to limit her sugar intake, though."

I waved my hand in dismissal. "Yeah, yeah, you and Claire both. That's the best part of being an aunt—load 'em up and send 'em home." His look shot lasers at me over the rim of his cup, and I snickered. We fell silent. "I'd like to spend some time with Daisy." My request tumbled out, unplanned, and surprised me a little.

"Any time you want. She's with my mom now. But she's going back soon to close things out there—my mom, not Daisy. The housing market is remarkable for the seller right now so it shouldn't take long. She wants to meet you. Says she wants to meet Violet's daughter."

"To be sure I'm not like her?"

"Drop the self-pity," he scoffed. "It's not like that. She felt a kinship with your moth—Violet."

"I'll have to think about it. Guess I don't see what harm it could do," I added quietly. I looked out the window and thought about how my life had changed so drastically in such a short period of time.

Around the corner from the shelter and into the alley strolled Pam. I was just about to say something to Max when Pam looked up and saw me watching her. She raised her hand, put her thumb up, and her forefinger pointed at me, acting as though she had a gun. She made to shoot me with it then blew her finger as if blowing the smoke from the gun barrel. Harmless, but disturbing, nonetheless. I nodded toward her, and Max turned to look. "You may want to let Pam know that I'm not a threat. She apparently doesn't know that you and I are family."

He turned his back to her again, his eyes pained, yet not letting go of what I said. "You're accepting it now? That we're family?"

I was just as surprised as he apparently was. I cocked my head to the side and looked back outside. Pam was gone. "Huh. Yeah, I guess I am." I narrowed my eyes at him. "Kind of."

16

On the way back to my grandmother's, I filled her in on the incident with Max and about Pam's odd behavior. "What do you make of that?" I asked her. "Have you seen her there before?"

"A couple of times just recently. She's never given us a reason to be alarmed. But what she did to you certainly was odd. You should take care, dontcha know. A jealous woman isn't anything to dismiss lightly."

I grimaced. "Nothing to be jealous of."

"Well, it sounds like she doesn't know that. It appears she thinks you're a new woman in her husband's life."

"Yeah, it certainly appears that way, doesn't it?" We fell silent a moment. "Max'll let her know, I'm sure."

When we pulled into Nana's drive, Levi was on the ladder in front of her garage, taking down the last of the lights. He looked different in tennis shoes, jogging pants, and a hoodie with a turtleneck underneath. He was usually in jeans, boots, and a black leather coat. His usual Underarmour beanie covering his shaved head looked oddly out of place.

"Who's the hottie on your roof, Nana," I said, grinning as we got out of the car. "I've never noticed Santa to be quite so cute."

Levi laughed, dimples in his whisker-stubbled cheeks and chin making my stomach somersault.

"Rose, why don't you get in out of the cold. Melanie, you should probably stay out here. Whenever you're around, it's warmer." He winked at me.

I laughed, and Nana half-groaned, half-laughed. "Oh, brother," she said, shaking her head. "You kids be careful out here. There are ice patches everywhere."

As soon as the door closed behind her, he said, "I love being around Rose. She makes me feel young. She's the only one who calls me a kid."

"Yeah? You like that, huh? Want me to start calling you kid?"

He laughed again. "No. That would be disturbing coming from you."

It felt amazing to laugh. It had been a few days but felt like weeks. The heaviness lifted, and the urge to have a little fun took over. "Hey, Levi?" I asked as he descended the ladder.

"Yeah?" he said as he reached the ground and turned toward me—just in time to get a snowball in the chest. His eyes registered shock, then mischief. He walked toward me slowly, and I backed up, laughing. "Come here," he said, his eyes sparkling.

"Uh-uh," I said, giggling as I continued backing up toward the door.

"What, you can give it but can't take it?" He grinned, continuing slowly toward me, stopping to scoop up a handful of snow and form a ball.

I turned and bolted for the front door, but before I knew what happened, I was sprawled on the ground, rear end and left hip throbbing. "Ouch! Found the ice patches!" Before I could move, Levi was by my side.

"Don't move," he instructed.

I groaned. He touched my leg, and I flinched. "Ouch!"

"ER, baby," he said, frowning.

"No."

"Yes," he argued. "Can you move your leg?"

I tried. "Yes, but my knee hurts." I hated to be a wimp, and my pride was all but broken, but man, did it hurt!

"Blondie, if you didn't have bad luck this week, you'd have none at all. I'm going to take you to the ER. You need to have this looked at."

I hated to agree with him on this, but I couldn't disagree. I wasn't sure I hadn't broken something. "How about Urgent Care? I'll go to Urgent Care."

I circled my arm around his neck, and he helped lift me off the ground and walked me to his car. "I'll drive," I teased and winced.

"Stay here," he said, getting me settled in. "I'll go let Rose know."

"Like I'm gonna run away," I said under my breath.

Levi turned toward me, hand behind his ear, an eyebrow raised. "What was that?"

"You're hearing is too good. I just said she'll wanna come with," I said.

"I'm pretty sure that's not what you said, Ms. Hogan. But I'll let you off easy." He smirked. "I'll be right back."

"Let her know I'm fine, in good hands, and will be back soon to get my car."

"So bossy," he mumbled, shaking his head and walked toward the house, but not before I saw him smirk. Again.

***

Levi pulled up in front of the door at Urgent Care and helped me inside before he went back out and parked the car. I hobbled up to the front desk and got the required paperwork to fill out. I'd no sooner sat down with the clipboard and reached for a pen when I realized I didn't have my purse. I exhaled loudly, hoisted myself up off the chair, and hobbled back to the desk to grab a pen equipped with a gaudy artificial yellow daisy attached to the top of it. I instantly thought of Max's daughter and the irony that daisies were my absolute favorite flower. And Asiatic lilies. But I worked at changing my affection for lilies because those were also Violet's favorite.

"Can I help you?" the receptionist asked.

I blinked away the thought of Daisy and said, "Um, yeah. It appears I left without my purse, so I don't have my insurance information. Can you look me up on the computer and get it that way?"

"Do you have a co-pay?" she asked matter of fact.

"Yes. It's one hundred for Urgent Care visits."

She turned to an elderly woman in back of her, saying quietly, but not quietly enough, "Shirley, this lady forgot her card too."

Shirley rolled her eyes and shook her head as she looked at me, giving me a nonverbal scolding. Then, she said to the receptionist, again not quietly enough, "You'll have to do the same thing I told you for the other woman."

"But this one at least knows what her co-pay is. Can I just take that right away?"

"If she's got it, get it," said Shirley.

"*She's* right here, and *she's* got it," I snipped. I blamed it on the pain.

"She's got somethin' else too," Shirley said under her breath.

My leg was hurting, but there wasn't a thing wrong with my hearing. If anything, the pain made it all the sharper. I opened my mouth to say something, then clamped it shut again. Nothing good would have come from my lips right now. The pain in my leg was excruciating. I reached for my wallet, and it hit me again—

I didn't have my purse. I swallowed an expletive and said, "Yeah, about that co-pay —"

"I got it," Levi said from behind me as he pulled out his wallet.

"Saved again," I said. Tears threatened to spring from my eyes. That's all any of us needed right now is a waterworks show. "I'll pay you back."

He looked at me and winked. "Yes, you will."

The last thing I felt like doing was laughing, but I couldn't help it. His misplaced humor was just what I needed. I hobbled back to my chair as Levi took care of matters at the desk.

"Detective Wescott!" Shirley's voice carried over to where I now sat. "It's so nice to see you again." She sported a smile so wide it made me think of Mister Ed, the talking horse, from the old TV show Granddad used to enjoy.

"Whatever," I grumbled.

As I waited for him to finish up, I rested my head back on the chair. I heard Shirley laugh, then the door leading to the patient rooms opened.

"Pamela Winters," Shirley called to her, "I couldn't find you in the system. You'll need to pay for the visit out of pocket."

I shot up in my chair—my rear end, hip, and knee reminding me I was more than a little bruised—and looked at the woman.

"I don't have the money with me," Pam said to Shirley. "But I'm good for it. I promise. I'll go home and get my card and the money and bring it in." She looked around, spotted me, then pointed toward me. "This woman knows me and can vouch for me. Right, Melanie?" The smile she gave was foxlike.

I was without words—a rare occasion—as I watched the interaction unfold.

"She doesn't have her card either," Shirley said, looking from me to Pam as if we were playing her.

I took a deep breath and squeezed my eyes shut before opening my mouth. "Yes, but I am in the system, and my co-pay is taken care of." I was more than a little irritated.

Shirley looked from me to Pam, then said to her, "Okay, go home and get your card. You can bring it in later. Or tomorrow will work." Miss Personality shook her head and sighed before mumbling to her co-worker, "It's not as if we can hold her hostage or take back services already rendered."

When I glanced toward Pam again, the door was already closing behind her. Levi sat down beside me.

"Who was that?" he asked.

"Pam."

"Pam who? Is she a friend of yours? Looks like maybe she could use our help."

"No."

"No? At the very least, it looks like she could use a shower."

"No, I mean, she's not a friend. Pam is Max's wife." I told him about the encounter earlier that day at the shelter and again when Max and I were in the cafe. "I think she's harmless," I said. "You can bet, though, that she's not going to bring any money in. According to Max, she's hit rock bottom."

"Be on alert, babe. Addicts can be unstable people. The addiction makes them do things they ordinarily wouldn't do."

"Well, since she said I could vouch for her, and Shirley seemed to buy that—no doubt because of you and not her love for me—I'll be the one in the hot seat when Pam doesn't pay."

"I'll talk to Shirley. It will be fine."

"You'll have to. You seem to be the only one she likes." I slumped down in my chair, pouting. "You might want to suggest she get a different job, too. She's clearly not happy here." I looked out the door Pam exited through minutes ago. "How do you know her, anyway? Shirley." I turned to face him.

"Long story." He turned away from me, looking straight ahead, and crossed his leg over the other, foot resting on his knee.

"It's not like I'm going anywhere. It may be called Urgent Care, but there's no urgency in taking people back to see the doctor." I glanced around me. There wasn't another soul in the waiting area. What could be taking so long? "Well?" I asked him. "Tell me. It's not like I'm jealous over Shirley," I said. "She's old enough to be my mother. It was just a question to pass the time. Take my mind off the pain." My hip felt a bit better, but my knee throbbed like no other.

"I dated her daughter one time a while back."

I raised an eyebrow. "How long ago is *a while*?"

"A few years ago. It was nothing serious."

I raised an eyebrow. "Yeah? You might want to tell Shirley that."

He gave me a sidelong look, then picked up my hand and brought it to his lips, kissing the back of it ever so gently. "I'm not interested in what Shirley thinks. I'm only interested in what you think."

"Hearing her voice gave me some answers in this whole drama," I said.

He slipped his beanie off and frowned. "Shirley's? Why?"

"No, Pam's."

"How so?"

"It's the same voice that called me so many times asking for Daisy. That's what Max assumed too. That it was probably Pam."

He chewed on that then cocked his head to the side. "That'd make sense. If Daisy's her daughter, she probably hoped she could get you to let her see Daisy alone since she wasn't getting anywhere with Max."

"I'm not sure who I feel sorrier for, Daisy or Pam," I said. "I could tell how hard it was for Daisy not to spend some quality time with her mom. But Pam is just so pathetic."

"Drugs'll do that to a person. Unfortunately, I see it all the time."

"How do you not become jaded?" I asked him.

He shrugged. "Because there are people like you in the world who give me hope. And a life outside of the office," he said, winking at me.

"Melanie Hogan?" a woman called as she held the door open, leading down a hallway.

***

An hour and a half, several x-rays, and an ultrasound later, I walked out with a brace on my knee and one crutch.

Levi met me at the door. "Grade-one knee sprain and bone contusion," I said before he had a chance to ask.

"What's with the crutch?"

"To keep the weight off. I don't have to use it all the time, just when it feels like I need to. He said I could use it on you if you misbehave."

He chuckled. "I see they gave you something for the pain."

"We won't be able to go out with Claire and Cole tonight. I have to keep it elevated and ice it every twenty minutes."

"Let's just go to my place," he suggested. "Cole and I can get your car to your house tomorrow."

"Better idea," I said, grinning. I was feeling absolutely no pain, and it felt remarkable after sending me through the roof earlier. "Let's go to my house and have Claire and Cole come over."

He nodded. "Okay. Maybe we can get takeout from The Fishing Hole."

"It's a date. Can we get my car tonight, though? I have to work in the morning."

"Um, yeah, I don't think you do," he said, shaking his head. He put his arm around me and walked me to a chair by the door. "Stay here, and I'll go get the car."

"I can walk out there. I got this here crutch to help." I held it up, nearly hitting someone coming in the door. "Oops, sorry," I said. I looked at the person and startled. "Max? What are you doing here?"

"Pam called and told me she saw you. I came to pay her bill and check on you." Lines around his eyes made him look tired and older than his forty-five years.

"I've got her," Levi said, reaching out to shake his hand. "I'm going to get her home so she can put her leg up and ice it."

"Where's your car?" Max asked. "I'm assuming you can't drive."

"It's at my grandmother's."

"Need help getting it to your house?" Max asked.

"Thanks. That'd be—"

"I've already got it taken care of," Levi interrupted. "Cole and Claire are on their way to get it. But thank you."

"Oh," Max said, looking from me to Levi. "All right, I'll just settle up Pam's bill and head back home to Daisy then."

As soon as he got up to the desk, I turned to Levi. "Why'd you lie to him?"

"I don't want him at your house until we're a little more sure with whom we're dealing."

17

As soon as Levi dropped me off at my house and got a fire going in the fireplace, Claire rode with him back into town to pick up my Jeep at my grandmother's. Cole was out on a call and wouldn't be done for another couple of hours. The entire evening spiraled into something completely different than we'd initially planned. But none of us complained. As for me, I hadn't broken anything, Claire's parents were still there to watch Syd, and we were all still able to hang out in front of a warm fireplace. Levi let me know as he walked out the door that he would be stopping by his house to pick up a couple of things before coming back.

I hobbled—surprisingly, with little effort—into the kitchen to make myself some chamomile tea, appreciating the effects of the pain meds. As the tea kettle started squealing its readiness, the thrum of snowmobile motors coming up from the lake drowned it out. Again, one on either side of my house and out to the road. They turned left, drove the ditch past Claire's house, and out of sight.

I'd just settled back on the couch with an ice pack on my knee, my leg elevated and resting on the coffee table, when they came back, this time both on the same side. I stood again and watched from the large picture window as a fresh layer of powdery snow whipped up behind the machines until they disappeared onto the lake and around a bend. My ex-husband had a snowmobile when we first moved out to this house, and he took it with him when he left me. At that time, I didn't want it anyway. But the idea of picking one up so Levi and I could go riding was an attractive one, I had to admit. Maybe next winter.

I must have dozed off because the sound of Claire's voice sent me into a panic. "Dang! You scared me, girl," I said, hand to my chest.

"Sorry, hun." Her eyebrows drew together. "How are you feeling?" she asked as she crossed the living room floor in long strides and sat down gently beside me.

"No need to be so careful. I won't break. It's still feeling pretty good thanks to the drugs they gave me." I thought of Pam. "Scary enough, I can see how a person could like these a little too much."

"How often are you supposed to take them?" She picked up the bottle on the end table and looked at the label.

"Every four hours as needed. Think I'll switch to ibuprofen, though. Thanks for bringing my car home. You're the best."

"You're just saying that 'cause you're high," she said, laughing. "What can I get you? Hot chocolate, tea, wine— oh, guess not wine," she said, hand to her mouth. "Then you'd be super loopy."

"I don't want anything right now. How was my grandmother when you got to her house?"

"Worried about you. Levi promised he'd take good care of you."

"Yeah, he called into work tonight. He's staying here. I told him he didn't have to, but he insisted."

She lifted an eyebrow. "I'm surprised you're letting him take care of you. Did you hit your head, too?"

I scowled. "Don't kick me when I'm down."

"Hey, those snowmobiles are making a mess of the ditch at the end of my driveway. I saw fresh tracks all over your yard. Are they driving you crazy?"

"Nah. As long as it's not at night while I'm sleeping, I don't care."

She nodded. "As long as it's just the two of us at the moment, fill me in on everything. Feels like we haven't spoken in days." She went into the kitchen, saying over her shoulder. "Hold on, though. I'm going to get myself some tea." Five minutes later, she was back. "Okay, go."

When I finished from beginning to end, I stopped and took a deep breath.

"Why don't you, Daisy, Sydney, and I go ice skating one of these evenings," she said. "The light from your back porch reaches almost to the lake. Between that and the moonlight, it's enough for us to see. It'll be fun."

I pointed to my leg. "Yeah, right. Unlikely."

She snickered. "Yeah, that could put a damper on things, I guess. Some friend I am."

I shook my head and grinned. "Truthfully, it's not such a bad idea. I want to get to know Daisy, and this would be a perfect way. The three of you can skate, and I can sit on that big ol' tree stump down by the ice rink. There's been a few light snowfalls since the rink was last shoveled, though."

"I bet Cole and Levi will shovel it off. It'll take them all of ten minutes," she said.

"I'll call Max tomorrow and see about getting Daisy for tomorrow evening."

"Let's see how you're feeling first. There's no rush. We can always do something else until you're healed. Take in a movie or something."

"But Daisy is from Phoenix. I bet she'd love ice skating. And what a fun thing for her and Syd to do together. Besides, you can't get to know someone when everyone's watching a screen, and you can't talk."

Headlights beamed through the kitchen window and danced off the picture window directly opposite from it across the house.

"Let's just wait and see how your knee does this week, okay?"

"I'll be sitting around all day tomorrow with my leg up and icing it. I'll be totally stir crazy by tomorrow evening and ready to get out."

"Tomorrow evening will be pushing it," she insisted. I stood to see who it was that pulled up in the driveway. "Hey, aren't you supposed to be using your crutch?" Claire asked from behind me.

"Only if I feel I need it. I don't right now."

186

"You're not going to make this easy, are you?" she asked, following me into the kitchen.

"I'm not going to baby it if that's what you mean. You and Levi need to stop micromanaging my healing process," I grumbled as I opened the door for Levi. His arms were empty. "Where's the stuff you picked up from your house?"

"In my car," he said, leaning over to kiss me. "What are you doing up and around? Shouldn't you be resting?"

I took a deep breath and exhaled, giving me enough time to get it together. Finally, I said, "Listen, you two, I have a bone contusion. A bruised bone. And a grade-one knee sprain. That's the lowest level. I didn't break anything. Now, if the two of you are going to treat me like I'm dying, go home because that doesn't help."

"We just care," Claire said, pouting.

I looked at Levi, a hint of a smirk playing on his lips. "What?" I asked.

"Someone's pain killers are wearing off, and she's just a little irritable." He pinched his thumb and forefinger together.

"No," I explained, struggling to be patient, "someone just doesn't want to be coddled." I harumphed. I took a breath and exhaled slowly. "Okay, fine. I might be a little irritable."

"Cut me some slack," Levi said, putting an arm around me, leading me back into the living room. "I'm feeling guilty. Your injury is my fault."

"Quit feeling sorry for yourself," I teased, pinching his rear end. "My lack of grace has nothing to do with you."

Headlights cut through the room again. "Finally," Claire said. "I don't think I'll ever stop worrying about him when he's out there. I mean, Birch Haven is a relatively safe town and all, but—"

"Says she two days after a homicide at our front door," I said.

"True. As long as Cole's in the same town as you, I have reason to worry," she said.

"Hey!" I exclaimed. "I take offense to that."

"But you can't deny it," Levi said. "You have brought a certain element of—well, let's just say danger—to town the last few years."

"You're welcome," I said, shooting him a look.

"For what?" he asked.

"Keeping Birch Haven's finest in business. Who knows, if it wasn't for me, there might not have been enough work for you to return to your job when you moved back here." Levi had recently returned to Birch Haven after moving to the East Coast to be near his son for nine months. A long-distance relationship was challenging but safe since I didn't have to worry about my independence being threatened. I was getting used to having him around a lot more, though. Ironically, that in itself scared me.

"Hey, Claire!" I called to her when she disappeared into the kitchen to open the door for Cole. "As long as you're in there, grab me a couple of ibuprofen and a fresh ice pack from the freezer."

"I'll get it," Levi said, starting to get up.

I grabbed his hand and pulled him back down. "I need ibuprofen and you. Claire can get one, and you give me the other." I grinned at him.

He cupped his hand behind his ear. "Wait, what did you say?"

"I said let Claire get the ibuprofen."

"Before that."

"I told her the ice pack is in the freezer."

"No, no," he said, shaking his head. "You don't get to weasel out of it that easy. You said you need me. I heard it."

"You must have misunderstood."

"Oh, no, I understood perfectly." He beamed, quite pleased. "Mind saying that again so I can record it? For proof."

"Yes, I mind," I said and laughed. "What a silly question."

Claire handed me three ibuprofen and a glass of water. "What's so funny?" she asked as Cole trailed behind her.

"Levi thinks he is, but he's not."

"Melanie admitted she needs me."

"Yeah, right," Claire scoffed. "Miss Toughie doesn't need anyone."

"Until now," Levi corrected her.

The banter and the laughing were better medicine than the pain killers. We talked about snowmobiles, ice skating, the salon, the police department, and about Rubie and Scott. Both Claire and I agreed that the salon was abnormally quiet without Rubie there. In contrast, Levi and Cole said Scott is so quiet they hardly know he's at work, much less gone. We all agreed that Rubie and Scott are proof that opposites attract.

Claire and Levi took turns getting me ice packs throughout the evening without missing a beat. And it hadn't escaped any of us that I was letting them, which caused a whole line of jokes. And Cole and Levi were more than happy to shovel the ice rink. It was almost as if the past few days hadn't even happened. Except they had. And part of my mind, though a small part, was hung up on Max and Daisy.

By the time Claire and Cole got ready to leave, the fire had died to embers. My head rested on Levi's shoulder, his hand solid and warm on my thigh, and I was fighting to keep my eyes open. As soon as the door closed behind them, Levi swooped me up in his arms and carried me upstairs, turning off the lights as we went. The last thing I remember is my pillow having the effect of a sedative, my flannel blanket and comforter pulled up under my chin. And the next thing I knew, I woke to the smell of coffee wafting up the stairs and into the loft.

The sky was beginning to lighten through my skylight. I turned, bumped my knee, and got a painful reminder of the injury. I looked at my nightstand, and there sat three ibuprofen and a glass of water. I smiled. I was getting spoiled very quickly. And I kind of liked it!

I stuck my leg out of the covers and removed the brace to get a look at my knee. It was black and blue, all right, but the swelling was well under control. I refastened the brace, put my feet on the floor, and gingerly put weight on my leg. Huh. Not too bad. The sound of Levi climbing the stairs prompted me to smooth my hair down and run a hand over my face, giving each cheek a little pinch for color: a trick my grandmother taught me when I was a teenager.

"I think I'm gonna make it," I said with a sleepy smile. "I could probably go to work today."

"Not a chance," he answered quickly. "I didn't take last night off to spend the day here by myself. Coffee and pancakes coming up."

"I'll come down. Just give me a minute to work out the stiffness." My body ached in places I didn't know I had, and as of last night, a giant bruise had begun forming on my hip.

"I'll be back up in about ten minutes." Then, after a peck on my forehead, he was back down the stairs.

I was halfway to the bathroom when my phone rang. I limped back to the bed and picked it up from my nightstand, answering without looking at the display.

There was silence on the other end. I took the phone away from my ear and looked at the screen. Blocked. I rolled my eyes and grumbled, "Not this again." After a beat, I repeated, "Hello?" Still nothing. "Pam, if this is you, Daisy is not here. Call Max."

"It's not Pam," said a muffled male voice.

I froze, put the phone on speaker, and sat on the edge of the bed. I grabbed my crutch and tapped the floor, signaling to Levi. "Who is this?"

"Someone you don't want to mess with. Lenny's money is mine."

"Who *is* this?" I repeated.

"Lenny owes me. If you know what's good for you, you and that brother of yours will leave his money alone."

Levi appeared at the top of the stairs and watched me carefully as he held up a note. *Keep him talking. Information.*

I nodded. "I'm not interested in Lenny's money."

"Smart on your part. You're already hurt. I would hate to see something worse happen."

"Are you threatening me?" I asked. I heard the fear in my voice and was disappointed. I didn't want him to know he'd gotten to me.

"Threat, promise; tomato, tomahto."

"How do you know me?" Silence. "I have a detective from the Birch Haven Police Department here." The line went dead. "Oops," I said to Levi, letting the phone drop on the bed. "Sorry."

"Don't be. You did everything right. But I had all I could do not to reach through the phone and wring his neck." His eyes grew stormy. "What did he say before I came up here? Did you recognize the voice?"

"No. But you heard it; it was garbled like what happens in the movies. He just warned me to stay away from Lenny's money. There are a lot of clues from that short phone call, though. First, he knows Lenny has money. Second, he knows I'm related to Lenny. Max too. He said, 'you and that brother of yours'. That means Max isn't behind any of this."

"I intend to find that out," he answered grimly.

18

I knew I was rambling, talking more to myself than to Levi. "It's got to be one of Lenny's henchmen. Someone he trusted with details of his personal life. I can't imagine that would be too many and could potentially narrow down the suspect pool."

"Oh, no, you don't, Melanie. You're not going to dig into this any further. The police department will. I'll call Walker right now."

"I don't understand why you can't be the one to investigate. I'm not their top suspect."

"But you are involved by way of association. That's a slight conflict of interest."

"Yeah, but then at least I could get the inside scoop."

"You'd have to pay for it, and the price is too high for you." He wiggled his eyebrows, and I laughed.

"You're such a rule-follower."

"Cops are funny that way, aren't we? Now," he said, all seriousness again, "I need to call in and report this right away."

"It's not like they can get the number. It was blocked."

"We can get a subpoena for the phone records. Get the number that way."

"*We?*" A flash of hope arose. Was it possible?

"Not you. We as in the police department."

There went that. "Fine. You'll keep me posted?"

"Babe, *I* won't even know unless I go poking around."

"So? What's the holdup?"

He took a breath and shook his head. "I'll see what I can do. Now let me make the call." He turned around halfway to the stairs. "Want me to help you downstairs first or come back up?"

"Neither. I can walk on my own." I slipped into my robe and looked at him as he stared at me. "What? I'm not an invalid. And I think I proved yesterday that I bruise but don't break." He wasn't amused. "Go," I said. "If I'm unable to make it down the stairs, I'll yell down for you to come help. But I'm going into the salon today." I shot my hand up, palm facing forward. "Before you get your undies in a bunch, I won't take any clients. I'll sit in the office with my leg elevated and iced. At least for one more day." I gave him the sweetest, most innocent smile I could muster.

"I'm supposed to believe that?" he asked with a snicker.

I did my best at keeping the innocence plastered on my face. "It's Tuesday. I pay bills and place orders on Tuesdays. You know, bookkeeping matters."

He shook his head and uttered something unintelligible as he went downstairs. As soon as I could hear him at the bottom, I picked up my phone. I needed more answers. The phone rang several times before it finally picked up.

"Yeah?"

As my grandmother would say, *Uffda*! "Max? Everything okay?"

He breathed with apparent relief. "Oh, hey, Melanie."

"I'll ask again, you okay?"

"Yes. No. Uh—yeah, I'm fine. Are you?"

"What's going on?" I asked.

"I got a—"

"Phone call," we both said at the same time.

"You too?" he asked.

"Yeah." *That validates what I thought. It wasn't Max.* "Do you have any ideas who it could be?"

"Someone who worked for Lenny."

"Who?"

"I don't know who," he said.

"Then how do you know—"

"Who else could it be? He said the money belongs to him, that me and, quote, that sister of yours, unquote, better leave it alone."

"Yeah, I got the same message. Here's what I think; I agree with you. It must be someone that worked for Lenny. This person knows Lenny has money—which, how much, we have no idea—or at least I don't. This person knows Lenny has two kids. It must be someone he trusted with his personal life. Someone in his position doesn't let just anybody in on that information. Which means—"

"It's someone high up in his circle," he finished for me.

"Yup. And when we find out who called us, we'll also know who his killer is. Someone is desperate to get that money."

"*When* we find out? How do you propose we do that?"

"I can be very resourceful. Besides, I've had my share of mysteries to solve in the past few years."

"Yes, that's been insinuated numerous times. Should I be worried?"

My antenna prickled. "I don't know, should you?"

"It sounds like you get yourself involved in some shady business."

My anxiety relaxed again. He had a point I couldn't deny. "None of it has been my fault."

"Says every person ever in the prison system."

I snickered. I was more convinced by the day that this man that waltzed into town was, indeed, my brother. I heard Levi ascending the stairs. "I have to go. Let me know if this clown calls you back again."

"You do the same."

I hung up as Levi reached the top step.

"Who was that?" he asked.

"Max. He got the same call that I did."

"You can't yet be a hundred percent certain you can trust him, Melanie."

"The person warned me to stay away from Lenny's money. Max is all too eager to share that money despite my not wanting it."

"You need to be careful. How do you know he isn't offering up half the money only to take the suspicion off him? If you're gone, he wouldn't have to share it at all. Just give me a little more time to investigate him, okay?"

I frowned. "I hadn't even thought of that." My mind traveled down some pretty dark roads before I brought it back to the room. "You haven't found anything yet, though, right?"

He sighed and tipped his head back. "No."

I sighed with audible relief. Knowing Levi as I did, he would have bent over backward to turn over every stone. "Why does it sound as though you wish you had?" He didn't respond. "Look, I told you I'd be careful," I said, getting up to follow him downstairs.

He turned around. "Yeah, well, your idea of careful and mine are completely different."

"Can we just call it motivated? That sounds better."

"Motivated?"

"Yes. To get answers and protect my friends and family," I said.

He took a deep breath and shook his head slowly as he reached his hand back for me to take hold of. "How creative."

***

By the time noon arrived, I was already stir crazy and thought I'd go mad if I didn't get to the salon. Most people would love a chance to stay home and maybe in bed for a day. But I wasn't most people. Far from it. I loved my salon and the people I worked with there. Much to Levi's surprise, I didn't argue with letting him drive me. I'd called Claire ahead of time and arranged to hitch a ride home with her.

"Don't even think about taking any appointments," she'd said. "I already called them all and rescheduled anyway."

"Wouldn't dream of it," I'd fibbed.

She proceeded to tell me that a man called for me, insisting it was critical he talk with me. It was a matter of life and death. But Claire, the protector that she was, refused to give out my cell phone number. I guess the man was just as resourceful as I claimed to be because he'd found my number anyway. Assuming it was the same one who'd called both the salon and me. And Max.

Pulling into the parking lot, Levi reached for my hand. "Try to stay out of trouble today," he said.

I opened my eyes wide and touched my hand to my chest. "Me? How insulting that you should even have to say that."

He smiled. "Yeah, shocking, isn't it? Promise me you won't overdo it."

"It honestly feels a million times better than it did last night. All that icing helped."

"Yeah, well, as I said, just make sure you don't overdo it, or the healing will go backward instead of forward. I'll let you know if I find anything more out on Max today."

"If you haven't found anything yet, how can you find *more*?" I snickered at the look he gave me. "Be sure and get some rest before you go into work tonight, mister."

"Headed there now." He leaned over and kissed me, lingering, his aftershave tingling my nose and my stomach.

"Be careful. Talk to you later."

I got out, shut the door, and waved as he drove off. The mailman walked up to the door at the same time as I did. He handed me the stack of mail, gave me a salute, and off he went to the business next door.

Babs was ringing up a client, Connie was standing in front of a mirror fixing her hair, and Claire was finishing up a hair color client. Though it was a quiet day, the place still buzzed with an energy to which I was addicted. These walls have held endless conversations, fun, and laughter.

After greetings and hugs, I went to the office and shrugged out of my black leather coat, hat, and mittens. It was a perfect day to do some bookwork and check the status of product shelves. I'd told Levi a little fib when I said I *always* did the bookwork on Tuesdays; it got done on an as-needed basis, regardless of the day. But it was the only plausible excuse I could think of to get out of the house. At the beginning of our business venture, Claire and I had agreed on duties, and bookwork was mine. Thankfully, I enjoyed it. I was much more detail-oriented than she was, and I didn't stop until I got things to balance out to the penny.

I shuffled through the mail. Invoices for Redken and Joico products, the electric bill, the water bill, and a bill for an ad we'd taken out in the newspaper. "Bills. All bills," I said, tossing them aside. I reached for two envelopes that slid off the side of the desk, catching them between my fingers. I set them on top of the others when one of them snagged my attention. It was addressed to me in block letters, but there was no return address and no postage stamp.

"That's weird." I turned it over to look at the back, then the front again. The mailman wouldn't have gotten it in his mail to be delivered if there wasn't a postage stamp. The hair on the back of my neck prickled. I stared at it for a moment before slowly sliding my nail under the flap. I unfolded the slip of paper, revealing a message from words cut out of what looked like a magazine.

Melanie, this is a warning—you and your brother need to stay away from Lenny's money. If you know what's good for you, you'll walk away and not look back or unfortunate consequences will fall upon both of you. And that little niece of yours. Walk. Away. Don't. Look. Back.

I gasped, then limped out to the salon. "Did anyone see the mailman today?"

"What, you hit your head when you fell, Melanie?" Babs asked. "You brought the mail in with you."

"I know. But did you see the mail carrier? I don't think I've seen this one before."

"Well, gosh," Claire said, setting the hair foils back down that she had been putting away, "I don't pay much attention to who it is that drops the mail off. Especially if I have a client in my chair."

"Same here," Connie added. "I just know he or she drops it on the front desk."

"I've noticed a couple of different ones but couldn't pick them out of a crowd," Babs said. "Sometimes they say hi, and sometimes they don't."

"Melanie, what is it?" Claire pushed her sleeves up, looked at the paper in my hand, and then met my gaze.

I glanced around the salon. "I got a letter: no postmark, no stamp, and no return address." I held up the letter, and all three rushed over to me to read it.

"You know, Melanie," Connie said, shaking her head, "I remember back when I almost quit because of the dangers and the stuff that happens around you. Now I've come to expect it and worry if we go too long without it."

"Dang, Connie," Babs exclaimed, "why don't you tell her how you really feel?"

Listening to the two of them, essentially trading places in character for the moment, made me smile.

"What are you going to do?" Claire asked.

"First, I'll call Levi."

"I thought he's not on the case," she said, frowning.

"He's not. Officially. But he can do whatever he needs to do with it and give it to whoever. As soon as I'm done with it," I added.

Her eyes narrowed. "Do I want to know what you're planning to do?"

"Heck, I want to know what I'm planning to do," I said, looking at her without seeing her. The wheels of my mind spun furiously at how to solve this. I tapped the letter on the palm of one hand as I pondered. "You know, whoever crafted this and called this morning is stupid. If the money doesn't go to family, it goes to the government. So it doesn't matter to this guy whether I take the money or not. Which I'm not planning on, by the way," I said, looking at each of them pointedly. "It's dirty money."

"Still spends the same," Babs said, shrugging. "I say take it. You've earned it after what that scumbag has put you through."

"Hello!" Connie sang quietly, giving her a little shove. "That scumbag is her father. A little respect, huh?"

Now they were back to themselves again. I absently enjoyed their interaction a moment and shifted my weight when an ache reminded me of my knee. This not being able to drive thing was becoming quite an inconvenience. How could I do anything if I was held hostage without a car? "Claire, when does your next appointment come in?"

"Fifteen minutes. Not enough time to take you anywhere."

Sometimes it was spooky how she or Jack could read my mind. "How do you know that's what I was going to ask?" Unnecessary question, that one.

"Because I know you," she said, slowly shaking her head and sighing. "Oh, how I know you."

"Don't make that sound like it's such a burden. If you can't take me, can I borrow your car?" I asked sheepishly.

"Nope, sorry. I won't enable you to do what you're not supposed to."

"If I'm the one driving, you aren't really enabling, though."

"Melanie Hogan," she said, laughing, "get your butt back to the office and put your leg up."

"I need to go get some ice."

"No, you don't," Babs said. "I'll get it."

"You ladies are impossible," I grumbled, limping back to the office. I dropped into the chair and propped my leg up on the desk. I had to admit it felt good to get my weight off it.

After mulling over what to do with the letter before turning it over to Levi, I finally gave in. There was absolutely nothing to go on. Maybe Levi could at least get prints from the envelope. I picked up my phone to call him when it rang, startling me. I looked at the caller ID.

"Hey, Max."

"Melanie, you have to help us!"

My heart rate spiked north of safe. "Daisy? Honey, what's wrong?"

"Someone is chasing me and daddy!"

19

I bolted upright in my chair, dropping my leg to the floor, wincing when it hit. "Daisy? Where are you?"

"Driving on the road."

"What road, honey? Can you put your dad on?"

"He can't talk," she said, her voice trembling. "He's driving really fast and if he talks on the phone we'll crash. We're trying to get away from the bad guys."

"Guys? There's more than one? Do you know who they are?"

"No," she said. "Daddy, drive faster!"

"Daisy," I said as calmly as I could, "put me on speakerphone, okay? Do you know how to do that?"

"Okay, you're on speaker."

"Max, where are you?"

"Highway 3. Headed north."

"Did you call 911? Please tell me you called 911." I held my breath.

"No, I didn't call them. They just turned off on a side road," he said.

"Did you get a license plate number?"

"No, I was a little busy getting away from them."

"Them? Did you recognize anyone in the car?" I asked.

"No. Tinted windows. But I do know it was a dark-colored sedan."

"Owned by every criminal in the world," I said, sarcasm apparent. "Where are you headed now?"

"The bank to fill out some paperwork for the drugstore purchase. But I need to permanently get rid of this guy and get Daisy someplace safe first. What, honey?" Correctly assuming he was addressing Daisy, I waited for the two of them to talk through Daisy's panic. I listened as she told Max she wanted to get her mom and go home, and to Max, as he tried to console her as best he could.

"Hey, Max?" I said, trying to get his attention. "Max!"

"Yeah?" he answered.

"Can you guys come to the salon?"

"I don't think we should. That would only draw him to you."

"Like he doesn't already know where to find me?" I said in disbelief. "Are you serious? He left a dead body for me to stumble upon, for crying out loud. I think it's safe to say he already knows where to find me. Bring Daisy here. She can stay with me at the salon for a while where there are a lot of people around. It might help take her mind off things. Besides, it'd be a whole lot more fun for her here than at the bank."

"Are you sure? I can bring her to my mom." With everything happening, his voice remained eerily calm. Did nothing rattle this guy?

"Yes, I'm sure. I'm kind of laid up with my bum knee today anyway. We can keep each other company." My spirits brightened at the opportunity to get to know the cute little girl with the freckles and pugged nose, who I was more confident than ever was my niece. "Drop her off and go get yourself a cup of coffee somewhere. And call the police to let them know what happened."

"Tell them what? I didn't get a license plate, and I can't give them a description of the person or anything else. Only that it was a dark-colored sedan. Which, by the way, you let me know was of no help."

Geez! This guy sounds like me! It obviously runs in the family. "Well, drop off Daisy with me and go get yourself a cup of coffee on your way to the bank. Well, maybe go to the bank first."

"Yeah, I guess I could do that. But I'll get coffee first, before the bank."

I rolled my eyes and pinched the bridge of my nose. This brother stuff was going to be a giant headache. "Whatever. See ya in a few."

After we hung up, I heard Claire and Connie both talking to customers. Babs came into the office with a bag of ice.

"Here, your majesty," she teased. She still wore her studded leather coat. The diamonds in her nose ring glistened.

"What, you just come in without bowing? How is that any way to treat a queen?"

"You know, Melanie, in all seriousness, if this stuff keeps up, instead of doing other peoples' hair, you'll be getting your hair done by my cousin."

I frowned. "What are you talking about?"

"My cousin I told you about—Andie. She's the one who does hair at the mortuary. Temporarily, anyway."

I shivered. "Let's hope not. All the more reason to find out who's trying to scare Max and me away."

She opened the ice pack box, poked and prodded the pack until the packet inside popped, releasing the cold, and then plopped it on my knee. "Isn't that supposed to be elevated?"

"Bossy much?" I asked. "It was elevated. Until Max called. Someone was chasing him and Daisy." I shot my hand up. "Before you ask, no, he didn't see who it was." I hoisted my leg back up on the desk and resituated the ice pack. "He's bringing Daisy here to hang out with me for a while. Poor thing was scared to death."

Babs's mouth hung open, her arms crossed in front of her. "Man! This stuff just follows you. I swear you're cursed."

"Thanks," I grumbled.

The bell jingled above the door, followed by Claire's sweet voice. "Babs, Bonnie is here for her shellac mani and pedi."

She bowed and exited, leaving me laughing again and thankful I'd come here today.

***

Daisy and I spent the afternoon drawing—or rather she drew, and I admired. We even played some games on the computer—or rather she played, and I watched. All in all, we had a productive time getting acquainted with one another, and having a niece was turning out to be more than just okay.

"Do you know my mom?" she asked after Max called, letting us know he'd be there in ten minutes.

"No. I only met her briefly."

"Where?" she asked, eyes filled with hope and curiosity. She clasped her hands in front of her.

"Umm…" I scrambled to come up with an answer that didn't let on where I'd met her, but something that wasn't a lie, either. I also didn't want to tell her I'd seen her at the Urgent Care clinic, or she would worry. *Oh, what to say.*

"You don't remember?" she asked, eyes wide.

I pursed my lips as if trying hard to recall. "I think it was just in town one day. While I was running some errands."

"Where?"

Oh boy! "Umm—well—I was in a cafe having coffee with your dad, and I saw her through a window. I knew it was her because of your dad." *Whew!*

She appeared to mull this over while I held my breath, hoping she left it at that.

"Did they talk?"

"No, honey, they didn't. Not while I was there." It was time for a diversion tactic, which I'd gotten quite good at with Sydney. "What do you say we get you another hot chocolate before your dad gets here?" I pushed my chair back to stand up, but Daisy didn't move.

"I wish my mom would come home. I think she wants to."

I sat back down and took her hand, so tiny in my own. I looked at her child-like fingers, the long, oval nail beds. "I bet you miss her." She nodded. "You have a pretty darn good dad, though. That must help a little, huh?"

She shrugged. "Do you get to see your mom?"

I flinched at the left-field fly ball. "My mom left when I was just a little girl. My grandmother and granddad raised me."

"Did that make you sad?"

I smiled at her. "My grandmother is the best woman in this world. Would you like to meet her someday?"

This pried a hint of a smile from her lips, but one that didn't quite reach her eyes. "Yeah. How come you didn't live with your dad like I do?"

Now that was a question that had all kinds of answers. None that I could tell this sweet, little girl. For starters, I couldn't imagine having been raised by that monster. Odd but powerful gratitude filled me that Violet took me away and left me with my grandparents without letting Lenny know he had a daughter. At least that part she did right. "I didn't know my dad," I finally said.

"How come?"

"Well—um—I—" My mouth and my brain were having a terrible time connecting. Too many questions for which I hadn't prepared. I should have known better after spending as much time as I do with Syd. You'd think I'd be a genius at this by now. But nope. Finally, I simply shrugged. "My mom never told me who my dad was. And my grandmother didn't know either." I looked deep into her eyes. "That's why it's so important that your dad is there for you. That he loves you so much."

This got a genuine smile, and she did a little jump on the edge of her seat. "My dad is the best. I'm sorry you didn't have one, Melanie."

I smiled at her and said quietly, "Yeah, me too. But I had my grandmother and granddad. They were the best."

"My grandpa was the best too." Her eyes lit up.

"Um—your grandpa?" Had Max told her about Lenny? And had he let the two of them meet? I was shocked, to say the least.

"Yeah, Grandpa George."

I took a breath of relief—Max's stepdad. I wasn't ready to have the conversation about Lenny with her. The last few questions were hard enough. "Yes, your dad mentioned him."

We both stood to leave the office when she turned and looked at me. "My dad said that you're his sister."

I cocked my head to the side, absorbing such innocent but profound words. Finally, I smiled, "Yeah, I guess I am."

"How?" she asked.

I chuckled and tucked a strand of blond hair from her bob haircut behind her ear. "That, my little one, is a question you'll need to ask your dad."

The bell above the door chimed. Babs's voice called out, "Melanie and Daisy are in the office. Head on back."

At least she was a little nicer than the first night we'd all met him. He probably hadn't known what hit him that night. And I was surprised he hadn't turned and high-tailed it out of there.

"Melanie?" Daisy said, turning again to look at me.

For the first time, I noticed her eyes were just slightly wideset, making the freckles on her little nose more visible. "Yeah, sweetie?"

"I'm glad you're my aunt. I've never had an aunt before."

I laughed softly. "I'm glad you're my niece, too. I've never had one of those before either."

"This is gonna be fun." She grinned.

"It sure is," I said.

"What's going to be fun?" Max said, turning the corner into the office, nearly bumping into Daisy. He tucked his hands into the front pockets of his dark-blue jeans.

"Girl talk," I said.

"Having an auntie," Daisy said at the same time. She wrapped her arms around Max's waist.

"What happened to your leg, anyway?" Max asked, pointing to the brace on my knee. "Didn't exactly have the chance to ask you at the clinic. Your guard dog was there."

I shot him a visual arrow. "That's rude."

"It was," he admitted. "Sorry. Can't blame the guy, I guess."

"Ya think?" I shook my head. "I fell on some ice yesterday."

"She's going to take me ice skating, Daddy," Daisy said.

"Yeah?" he said, looking at me, brows furrowed. "You fell on ice, and you want to take my daughter ice skating?"

He smirked, and I narrowed my eyes at him. "Like living dangerously, do you? Because *you* are skating on thin ice right now."

"How are you going to do that?"

"Well, with your permission. But the ice is safe."

"No, I mean, how are you going to ice skate?" he asked, pointing again at my knee.

"Claire's daughter is the same age, so they'll go with us. Sydney and Daisy can skate. And probably Claire. She's pretty good. I'll be a spectator on the sidelines. Every sport needs a spectator, right?"

"You sure? I can come with if that would help. Make that two spectators."

"Girls only, Dad," Daisy said, tugging at his arm.

"You heard her," I said, grinning. "Girls only."

"Yup, girls only," Claire added, now standing in the doorway behind Max.

"Where's the rink, here in town?" he asked.

"At my house. On the lake. Cole and Levi shoveled a small area."

"All right, then. When is this girls party supposedly happening?"

"Why not tomorrow after work?" I said, looking from Claire to Max and back to Claire. "It's supposed to be a bit warmer tomorrow. And nighttime is the best time to skate by the light of the moon under the stars. If it's cloudy and there's no moon or stars, the light in the back of my house shines almost to the lake." I looked at Max. "If you can have her here by five-thirty tomorrow evening, I'll take her home with me and bring her back to town when we're done. Probably around eight or so?"

"Miss Claire, can I sweep the hair for you from your last haircut?" Daisy asked.

"Well, gosh, I already did it," Claire said before opening her eyes big and bending over to Daisy's level. "But I tell you what, why don't you come with me, and we'll see if Babs or Connie need help with anything." She held her hand out, and Daisy grabbed it.

"Five minutes, kiddo," Max said. "We have to get going. Gramma needs to run some errands, and I told her I would drive her. Thanks for taking her this afternoon,

Melanie," Max said as soon as they left. "It's good for her to have a positive female role model."

"Well, calling me a positive role model is pretty presumptuous, given that you've just met me and all." I worked to suppress a grin.

"I figure you've got to be okay if you're dating a lead detective at the police department. It's not like you can have a criminal history."

If you only knew. The past couple of years I'd gotten myself into some pretty good jams and had nearly attained that criminal history he spoke of, due in large part to my own birth mother and now my father. Or rather the sperm donor. He wasn't a father. Someday I'd have to fill Max in on the troubles I'd been in. But not yet.

"Have you ever wondered if we have any other siblings out there?" I asked. "I mean, what are the chances that our mothers are the only ones that had children by that man?" I wrinkled my nose. "That thought's disturbing. I don't want any siblings."

"Thanks," he said dryly.

"Don't get all bum hurt. I haven't decided yet about you, so there's still hope," I teased.

He chuckled, a rare break in his calm, almost flat, persona. "Fantastic. And no, I don't believe there are any more of us out there. According to my mom, Lenny made sure of that. And she did some legwork to check it out. Didn't uncover anything."

"Hm. I hope you're right." I pondered it for a minute. "Hey, what were you doing out on Highway 3 when whoever it was chased you?" I asked.

"Going to your house."

My breath caught. I hadn't yet told him where I live. Of that, I was sure.

20

Not only had I never told him where I lived, but as far as he knew, I would have been at work. Why would he be going to my house while I wasn't there?

"Why?"

"Why what?" he asked, frowning.

"Why were you going to my house?"

He studied me a moment. "You don't trust me, do you? You think I'm up to something."

"Why wouldn't I? Look who your father is."

"And yours," he answered wryly.

He had a valid point, but I still needed to know. "It was just a simple question, Max. Why were you going to my house when I was at work?"

"To see where you live. Because for some godforsaken reason, you're trying to keep me away. And yet you want me to trust my daughter with you? Exactly how does that work in your world? I can't know where you live, and yet you want to take my daughter there."

Again, he had a perfect point; I couldn't deny it. It made no sense at all. I was ashamed that I'd assumed one-sided trust was okay. "I'm sorry, Max, you're right. But if you knew what I've been through the past several years—"

"You're not the only one with a history that's been hard, Melanie. Not the only one who's been burned. Given what I've been through with Daisy's mom, a woman I trusted with my life and the welfare of our daughter up until recently, frankly, I don't know that I can trust *you*."

"That's why you wanted to come out to my house with her," I stated more to myself than to Max. And here I thought it was something sinister. I'd let my imagination get the better of me. Again. "Max, listen—"

He shifted his weight, took a breath, and tipped his head back, rubbing the back of his neck. He looked back at me. "I know this whole thing is new and won't be easy on either one of us for a while. Quite possibly never. But I'm willing to give it a shot. Are you? Because I'm not going into this alone."

I sighed. "I'll do my best. That's all I can promise."

"That's all I ask," he said, shaking his head slightly. "I have to get going."

"Hey, Max?" He stopped and turned. "Want to bring Daisy out to my house tomorrow? About six?"

"Yeah, that'd be good. Text me your address. I know the general vicinity but not the exact address. At least that's one thing that wasn't easy to find on you."

I nodded. "But you heard what Daisy said. It's for girls only. You'll have to stay in the house or drop her off and come back." I smiled at him.

He shook his head, one corner of his lips curving upward. "Wouldn't dream of intruding on girl time."

I watched as he walked out then decided to follow. Thank goodness it was a slow day for business. The girls popping their heads in, and even occasionally joining in with Daisy and me, made it fun for her. And I didn't feel an ounce of guilt for not helping in the salon. That had never happened before.

As soon as Max and Daisy were out the door, and before any of the ladies could object, I quickly slipped into my coat and wrapped a scarf around my neck. "Headed to the grocery store," I said. "Any of you want anything?"

"How's that knee feeling?" Connie asked.

"Better, actually." I fished my gloves out from my pocket and worked my fingers into them. "I haven't had to take anything for pain for quite a while." I snagged my crutch and tucked it under my arm.

"Well, be careful," Claire said. "I don't need to remind you of the dangers of ice patches."

"Yes, Mother."

"Want me to go for you when I finish up here?"

I looked at the client in her chair and back at Claire and shook my head. "Um, no, my friend. You do your thing, I'll do mine. I'm sure Ann will appreciate it."

"I said after I finish." Claire rested her hand on Ann's shoulder. "I wouldn't just leave you," she told her.

"No, I'm good," I said. "I need to get out anyway. I'm going crazy sitting around."

"To be honest," Babs said, "I'm surprised you've been as good as you have. I think that little girl was good for you today."

I smiled. "Yeah, I agree." I started walking for the door and stopped, turning. "Hey Babs, you know your cousin that works for the Birch Haven Funeral Home?"

"Andie? What about her?"

"Yeah. Can you find out if that's where they took Lenny?"

"Wouldn't they fly him back to California?" Claire asked.

I shrugged. "I don't know. That's what I want to find out. But they would have done the autopsy here."

"Who's planning the funeral?" Babs asked.

"No idea. I guess I could ask Max if he knows."

"I'll call Andie as soon as I'm done here," Babs said.

"Who's Lenny, and how did he die?" Ann asked, reminding me there were other people than just us in the salon.

"Some guy Melanie knows," Claire jumped in. "He was visiting from California and died in Birch Haven."

"Oh!" Ann gasped. She rested her fingers against her lips, the fire-engine red nail polish matching her lipstick. "Is that the guy they found dead right here outside your salon?"

"How did you find out about that?" I asked. "I didn't see anything in the paper yet."

"It's a small town, sugar. Word gets around. There are three methods of communication in Birch Haven— telephone, telegraph, and tell a Birch Haven local."

We all busted out laughing. "I'll have to remember that one," Babs finally managed to get out.

By the time we finished, it looked as if we all just had a good cry. Connie held her side and Claire her stomach. Babs blotted her mascara with a tissue.

"Okay, ladies," I finally said, "I'll be right back. I'll let you know if I hear anything from any of the locals at the grocery store."

Despite feeling little pain this afternoon, hobbling on a bum knee with a crutch to the other end of the strip took some time. And making sure I didn't slip on the floor of the store, wet from melted snow, took some concentration.

As I rounded the corner to the protein bars, a large, bald man, looking like he was more muscle than anything else beneath his Los Angeles Rams coat, stood at the end of the aisle. From the back, he could have been mistaken for Levi.

He locked eyes with me, and I turned away. When I braved it to give a sideways glance, he was gone. His demeanor—downturned lips, tight jaw, narrowed eyes, and arms slightly bowed out—gave me the creeps. Like an adult on the pony-chair we had at the salon for kids' cuts, he looked sorely out of place.

I proceeded to the drink aisle and peeked around the corner before turning. Empty. I started my trek toward the smartwater when he turned down the aisle toward me. After another menacing look, he grabbed a six-pack of Coke, lingered a moment, then left.

I placed my items on the belt at the checkout with trembling fingers, my eyes darting around the area until I had my bag in hand and made for the door. I took a deep breath, feeling a little silly. The guy was probably having a bad day or maybe just hated women. Whatever his problem was, it was unlikely it had anything to do with me. Regardless, this chocolate-peanut butter protein bar had better be worth it.

I jaunted as quickly as I could back to the salon while still keeping aware of my surroundings. When I got there, the ladies were cleaning up, preparing to close.

"Timed that one just right," I said as I sat my bum in my stylist chair. I took a swig of water then munched on my protein bar as I watched them. "Every job needs a good supervisor. I volunteer for the job."

"You're kind of annoying when you're laid up," Bab's said.

To show just how true that was, I continued to comment until Claire sprayed me with a water bottle. I ducked, put my arm up to block the water, and scowled. "Bully," I said under my breath, which earned me another splash of water.

On the way home, Claire and I finally had time alone. As close as we lived, often the span between moments spent together, just the two of us, was too long. And with her parents visiting, it compromised that time even more. They were wonderful people and treated me like their own daughter, but I wasn't disappointed they were heading out the next day. Sydney wasn't thrilled about it, from what Claire said, but why would she be? They treated her like a princess. What little girl wouldn't love that?

"Have you talked to Rose today?" she asked me.

"A couple of times. She had to make sure I was following the doctor's orders."

"Well, I, for one, agree with Babs. I can't believe you are."

"I think there's so much that's been dropped on me the past couple of days that I don't know what's what anymore." I thought about the guy from the grocery store. "I feel jittery, looking at everyone as a possible suspect." I cast a glance at her then back out the front window. "I can't stand to be laid up. I'm not going to take a chance by doing anything that will prolong the healing."

"Good girl," she said. The headlights of an oncoming car lit up her face, showing her white teeth.

"Thank you, Mom."

"What else is on your mind?" she asked.

"You don't think I have enough on it already?" I shook my head slowly and looked out the side window. "Feels like I have mental whiplash."

"You do," she agreed. "Have enough on your mind, that is. But I know you. What are you thinking?"

"Max is bringing Daisy out to my house tomorrow night."

Her head jerked toward me. "He's what?"

I grabbed the dash. "Watch the road!"

Doing as she was told, she asked again, "He's doing what? Levi is going to have a cow, you know."

"This isn't Levi's call to make. He needs to trust me." I felt Claire's attention on me. "Watch the road, please. Max is trusting me with his kid," I explained. "I'm not sure if that's stupid or if I should feel honored. I mean, he hardly knows me. Would you trust Sydney with someone you don't know?" I looked at her as she shook her head.

"Nope."

"See? He's taking the much bigger chance here. The least I can do is meet him halfway. How can this have a shot if I don't at least try?"

"You genuinely like this guy, don't you?"

I shrugged. "I guess."

"To say I'm surprised is an understatement. You don't just let people in like this. It's kind of freaking me out."

"If he's family, I have to. Wouldn't you?"

"Yeah, but—"

"Claire, he's got way more to lose than I do. He's the one who knew about Lenny's inheritance and is willing to share it. Not that I want it. But the fact that he's willing to says a lot. He has nothing to gain by finding me, and yet he did."

"It sounds like you've thought about this from all angles."

"A ton. I've tossed it over every which way and can't come up with any reason whatsoever that he would want to harm me. Nothing. And you know how suspicious I am about people. No matter how I look at it, he's the one who stands to lose anything at all. And yet he's stepping out on the proverbial limb anyway." We were quiet while Claire seemed to ponder what I'd said. "The only sad part is that it's Lenny's blood that connects us. The fact that it's his DNA we share does alarm me just a little bit. Though, Violet's isn't a whole lot better," I snarked.

"It shouldn't alarm you."

I snapped my head around to look at her. I hadn't anticipated that she would find a reason to refute my concern quite so easily. "Why not?"

She took a deep breath before she spoke, perhaps weighing whether to say it or not. "Melanie, Lenny wasn't born bad. Children are inherently good. Somewhere along the line, for reasons we don't know, he turned evil. But that has nothing to do with his blood or DNA, as you fear. Now had you both been raised by the guy, that'd be a different story."

"More like a nightmare."

"Who knows what his childhood was like?" she continued. "He might have had a father who taught him to be the way he is. Or even his mother. He might have been part of the foster system. We know how that can screw up a kid. Somewhere, somehow, he lost his innocence, the goodness he was born with. You and Max didn't inherit that part, but rather who he was before this stuff." She glanced over at me. "And whether you want to admit it or not, maybe you've already thought about it, but Violet gave you a huge gift by not letting Lenny be part of your life."

I stared at the countryside rolling by under the light of the moon, absorbing Claire's words. Finally, I said quietly, "I had no idea you had a degree in psychology."

"Are you mad?" she asked, biting her lower lip. "I hurt your feelings, didn't I?"

"Nah. All of what you said is true. I just didn't know you'd given it so much thought."

She sighed, relieved. "Of course I did. You're my best friend. There's no way I can just sit back and not think all this through, so I know what I need to do to protect you."

I shook my head. "What have I ever done to make you and Levi think I need protection?"

"We both know you well enough to know you think you're tough, and you put on a good facade. But sometimes, my dear friend, you're your own worst enemy."

"I suppose I am," I mused, staring out the window again. "What does Sydney think about having a sitter again after school now that your folks are leaving?"

"Ha!" she laughed. "Nice subject change. And we don't call it a sitter. She said that's for babies. I swear she thinks she's an adult. And sometimes she sounds like it."

"It will be fun to get her and Daisy together tomorrow evening."

"I think it's cool that Syd, Daisy, and Jackson are all close to the same age. We'll have to get all three of them together before Max and Daisy leave."

"They're not leaving."

"They're not?" she said, her voice raising an octave.

I grabbed the dash again. "Keep your—"

"Eyes on the road," she said. "I know, I know. And I am. Stop nagging. What do you mean he's not leaving?"

"Max is buying the old drugstore on Maple Street. The owner is retiring after fifty years of owning it."

"Wow! What do *you* think of that? Of him moving here," she asked.

"What I think doesn't matter. He's moving here whether I want him to or not."

"Do you? Want him to move here."

I thought about it for a minute then looked at her. "Yeah, I do." I smiled to myself. "I have a brother and a niece, Claire. I think I'm growing more used to it and might even like it a little bit."

"By looking at you, I'd say you like it more than just a little bit."

We turned into my driveway, and she drove up right in front of my house. "Want help getting in?" she asked.

"Heck no. I'm good. But thanks anyway." I opened the door, got out, then bent over to look across the car at her. "Unless you want to come in."

"I better get home and spend the evening with my folks before they leave."

"I get it." I blew her a kiss. "Thanks for the lift. Love ya!"

"Love you too. Stay off your knee as much as possible."

I gave her a salute, stood, and shut the car door. She waited to leave until I'd closed the house door behind me. A couple of quick honks followed.

After closing all the curtains, except the large one that faced the lake, I headed up the stairs to change into a pair of yoga pants and a hoodie. I grabbed my book off the nightstand and made my way back to the living room. I was pleasantly surprised by how much better my knee felt tonight. I dropped my book onto the couch and went to the kitchen to make some popcorn and grab a can of orange seltzer water. When the popcorn finished popping, I poured it into a bowl, dropped a handful of M&Ms into it, and headed back to the living room.

I stopped in front of the window and gazed out over the lake, appreciating the serene beauty. The moon was bright, and millions of stars speckled the sky. Between that and the light from the snow-covered ground, it looked more like dusk than the evening hours' typical darkness. I watched as four snowmobiles zigzagged across the lake, chasing each other, white dust from the snow kicking up behind the machines. It was beautiful and mesmerizing.

A fish house a few yards out from the shoreline housed evening fishermen. Lantern light illuminated a small window and a crack in the door. Two snowmobiles were parked alongside it. Levi and I had drilled a couple of holes in the ice a few weeks ago, and we planted ourselves on two upside-down five-gallon pails for chairs. I caught the first fish and claimed the victory until I realized I had to touch the slimy thing to get it off the hook—a measly little perch. And I couldn't help but feel sorry for it. I dipped it back in the water, hoping it would free itself and swim away. Levi had grabbed the line and pulled it up. "What are you doing?" he'd asked incredulously.

"Letting him live," I'd said, pouting.

The excursion ended with Levi taking the fish off, tossing it back in the water, and me happily watching it swim down the hole and out of sight. I smiled at the memory, jarred out of it by my phone.

"Hello?"

"Melanie, it's Max."

"Please don't tell me you've changed your mind on Daisy coming over tomorrow evening." I crossed my fingers.

"No. But if it's all the same to you, I'll probably just wait in the house for you guys. Or I should say girls," he added, "since it's girl's night and all."

"That's fine. I told you you could. Is that all you called for?"

"No." He hesitated. "I got a phone call from Lenny's attorney."

"What'd he want? And speaking of Lenny," I said before he could answer, "is he at Birch Haven Funeral Home, or was he flown back to California?"

"He's here."

"Why?"

"We've decided to bury him here."

"*We*?" I asked.

"My mother and me. No one else came forward to bury him." I was silent. I didn't know what to say. "Hello?"

"Yeah, I'm here."

"You're more than welcome to help. I just didn't think you'd want to."

"You're right; I don't." *Did I*? "Why did you decide to bury him here when California is home to him?"

"He's got nothing left or anyone in California, except for his goons. One of whom is probably his killer. I'm here, you're here—it just seemed the logical place for him to rest."

"Rest," I mumbled. "That's an odd word for death. Anyway," I said, "what did his attorney want?"

"He said he needs to meet with me. I've made an appointment for tomorrow at noon."

"Need me to watch Daisy?" I asked.

"No. My mom has that covered. I'm calling to see if you want to go with me. You're just as much an heir as I am. And before you say again that you don't want his money, it's not just about the money."

"What is it about then? Because you're right, I don't want his dirty money."

"We don't know what he all has for assets. For all I know, all his money is tied up. Although I hope it's not since I'm buying the drugstore and counting on some of the money for help."

"I don't know, Max..."

"I'd like for you to go, Melanie. But obviously it's your decision."

I thought a moment longer. "Fine. I'll go."

"It's at Swanson, Swanson, and Hebert."

"I know where that is. I'll meet you there."

As soon as we hung up, I regretted my decision. What did I just get myself into?

21

I woke before my alarm sounded and shut it off. I wouldn't be falling back to sleep anyway. After tossing and turning, I finally decided to call it quits and get up. I hadn't slept well because I had been too wound up fighting the urge to call Max and cancel. Yet, something greater pulled me to keep my commitment.

When Levi called late last evening, I'd told him about Max's plan to bring Daisy to my house the following evening and about meeting Max at Lenny's attorney's office. As expected, he had been pensive about my decision to give Max my address and curious about the appointment with the attorney. When I'd presented my argument to him, the same one presented to Claire, defending my position to give Max my address so he could bring Daisy out, he surprised me by being okay with it. But he didn't pass up the opportunity to bring up the possibility of staying with me until we knew it was safe. I had insisted that wasn't necessary, that he worked nights anyway, so the suggestion was a moot point. He had grown quiet, after which he'd told me we needed to talk over a few things. I had an idea what those "things" were and didn't look forward to that conversation. That, too, had kept me awake.

I wrapped myself in my robe and kicked on the furnace, taking comfort when it started to hum. Last winter, my furnace had gone out on a weekend which cost me a pretty penny to get someone out to fix it during nonoffice hours. Since then, every time I kicked it up in the mornings, I breathed with relief when I heard it turn on.

I went downstairs and started my coffee pot manually since it wasn't scheduled to begin on its own for another half hour. Despite having to reschedule about half of the day's appointments not to overextend the time on my knee, I looked forward to going to work. But anxiety began to take up residence as I thought about the day's events. The two things I looked forward to were work and ice skating that evening. All the stuff in between was debatable, depending on the outcome.

After finishing my morning devotional and a hot shower, I pulled a long-sleeved black thigh-length sweater over my head, donned a pair of black leggings—complete with the knee brace—and opted for my flat-heeled black slouch boots instead of my typical high-heeled black ones. I wasn't sure my knee was ready for heels. Fifteen minutes for drying my hair, applying light makeup, and slipping into my black leather coat with a scarf and gloves, and I was out the door. Claire called when I was halfway to the salon. I put her on speakerphone so I could concentrate on the icy roads.

"I'm picking you up, right?" she asked.

"No. I'm already on my way."

"Why didn't you wait for me? I was looking forward to another drive together. It's kind of silly that we don't carpool more often anyway."

"Carpooling would work if you were able to leave the house earlier. I like to get to the salon sooner." Which wasn't a lie. Claire always arrived well after me. "You have Syd to get ready. I don't."

"But today, my parents brought her to school before they left for home."

"How was I supposed to know that? I don't watch your house with binoculars to know what you're doing, you know." I chuckled. "I should do that, now that I think about it. It could be my evening entertainment."

She laughed. "Yeah, right. You'd fall asleep from boredom the minute Syd goes to bed."

"See you when you get in." Before she hung up, I said, "Wait! Before I forget, I have to leave for a while at noon today. I shouldn't be gone long."

"Where are you going?"

I filled her in on my call from Max the evening before. "Levi is pretty intrigued."

"I bet! So am I. What did Levi say about you giving Max your address? You did tell him, didn't you?"

"Yes. He would've found out anyway. And I didn't want to keep it from him."

"What'd he say?"

I signaled to turn onto the main road through town. "Said he trusted me to make the right decision."

"Really," she scoffed. "Why am I skeptical of that?"

"Then he proceeded to tell me that he could stay at my house for protection. Until we're sure there's nothing to worry about. I told him no."

"You what?" I could almost see her frowning like I'd lost my mind. "Why would you do that? I swear, Melanie, sometimes I think you're intentionally sabotaging your relationship with that man. You realize that every woman in Birch Haven would die for him to notice them, right?"

I exhaled long and slow. "I'm scared, Claire. Plain and simple. Sheer fear. That's it."

"And you think the answer to that is to chase him away? You make no sense."

"No, that's not the answer."

"But that's precisely what you're doing." Her words were riddled with exasperation.

"What about Cole? He hardly ever stays at your house." The childish *so there!* sentiment wasn't lost on either of us.

"Really, Melanie? I'm not the one in danger; you are. Besides, that's different. I have Sydney there. I can't have him stay when she's home. It wouldn't be right."

She had a point, and I sighed. "I know. I worry that if he's around too much, it will suffocate my independence. And I worry that he'll eventually leave. I know you think that's stupid, but—"

"I don't think it's stupid, but it's not exactly fair to just assume he's going to do you dirty. Or to assume he's the same as Cain. The man couldn't be more different from your ex."

"I know." I pulled into the parking lot and left my car running while I stayed put. "I love him to death, but —"

"But what? And please don't say you love him to death. That can't turn out well for you."

"Haha. Very funny."

"Tell ya what, if I don't get out of the house, I'm gonna be late. I'll talk to you as soon as I get there."

"Goodie," I said dryly.

***

The salon hummed with life again, the norm for any day. Why yesterday was so quiet wasn't exactly a mystery, I guess, with Rubie gone and my clients rescheduled.

Before I knew it, eleven-thirty approached. I finished up drying my client's hair, rang her out at the register, and slipped into my coat, telling the ladies I'd be back as soon as I could. My next appointment wasn't until two.

"Hey, Melanie," Babs said when I'd reached the door. "I talked to Andie. She said Lenny is there. That he's getting buried in Fairmont Cemetery in Birch Haven."

"I heard," I said. "Do you think she would be open to talking with me?"

"Sure. I already told her you'd be calling her. I just assumed." She snickered. "I'll text you her number."

"Thanks," I said, pushing the door open. "See you all as soon as I'm done."

The drive to the attorney's office took less than ten minutes. I looked for Max's car in the parking lot, spotting him in my rearview mirror as he pulled in behind me. After turning off my car, I sat still for a moment, collecting myself before walking blindfolded into the unknown. I couldn't help but feel I had no business being here. That this was all because of a man who hadn't only attempted to kill Violet but had also attempted to frame me to get back at her. A man who did everything he could to destroy my life. I stifled a scream when Max pulled open my car door.

"Just going to sit there all day?" he asked.

"Maybe. If I want to," I said, narrowing my eyes.

"Come on," he said, holding out his hand for me to take. I brushed him aside and swung my legs out, standing slowly so as not to lose my footing on the ice.

"You're one of those," he commented as he walked away.

"Wait," I said, a word brushed with irritation. "One of what?"

"I was just trying to help you. Go ahead and fall on your butt again if you want."

"Sorry," I said, my cheeks feeling warm. "I'm just not used to — to —"

"Help? I've figured that out. Come on. Let's go in." He shook his head and muttered, "Poor Levi." When we got to the door, Max reached for the handle and turned to me. "Do I dare open it for you, or should I let it shut in your face?"

"Whichever you prefer," I said. He pulled it open and stepped to the side, allowing me to pass by.

"Thank you."

"Don't mention it."

The front desk was empty, but music played from somewhere in the room. Two hallways led away from the main reception area. I glanced down both and looked at Max. "There's no one here."

"I'll be right there," boomed a voice from down one of the hallways.

I looked up at Max with an arched eyebrow, and he shrugged. I took in the walls, decorated with artwork of city lights and traffic. A display case lined one complete wall, filled with all sorts of gambling memorabilia. I noticed Max taking it all in as well, his face devoid of all expression. Per the usual.

Finally, a squatty, balding man appeared from the room behind the desk. "You must be Max," he said, popping the last of something in his mouth. He licked his fingers, wiped them on his slacks, then reached out to shake Max's hand. My stomach turned, and I quickly looked the other way so I wouldn't have to shake his hand. "Who is this?" he said. I turned to see him looking at me. All of me. My skin crawled.

"This is my half-sister, Melanie."

"So this is Melanie," he said, his beady little eyes looking me up and down. I squirmed and resisted the urge to straighten his toupee. "The name's Barry." He reached out his hand, which I didn't take.

"How is it Lenny had an attorney here when he lived in California?" I asked, straight to the point. I wanted to get this over with and get the heck out. I regretted my decision to come with Max at all.

"We have satellite offices around the country," he said, pulling up his pants with one hand. "Some in much smaller towns than this. I'm not *the* attorney for Lenny. I'm a partner."

"I bet," I mumbled. Max shot me an amused look.

"Let's get on with it, shall we?" Max said, rescuing me. "It shouldn't take long, should it? Melanie has to get back to work."

"Come on back," he said, motioning us to follow him. "Sorry about no one at the front desk. Mae has the day off to be with her kid. He's going through some sorta trouble. I told her to give him the boot, but she doesn't listen to me."

"Do you have children, Barry?" I asked.

"Nope."

"Shocker," I murmured. Max elbowed me.

Max and I each took a seat in a chair across the desk from Barry. I watched as he opened a large manilla envelope with his fat little greasy fingers, licking his index finger as he flipped through the papers. I shuddered.

"At the time Lenny made out the will a few months back, he only knew about Max, not you, Melanie. So initially, he signed almost everything over to Max. That bein' said," he flipped through to another page, "his attorney found this letter among his effects."

"What does it say?" Max asked.

"Apparently, he found out about Melanie but hadn't changed his will yet. The letter states his wishes are for all of his estate to be split evenly between three people. But it's not a legally binding letter. Legally, the inheritance will be split two ways."

Three? I inhaled sharply when he said the word, nearly missing the rest. Max and I glanced at each other. Did we have another sibling?

"You said three? Who's the other?" Max asked. I held my breath, afraid of the answer.

"Daisy. His only granddaughter," Barry said. "Hers is to be put into a trust until she turns twenty-one. Upon your passing, Max," he said, looking at him above the rim of his glasses, "should that happen, your share, whatever is left of it, will go into the trust for Daisy."

I breathed an audible sound with relief. One sibling was all I wanted.

He looked at Max over the top of his glasses—a smudge right in the center of one lens—then to me. "Should you want to contest the will, you can."

"No."

Barry put his hand up, palm facing me, "Not so quick. If you provide proof of paternity, along with the letter, you have good cause—"

"I'm not going to contest it," I insisted, pushing my shoulders back slightly. "I don't want the money."

"You both may want to think about this before jumping to any decisions."

"I have." My jaw felt tight, and there was the tiniest twitch by my left eye.

"As have I," Max said. "I will be giving Melanie a third."

I shot him a dark look. "I said I don't want it."

"Chill," he murmured, shaking his head.

The rest of the meeting consisted of Barry rambling on about probate law in his sleazy voice and addressing Max's questions on Lenny's assets. I focused on the bookshelf that lined the wall behind him and the parking lot outside the window. I caught an occasional sentence, few of which were from Max.

Forty minutes later, Max and I walked out of the office. Again, he opened the door for me, and this time I was so preoccupied, I hardly noticed. Not enough to say anything, anyway. I inhaled deeply, letting the fresh air clear my lungs and my head.

As soon as we reached my car door, he whistled. "That's some serious money," he said.

"Ya think?" I was still stunned and unable to say any more.

"About your third —"

"I need time to process all of this, Max. I'm not ready to talk about it."

"I didn't think you were paying attention most of the time," he said as he glanced at a tall brunette who passed us.

"We women are multitaskers." I elbowed him as he continued to watch the brunette. "Put your tongue back in your mouth. You're still married."

He stopped, opened his mouth to say something, then closed it again. I thought I saw a trace of a smile but couldn't be sure. Finally, he said, "I wasn't looking at her."

"Liar."

"I'll see you this evening when I bring Daisy out."

***

The rest of the afternoon, I was only partially present. Even the salon didn't have the power to snap me out of it. Finally, at four-thirty, I slipped into the office and called Andie. I got her voicemail and left my phone number, asking if she could please call me back at her earliest convenience. Five minutes later, my ringtone played.

"Hello?"

"Is this Melanie Hogan?" said a sultry voice.

"It is. And you must be Andie."

"Yup. Babs told me you were probably gonna call. How can I help you?"

I tried to visualize her and wondered if she looked anything like Babs with her tattoos and piercings. "You sound just like your cousin."

She chuckled. "That's what everyone says."

"I wondered if I could ask you a couple of questions about Lenny Martin."

"Sure. I don't know what I can tell you, though. I only do the hair and makeup to make the client look presentable for a funeral. It's just a part-time gig."

"I understand. I mean, I don't, really," I added. "It sounds a little—"

"Morbid?" she said, laughing, which also sounded a lot like Babs.

"No, just—"

"It's okay. Most people think it is and wonder how I can do what I do."

"How can you?" I asked, wanting to understand.

"Ask Babs to fill you in. It's a story that would surely make you think I'm crazy if I told you over the phone. Question away. I'll answer what I can. But I'll tell you right off the bat, if you're going to ask if you can see him, you don't want to until he's ready. Trust me."

"I already did see him. Kind of."

"That's right. You're the one who found him, huh?"

"Yes. However, I didn't see his face. Just from the back."

"Well, trust me when I tell you that you don't wanna see his face. I did what I could so far with the makeup. I'm darn good at what I do, but even I'm not that good. Whoever did this had some serious strength. And anger. Just my opinion."

"Has anyone been in contact with the funeral home? To see him or for anything else?"

"Just his son and his son's mom. Sounds like they're planning the funeral."

"That's what I heard. From Max, his son. Anyone else?"

The line went quiet. Finally, she said, "No, no, I don't think so. Not that I can remember."

"Okay, then. Thank you—"

"Oh, wait!" she exclaimed. "I totally forgot. There was someone else."

My heart sped up. "There was?"

"Yeah. A woman. She had brown, shoulder-length hair. Kind of a bob-style with bangs. Bright red lipstick and tons of makeup, fur coat, and all that jazz. Except I couldn't see her eyes. I thought it was weird because she had on dark glasses and kept them on the entire time. I saw her talking to Mr. Morgan, the funeral director, when I passed through. He introduced me to her. Kind of reeked of fake money."

"Fake money? How do you mean?"

"Someone trying to pretend they have a lot when they don't. Fake fur, cheap perfume—you know the type. I mean none of that is bad, but the pretending to be who you're not…"

I couldn't imagine the woman Andie described fit the description of Max's mother, but I had to ask. "It wasn't the son's mother, Sharon, was it?"

"No. I remember her. Nice looking lady."

"Did you get her name? The fake lady."

"No, can't remember her name, but it wasn't Sharon, no. It was something more exotic. But Mr. Morgan introduced her as the deceased's daughter-in-law."

22

When I hung up from Andie, I sat there, unable to move. Lenny's daughter-in-law? The description was far off from Pam. That means Lenny had another son out there somewhere. But why didn't the attorney know about him? Something was fishy. If we could get a few minutes away from the girls, I'd have to fill Max in this evening. Between the two of us, maybe we could make some sense out of this and figure out who it could have been. It could easily have been a decoy placed there by the killer to get the money.

My mind wandered to the money. When the attorney pushed the documents across the desk at us, detailing the amounts, it felt like he'd punched me. How does someone acquire that much money and so many assets? Max had told me that it was a significant amount, but even he hadn't expected what we saw.

"Melanie!" Connie called, "Susan is here for her cut."

"Coming," I called back. I pushed the chair away from the desk and stood, stretching my knee a bit before continuing. Susan was my last appointment for the day and one I rescheduled from yesterday.

"Come 'ere, you," she said the minute she saw me. She enveloped me in a hug. "You poor, poor thing," she cooed. Finally, she released me and held me at arm's length, looking at the brace on my knee then into my eyes. "Good thing you didn't break anything, tiny as you are," she said. "You sure you're up for this? 'Cause I can come back next week, you know."

"That's very thoughtful of you," I said, "but I'm good. Promise."

She went to my stylist's chair, grabbed the cape, and began to put it on herself as she sat down. "You're a tough cookie, aren't you?"

I gave her a victory grin and said loud enough for Claire to hear me. "Yes, as a matter of fact, I am a tough cookie, Susan. Could you tell Claire that?"

"You just did," Claire said, laughing. She spun her client in the chair and whipped off her cape, setting her free into the world with gorgeous caramel-honey hair color. "The problem is she thinks she's tougher than she is and gets herself in trouble because of it."

"Not true," I said, patting Susan's shoulder. "She's not telling you the truth."

Susan chuckled and looked at me in the mirror before us. "Your reputation for trouble is already out there, honey. You do tend to find yourself in heaps of it."

My eyes opened wide, my mouth forming an "o." "Claire paid you to say that, didn't she?"

"I so did not!" Claire exclaimed. She had the most beautiful laugh. It made the worst day a good one. And she did it often. It was rare that Claire wasn't happy, happy, happy. Sometimes it was even irritating.

"Did you call Andie?" Babs said as she got her coat on, readying to leave for the day.

"I did." I led Susan back to the shampoo bowl. "Thanks for giving her a heads up so she didn't think I was some freak."

"Oh, she probably still does," Babs said and grinned.

"Aren't you guys all a barrel of laughs," I said, shaking my head. "You've all been inhaling too many color and artificial nail fumes."

"That or you haven't been inhaling enough," she said with a wink. "See ya mañana."

"Adios," I said. I finished rinsing the shampoo from Susan's short, processed hair and rubbed in a good dose of conditioner. I heard my phone playing from the office.

"Want me to get it?" Claire asked.

"Yeah. If it's Levi, tell him I'll call him back as soon as I finish here."

"If it's anyone else?"

"Tell them I'll call back as soon as I finish here." I smiled at her, and she laughed.

Seconds later, she came out of the office, talking on my phone. "It's Max," she mouthed. I watched her as I finished rinsing Susan's hair and towel dried it, wrapping her hair in the towel just so. When Claire hung up, she said, "Max is going to be a little bit later than expected. But that works well since we'll be getting home later than expected anyway."

"You can leave now if you want," I said. "You don't have to wait for me."

"Connie and Babs are gone. You'd be alone," she said.

"I'll be fine. Susan is here."

"You're the one who set the no-one-here-alone-after-dark rule. I'm not leaving you to lock up by yourself."

"And there's a killer out there," Susan said, her eyes wide. "No, absolutely not! You shouldn't close up alone."

"You know about that too?" I said, shaking my head. "It's a wonder I have any business at all."

"Honey, who doesn't know about it? This is Birch Haven, after all," Susan said.

"That it is," I said, slowly shaking my head.

***

Twenty-five minutes later, Susan left; I locked the door, cleaned my station, and dropped the money in the floor safe. I would balance it out and deposit it in the morning. Claire had already tossed a load of towels in the washing machine. We'd transfer them to the dryer in the morning as well.

"Ready?" I asked Claire, who was putting an Aveda product order together.

She set her pen down and stood. "Yup. Let's rock and roll." She grabbed her coat and tied a scarf around her neck. It was a multicolored one you could see from miles away, matching the signature headscarves she wore nearly every day to tame her wild black curls. "I'm gonna stop at Harvey's drugstore and pick up something Syd needs for school. It'll only take a minute."

I gave her the thumbs up, locked the door, pulled it to double-check that it clicked, and headed to my car. My knee was a bit achy this evening, and I hoped I hadn't overdone it. Setting the healing process back wouldn't work for me at all. I had too much to do. Like catch a killer.

On the way home, I replayed in my head the conversation from the attorney's office and the one with Andie. I had to find out who the woman was who went to the funeral home. And I had to find out what she talked to the funeral director about. I picked up my phone, pressed the home button, and spoke my request. "Call Birch Haven Funeral Home."

A second later, the female robotic voice said, "Calling Birch Haven Funeral Home."

The voice always creeped me out. Claire always raves about wanting an Alexa. I told her if she ever gets one, I'll never come to her house again. Call me a conspiracy theorist, but I, honest to God, believed people could listen in on those babies. And that they *do*! Claire told me I had nothing to worry about unless I was a serial killer planning my next murder. Otherwise, no one gave two hoots about what anyone said in my home.

The phone continued to ring until finally, someone picked up.

"Birch Haven Funeral Parlor. How may I help you?"

Funeral *Parlor*? I grimaced at the odd word. "I'm calling for Mr. Morgan. Is he in?"

"No, he's not. We closed a half hour ago."

"I see. He didn't stay late?"

"No, ma'am. Was he expecting you?" she asked with a nasal voice.

"No. I mean, I didn't have an appointment if that's what you mean."

"Is there something I can help you with?"

"Um, no, thank you. I need to speak with Mr. Morgan." This lady wouldn't know what the woman who claimed to be Lenny's daughter-in-law talked to Mr. Morgan about.

"You'll have to call back tomorrow then. He's in the office by eight."

"Okay, thank you." I was just about to hang up when I said, "Wait! Ma'am?"

"Yes?"

"Can I leave you my number in case you talk to him this evening? It's about Lenny Martin."

"You can, but I won't be talking to him," she said. "I assure you Mr. Morgan doesn't check in with me once he's left the office."

"Just in case. I mean, what can it hurt, right?"

She sighed in resignation. "Okay, sure. What's your number?"

I gave it to her slowly, then repeated it.

"Got it the first time," she assured me. "I'll be sure to give it to Mr. Morgan should he call."

"Thank you so much."

"No bother at all," she said in a tone that let me know that's precisely what it was—a bother.

Oh well. I turned into my driveway to see the warm glow of the kitchen light through the curtain welcoming me as always, melting away any concerns. Almost. Although I had a detached garage and a jaunt to my house, I parked in it anyway to avoid plugging in my car. In Minnesota, if you left your car outside and didn't plug it in during the winter months, you'd find yourself with a dead battery come morning. And as easy as plugging it in was, sometimes parking in the garage was just easier. Having an attached garage built this spring was a top priority.

Taking each step carefully, I climbed my steps and unlocked the door. The scent of pine tickled my nose and warmed me. The pine from a Christmas tree was the best, but the oil diffusers were an adequate replacement after the tree was down.

After shrugging out of my coat, scarf, and gloves, I flipped on lights as I walked through the house, then kicked on the furnace. A couple of snowmobiles zoomed across the lake, heading toward the far side. I looked forward to seeing the orange sailboat that I'd come to think of as mine sail past my house each morning come summer. But for now, the snowmobiles would have to do. As much as I loved living out in the serenity of the country, it was nice to see other people enjoying it too.

I'd no sooner changed into my sweatpants and a hoodie when I heard the engine of a car in my front yard followed by two car doors. Two car doors indicated that it could be either Max and Daisy or Claire and Sydney. I heard a key turn in the lock.

"Hey, Claire!" I called down the stairs from my loft. "I'll be right there."

"I'm here, too, Aunt Mel," Syd's voice carried up to me. I smiled. *Aunt Mel.* Now I would have two little ones calling me Aunt Mel. How special was I? My chest inadvertently puffed out just a tad.

"Down in a sec," I called again, hurrying as fast as I could to grab my snow boots from my closet. I hobbled down the stairs.

Sydney had her skates draped over her shoulders, big, bright, green pompoms affixed to the laces. "Well, aren't you just the cool one with your pompoms on your skates? And they even match your mittens." I leaned over and hugged her.

"Mom said I have to be careful with you because you're hurt. And she said you got hurt because you're old."

Claire let out a loud whooping laugh. I shot arrows at her with my eyes. "She did, did she?"

Sydney giggled. "Yup. But don't worry, I told her you're not old."

"Just fragile," Claire said, still laughing.

"This is going to be a fun night. Maybe you, dear friend, should stay in the house with Max, and I'll take the kids skating."

"What's Daisy like, Aunt Mel? Is she nice?"

"Yeah, she's pretty neat. I think you'll like her." I hoped so. "After skating, we can come back to the house for some hot chocolate."

"With marshmallows?" She grinned, revealing new teeth trying to find their place in a new world.

My eyes widened. "Well, yeah," I sang. "What's hot chocolate without marshmallows?"

"Boring," she sang back.

"I'm not sure who's the bigger kid here, you or Syd," Claire said.

"I'm definitely bigger," I said, standing next to Sydney, moving my hand from her head up to mine.

"Not by much," Claire said.

Beams of light from headlights danced on the wall. "Looks like Max and Daisy are here."

"Is Daisy gonna go to my school?" Syd asked.

"I don't know, sweetie. She might end up going to Harrison. Depends on where they find a house."

Car doors slammed moments before there was knocking on my front door. I whisked it open, and there stood Daisy with the identical pompoms on her skates but in purple, gloves to match. Indescribable joy rose in me. I had a feeling that things were going to work out just fine.

As soon as Max came through the door, he rubbed his hands together. "We picked up some skates for Daisy in town today. Are you sure it's warm enough at the lake?"

"Yeah. We have a small barrel that we burn wood in for heat."

He cupped his hands and blew into them. "Alrighty then. I'll be hanging out here waiting."

"Why don't you head up to The Fishing Hole for a beer?" I suggested.

"Not the bar type," he said firmly, his pouty lips forming a thin line.

"It's more of a restaurant," I said. "Not your stereotypical bar."

"Not in the mood," he said, abruptly dismissing the suggestion.

I didn't know him well yet, but I'd guessed I hit a nerve. "You okay?" I asked.

He glanced at Daisy, who was chatting it up with Syd. Or rather, Syd was chatting incessantly, and Daisy was listening.

"Fine."

"Yeah?" I asked, giving him a sidelong glance.

"Not now," he said.

"Maybe we can talk later? I have something to tell you too."

"Do the two of you want to talk, and I can take the girls to the lake?" Claire asked.

"Not on your life," I said, slugging her in the shoulder. "You'll tell them stories and lies about me."

She clasped her hand to her chest, eyes wide. "*Moi?*"

I rolled my eyes and looked at Max. "She's not as innocent as she makes herself out to be." Except she pretty much was. Claire was perhaps the most naive woman I've ever known for living the life she's lived. It was both refreshing and endearing. But worried me sick.

"You ladies—and girls—" Max said, looking at Sydney and Daisy, "go and have fun. I'll just sit back and watch some TV while I'm waiting. Get caught up on the news."

"I can catch you up on news, and I don't even watch it," I said.

He raised his eyebrows then shook his head slowly. "Go. We don't have all night."

"Stay out of my stuff," I warned, not missing his amused chuckle.

Just as we were leaving the house, my phone played. I looked at the screen, but it wasn't a number I recognized. I felt torn between answering or letting it go to voicemail. What if it was Mr. Morgan? As much as I needed to get answers from him, I also needed this time with the girls, preferably without any possible surprising news hanging over us like a cloud. Besides, the receptionist was certain she wouldn't be talking with Mr. Morgan to give him my message.

"You going to get that?" Max asked. I looked at Claire, Sydney, and Daisy, already trekking through the snow toward the lake.

"Nah. It might be the funeral director, but I doubt it. Besides, now's not the time. That's what I need to talk to you about."

"Hmm," he said, brows knit, "Me too. And about school as well."

I held his gaze, torn between taking Claire up on her offer to stay and chat with Max while she took the girls skating, but then turned to leave. "I'll be back up in about an hour. Claire can occupy the girls for a few minutes while we talk. Right now, I have a very important date with some pretty important girls."

23

By the time I got down to the lake, Claire had already started the fire in the barrel. The girls began lacing up their skates. Claire helped tighten the laces on Sydney's skates, arranging the pompoms just so, while I helped Daisy. Because of my knee, I couldn't squat as Claire could, so I sat on the wooden bench, my injured leg out straight in front of me. "Come here," I said and waved Daisy toward me. Out of the blue, a snowball plopped on my hat.

Knowing exactly where it came from, I looked up at Claire and let out an evil cackle and began picking up snow. "Yours is the most pathetic snowball I've ever seen. You Minnesota aliens need a lesson from us Minnesota natives on how to make a good snowball."

"Bring it, my crippled friend," she said, laughing and waving me on.

Daisy and Sydney laughed and cheered us on, disappointed when I dropped my snowball rather than take Claire up on her challenge.

"I can't. I'll re-injure my knee."

"Excuses," she said, shaking her head. "You're just scared 'cause you know I can take you."

Typically not one to back down from a challenge, I again began scooping up a mitten full of snow when Sydney's voice stopped me.

"Hey, Aunt Mel, am I an alien or a native?"

I looked at Claire and readjusted my black mittens. "Your daughter just saved your skin." The girls giggled, and I looked at Sydney. "You, my dear Syd, are a Minnesota native girl through and through," I said, standing and pulling her over into a side hug.

"How come my mom isn't then?"

" 'Cause your mom had a life before you came along, you know. She was already living in Minnesota when you were born."

"Your dad and I moved here a few years before you were born," Claire said. "You know that story."

"Be thankful for that, Sydney," I said. "We Minnesota girls are much tougher and stronger."

"Yeah, in attitude," Claire said.

I looked over at Daisy, who had been taking it all in silently. "You okay, sweetie?" I asked, holding my hand out to her.

"Yeah," she said, taking my hand.

"Hey, Claire? Why don't you and Sydney head onto the ice. Daisy'll be there in a minute."

Claire gave a salute, and they began their short journey, ice skate blade guards on until they reached the ice. "Nice to have the guys shovel for us," she called over her shoulder.

I sat down on the bench and patted the seat next to me. Daisy sat down, keeping watch on Claire and Sydney.

"Hey, kiddo, what's going on?"

"I miss my mom," she said, pushing the snow around with her ice skates.

"I'll bet you do."

She refocused from her skates to me. "Do you miss yours?"

Oh, boy! Another curveball I hadn't seen coming. "I used to."

"You don't anymore?" she asked.

I shrugged. "It's complicated."

"My mom came to the hotel when I was there with Gramma. She tried to see me, but Gramma wouldn't let her. They argued, and my gramma made her leave."

"How did that make you feel?"

"Sad." She looked down at her skates and started pushing snow away again. "Sydney's lucky." She focused on Claire and Sydney, holding hands and going in circles, laughing loudly. Talk about rubbing salt in the poor girl's wound.

"Tell ya what," I said, standing up, "why don't I walk to the rink with you, and you can join them in their little circle. Deal?"

She grabbed my outstretched hand. I walked beside her and helped her over the edge of the snow that bordered the shoveled area.

"Did you skate back home, Daisy?" Sydney asked, skating over to her.

"Yeah. But we only have indoor rinks, not like this. And we rented our skates there."

"Come on," Syd said, grabbing her hand. "We can skate together."

I'd never been prouder of my little Sydney ever in her young life. I swallowed the lump of emotion in my throat as I watched the two of them. Claire zipped over to me, sliding sideways to a stop, shaved ice chips from her blades spraying up toward me.

I brushed off the front of my coat. "Hey there, hotshot, you have a pretty amazing daughter." We watched the two girls still holding hands, squealing with delight.

"You sound surprised," Claire said, chuckling.

"I think she takes after her Aunt Mel," I teased.

"Right!" She rolled her eyes. "Is Daisy okay?"

"Misses her mom." I told her what Daisy confided in me about her mom and gramma arguing. "She's confused why she can't spend time with her mom. I don't blame her."

"Maybe you could talk to Max about supervised visitation? I mean, I get that he doesn't want Pam to have time alone with Daisy when she's high. But maybe Max can talk to her about staying sober long enough to have a supervised visit."

"I'm sure he's tried that. I don't think he'd try to keep Daisy away from her mother unless he thought it was critical. Besides, he said it's ordered by the Court." We watched the two, now skating separately, one trying to do what the other was. Daisy was quite good and a natural. "She and I have so many similarities. So many commonalities. It's almost like we're connected."

"You are. By blood. It doesn't get any more connected than that."

"Go skate, you goon," I said, shaking my head.

"I was serious."

I nodded across the lake. "I want us to get some snowmobiles. Look at them. Doesn't it look fun?"

"How about cold and dangerous?" she said, watching them.

"Stop being a weenie. You and Cole and me and Levi could all go out on the trails. There are tons of them around here. We could roast hot dogs and marshmallows over a winter bonfire in the woods. Drink wine from a flask..." I watched her carefully then smiled. "I got you with the wine, didn't I?"

"Mom, come on!" Syd yelled. "Come skate with us."

"The queen summons." Claire laughed and was off, sailing across the ice.

I watched the three of them, feeling sorry for myself that I couldn't skate with them but grateful I hadn't done more damage to my knee than I had. I looked up at the house and saw Max standing in the large window, watching Daisy. I turned my attention back to the skaters. Daisy was now holding Claire's hands, turning in circles as

Syd had been doing earlier. My heart and soul needed this after the past couple of days.

I fished my phone out of my pocket with my mittened hands to check if I had any missed calls. Both Levi and my grandmother knew about our ice skating plans for tonight, so I hadn't expected a call from either of them. The person who called earlier hadn't left a message. Maybe I should have answered in case it was Mr. Morgan. I wanted answers. I spent a brief moment regretting that decision but pushed it aside, happy I'd chosen family first.

I started shivering, cold from standing still. The three of them skated over to me.

Claire rubbed her mittened hands together. "Brr! I think it's gotten colder since we started skating. We're ready for hot chocolate by the fireplace," Claire said.

"With tons of marshmallows!" Syd and Daisy said.

"Well, what are we waiting for!" I exclaimed. "Let's get those skates off and get up to the house." I looked at the window, but Max was gone.

"The fire in the barrel is almost out," Claire said. "But I'll go throw snow on it to finish it off."

After the fire was extinguished and skates replaced with boots, I steered them toward the basement door so the girls could take their wet clothes and boots off. I rarely used the basement entrance and used the basement itself mainly for storage. It was small and only stretched beneath half the house. I typically kept the door leading from upstairs to the basement locked.

We'd just reached the door, Daisy and Sydney in the front, when I said, "Hold up, girls. I have to unlock it." Busily chatting, Sydney reached for the doorknob and turned, stepping inside, while not missing a beat in the story she told Daisy. I froze and looked at Claire, whose brows were knit.

"Melanie, why do you leave this door unlocked?"

"I don't," I said in a hushed voice. "This door is never unlocked."

"Girls!" Claire said sharply, a tone I'd never heard her use before. It caused me alarm in and of itself. "Get back out here," she said.

Sydney turned around. "What's wrong, Mom?"

"Come on," Claire said, wiggling her fingers, waving them out.

"You girls wait out here while I look around," I said.

"Melanie, what's wrong?" Daisy asked, her wide eyes frightened.

I touched her upper back. "Probably nothing, sweetie. But I just want to check something out, okay?"

"Maybe Max unlocked it for us," Claire whispered.

I shook my head slowly. "Maybe, but somehow I don't think so. He doesn't have any idea I have a basement door since he's never seen the backside of my house."

"Men just have a sixth sense about those kinds of things, don't you think?"

I shrugged and stepped inside slowly. "Max?" I yelled. If nothing else, it would scare out whoever it was if they knew there was a man in the house. Especially if they had no idea whether he was armed. I had a gun in my house but kept it in a small wall safe in my bedroom closet. Not too helpful right now. "Max!" I yelled again, louder.

The lock mechanism on the upstairs door clicked, and he opened it. "Everything okay?" he called down.

I looked back at Claire and whispered, "It wasn't him. He had to unlock the door to look down here." I shuddered. "Can you come down here?" I asked him. "Bring your piece."

"My what?" he asked, his voice riddled with confusion.

Great. "Your piece," I said again. "You know, your weapon?"

"Daddy doesn't have a weapon," Daisy said from behind me.

Double great. I'd have to teach them both about a few things. But oddly, I was significantly calmer. If whoever it was hadn't come out, either they were long gone or better yet, they were never here, and I had somehow just left it unlocked.

I struggled to remember when the last time was that I'd used this door. Months. I shuddered again. I had to learn to be more careful. The door between the upstairs and down stayed locked, but a child could break that thing open.

"Melanie," Max said, now halfway down the stairs, "are you all okay?"

"Yeah," I said, feeling a little silly. Daisy and Sydney were now inside, both looking around the basement, eyes wide. "Go ahead and take off your boots and wet hats and mittens, girls. And brush the snow off your pants, okay? You can leave your skates down here until you go home."

"Oh, no!" Daisy cried. "I forgot my skates at the lake!"

"I'll go get them," Max said.

Neither Claire nor I protested. The girls scrambled up the stairs in a rush to get their hot chocolate.

"Do you recognize anything missing or out of place?" Claire asked.

I took another glance around more carefully this time, then shook my head. "No. Not that I can tell. But I'm hardly ever down here. I was probably just distracted when I put the Christmas stuff away."

"But did you use the outside door when you were down here?"

I shrugged. "I didn't think so, but I must have. What other explanation could there be?"

Claire wrapped her arms around herself and shivered. "I don't even want to think of another explanation. Maybe ask Levi if he can change the lock."

I frowned. "Why would I do that? I can change it myself."

"God forbid you should allow the guy to help you." She frowned and slowly shook her head.

"I do allow him to help. If I can't do something myself."

"I have one word for you, my friend — "

"Brilliant?"

"Stubborn. Bull-headed."

"That's technically three words," I said.

"Mom! Aunt Melanie," Syd hollered from the top of the stairs. "Hurry up!"

Claire snickered. "Once again, the queen summons."

"Go, servant," I said. "I'll stay down here and wait for Max to come back up so I can be sure the door is locked after he comes back in." I turned toward the door and looked out the window, just in time to see Max pick up Daisy's skates from the ground by the bench. And just in time to see a snowmobile zip along the shore, jump up over the bank, and hit Max broadside before it sped off into the night.

24

"Claire!" I yelled up the stairs. "Watch the girls!"

I pushed the door open and barreled out of the house as fast as I could, my knee reminding me of its injury. I trotted through the snow as quickly as my knee would allow, calling 911 as I ran. From where I was, I couldn't tell how badly he was injured, but as fast as the machine was going and the way it sent Max flying, I knew it couldn't be good. He hadn't moved since getting hit.

"911, what's your emergency," the voice asked.

"I need an ambulance." I rattled off my address. "A snowmobiler has just hit my brother. He's not moving."

"Is he breathing?" she asked.

"I don't know. I was up at the house, and he was down by the lake. I'm almost to him now. But the snowmobile walloped him hard!"

She kept me on the phone with her until I reached Max, assuring me that she had dispatched medical. "What is your name?" she asked.

"Melanie. Melanie Hogan."

"You said it's your brother, Melanie?"

"Yes. His name is Max Winters."

"Is the snowmobile on scene?"

"No, he took off right after he hit him."

"He? Do you know who it was?"

"No," I said. "There are a lot of snowmobilers around here. They use my yard to get from the lake to the road. But I don't know any of them." I finally reached Max and knelt on my good knee beside him. "He's breathing. My brother is breathing." I placed my fingers against the carotid artery on his neck. "He has a pulse. Max? Max, can you hear me?"

"Melanie?" the 911 operator said. "What's happening?"

"Max," I said again, fighting back tears of relief when he opened his eyes.

"What happened?" He groaned. "Ouch!"

"What hurts?" I asked, looking him over.

"My hip. My leg. Godfrey!" he exclaimed.

"I've got an ambulance coming," I told him, my hand on his shoulder. "Just lay still." I took off my coat and covered him with it.

"Daisy."

"Claire's got her in the house."

"Daisy?" the 911 operator asked. "Melanie, who's Daisy and Claire?"

"Daisy is his daughter. Claire is my best friend. Is the ambulance almost here? I can't hear them. It's freezing out here, and I can't move him." I stood up. "Oh, that's right! I stashed a few blankets in the boat shed. I'll be right back, Max."

I walked to the shed, the phone still to my ear. "I'm beginning to hear sirens," I told the operator. "I have to go.

Please make sure they know we're down by the lake." I slid my phone into my back pocket. My teeth chattered as I shivered from the cold and adrenaline. I reached for the doorknob, but it wouldn't turn. I let out a loud "*grrrr*" and kicked the door with my good leg. Why on earth did I remember to lock this one? The overhead door was locked too. I looked from the door up to the house, then back to the door. Running up to the house would take too long, especially given my present handicap. Max could freeze by then. The sirens got slightly louder. I turned my head and jammed my elbow through the window, reached in through the broken glass, and unlocked the door.

By the time I'd layered the blankets over Max, I heard the ambulance in my yard. It occurred to me that I hadn't called Claire and the girls. They were sure to be scared to death. I grabbed my phone and saw I had five missed calls from Claire. While talking to Max to keep him awake, I punched my finger on her name.

"Melanie, what's going on? What happened?" she answered in a panicked voice. "I have both girls in here crying, and I can't leave them.

"A snowmobile hit Max. But tell Daisy he's fine. It looks like he might have some broken bones, though."

"They're unloading an ATV right now with a stretcher attached to the back."

"Make sure Daisy knows he's going to be fine, okay? Thanks, Claire." She began talking to Daisy before we even hung up.

I tucked the blankets up under Max's chin and lay one under his head. His breathing seemed to be getting shallower, and he uttered an occasional incoherent word or two. I guessed he'd graduated from mild hypothermia to moderate. He was literally freezing to death! As was I. I could hardly feel my limbs anymore, and my body wasn't shaking quite as violently.

I vigorously rubbed his hands between mine, hoping the friction would keep him warm while I said the alphabet forward and attempted backward to test my own cognitive skills. Then I pinched myself hard to be sure I could still feel it.

Lights from the ATV came down the hill, and I stood on rubbery legs and waved my arms above my head. They zipped right up beside us, the two men working in tandem to assess Max's injuries before they moved him and to treat his hypothermia.

"Ms. Hogan," one of them said, "are you able to get up to the house?"

"Yes," I said, blowing into my cupped hands, "but I should stay with him." I nodded toward Max.

"You aren't going to do him any good if you're frozen. Besides, there's nothing you can do for him right now. We've got this. Go to the house. There's a fire truck on its way to check you out and make sure you're okay."

I nodded and headed toward the house, looking back at them working on Max, then up to the house window where Claire stood with the girls. I made a feeble attempt to wave. My legs felt weak, but the will to make it to the warmth of my home was greater, propelling me forward.

I was three-quarters of the way up when a fireman came toward me from the side of my house. He jogged toward me in boots and a parka, a knit hat on his head. When he reached me, he took one of my arms and circled it around his neck, holding onto the hand, circling his other arm around my waist, helping me along.

"Lean on me. We're almost there," he said. "Tell me your name."

"Melanie Hogan." My lips were stiff from the cold, and it sounded like I was drunk.

"What's your date of birth?"

"Umm...March."

"March what?" he pressed.

"Umm — twenty — twenty-fifth."

We went in through the basement door, and he sat me down on a chair, kneeling on one knee in front of me. He looked in my eyes with a penlight and assessed my overall condition.

"You've got some frostnip on your nose, cheeks, and fingers."

I touched my fingers to my nose and cheeks. "It all feels a little numb and tingly."

"It will tingle more as it warms. Be sure and stay inside tonight. If it gets worse, it means you have frostbite and will need to go to the doctor for further treatment."

Claire and the girls rushed down the stairs. "Is she okay?" Claire asked.

"Frostnip and mild hypothermia," the fireman said. "She needs to stay warm. And some warm tea would be good."

"I can get that right now," Claire said, already halfway up the stairs.

Daisy stood on one side of me and Sydney on the other.

"Where's my dad?" Daisy asked.

I put my arm around her waist. "The paramedics are taking good care of him." My lips were beginning to warm, making it easier to talk. "He'll have to go to the hospital."

"How am I gonna get home?" Her eyes were wide and filled with fear of the unknown. So many questions circled in those eyes.

"We'll call your gramma and see if she can come and get you. Otherwise, you can stay here with me tonight. How would you like that?"

"I wanna stay with my dad." Her jaw was set in a firm line.

I took one of her hands in mine. "Sweetie, you can't stay at the hospital. But I tell you what, whether you stay here or with your gramma, you'll be able to see him tomorrow, okay? I promise."

"Is school on break?" the fireman asked casually, finally done examining me and standing up.

"No. She and her dad are here on family business."

"We're moving here," she told the fireman. "Me, my dad, and my mom."

I glanced at her, deciding not to tackle that one tonight. None of us had the energy for it.

"Why doesn't she stay here and go to school with Sydney tomorrow?" Claire asked, coming back downstairs with a cup of tea. "I can bring them in the morning and talk to the office about it. I'm sure it will be okay. And that way, she can visit the school."

"I don't have the authority to say yes or no to that," I said. "We'll have to ask Max."

"I want to see my dad," Daisy said, her eyes misty.

I looked at the fireman. "Can she see him before they take him to the hospital?"

He looked down at the lake. The paramedics were fastening Max to the stretcher that pulled behind the ATV like a sleigh. One medic hopped on the ATV, the other appeared to do something else to the stretcher, then hopped on the machine behind the other.

"I'll go catch 'em and be sure she gets to see her dad," he said to me, then looked at Daisy and rested a hand lightly on top of her head. "I'll be right back."

"We'll be upstairs," I said. "Just come in through the front door."

We filed up the stairs, Daisy sticking close to my side. When we got to the top, I was surprised to see a deputy's car in the front yard. Then it occurred to me: Of course they would be there.

"Why are the police here, Mel?" Claire asked, brows knit.

"Whoever hit Max took off. Hit and run."

"Oh, yeah! I was so worried about you and Max that I hadn't even thought of that part."

"Me too. Worried about Max, I mean," I said. *Involved in yet another crime without doing anything wrong.* This pattern was picking up speed like a snowball rolling over a cliff.

The fireman came to the front door to get Daisy. "You stay here," he told me. "You can't be going back outside yet with that frostnip. You'll need to be careful with that from here on out, not just tonight. Be sure and keep covered as best you can when you're out for any extended periods."

I rolled my eyes and shook my head at the picture of my future. I'd own stock in the scarf and mitten industry before long. I wrapped my leather coat around Daisy's shoulders and slid a hat over her head before he led her out to Max. I watched the two of them from the window, relieved when Max reached up to Daisy and pulled her into a hug. She laid her head on his chest.

Claire stepped up behind me and rubbed my back gently. Sydney stood with her nose to the window on the door, taking it all in.

"This stuff—" Claire said with a sigh. "This stuff just follows you, Melanie."

"Ya think?" I grumbled. When the paramedics loaded Max into the ambulance, the fireman led Daisy back into the house.

"Mr. Winters asked if you would call his mother to let her know what's going on and to ask if she can come pick up Daisy."

"Sure, but I can keep Daisy with me, too." Given the circumstances, I wondered if she would be more comfortable with her grandmother. I looked at her, "Sweetie, if it's okay with your gramma, do you want to stay here tonight and go to school with Sydney tomorrow?"

"Yeah!" she said, without giving it a moment's thought.

"Here," the fireman said, "I wrote down her grandmother's phone number for you."

"How is he? Max," I asked.

"Hypothermia and a possible broken hip. Could be some internal injuries, but they won't know for sure until they get him to the hospital," he said.

My chest felt weighted down. I nodded. "Okay." The deputy finished talking with the paramedics, glanced in my direction, and then said something to them. "Great," I muttered.

"Something wrong?" The fireman, who had started out the door, turned toward me.

I shook my head. "No. Well, not that you'd want to hear about anyway."

"Okay, then, it looks like the deputy will have some questions for you."

"They always do," I mumbled and exhaled slowly. Thankfully he didn't hear me. That, or he didn't want to acknowledge it. Who could blame the guy?

25

I opened the door for the deputy and looked at his name badge—Deputy Olsen. He was either new to the department or hadn't had the misfortune of dealing with one of my past events. I'd meet the entire department soon if this didn't stop. As it was, the city police department was too familiar with me, and not because of Levi.

My phone rang. I looked at the display screen and put up a finger to Deputy Olsen.

"You have radar on me, or what?" I asked, trying my hardest to keep things light.

"What's going on, blondie?" Levi's voice soothed my soul like a cup of chicken soup. I glanced at the girls, now watching TV in the living room, my heart swelling with pride as my girl Sydney kept Daisy's mind off her father. Sydney knew what it was like to be without a father; hers died while he was in the military and on tour. "Babe?"

"Hey, I have Deputy Olsen here. I'll call you back when he leaves, okay?"

"I'm coming out."

"I'm fine," I assured him. I turned away from Deputy Olsen and stepped into the living room.

"It's not a problem," Levi said. "I just got into the station, and nothing is going on for a change. Except at your house."

"Levi, don't miss work again on my account. I promise I'm fine." Daisy looked away from the TV and at me. I walked back into the kitchen as silence fell over the line.

"Okay, then. Call if you need anything." The sting in his voice was palpable, and I felt worse than I had all night.

"I will. And Levi?"

"Yeah?"

"I love you."

"Back at'cha."

My chest felt heavier. What in the world was the matter with me? The guy just wanted to help me, and I erected that darn wall again. Pretty soon, he would stop trying to scale that wall.

I took a slow, deep breath and walked back into the kitchen. Claire and Deputy Olsen both stopped talking when I entered.

"Let's get this over with," I said. My anxiety was getting the better of me, and I needed time to collect myself and figure out what happened tonight. I motioned to a chair at the kitchen table. I took the chair opposite him.

"I'm going to go in with the girls," Claire said.

"What happened?" he asked. "Start from the beginning."

"Claire and I and the girls were down at the skating rink on the lake for about an hour. Max stayed up at the house. When we came back inside, Daisy remembered she left her skates at the lake. Max went down to get them, and I guess it was dark enough that the snowmobile didn't see him. The snowmobile hit Max, and he went flying. I ran down there—" I looked at my knee, now throbbing, and touched the brace lightly— "I guess I should say I *hobbled* down to the lake, got some blankets out of the boat shed to try to keep him warm, and then the paramedics and the fire department got here."

"Did the snowmobile have a headlight?"

I thought back, struggling to recall. "I don't remember. I think so."

"I've noticed there are several snowmobile tracks on your property. Do you own one?"

"Yes, there are, and no, I don't. Snowmobilers use my property to get from the lake to the road and vice versa. It's a straight shot."

"Do you know any of them?"

"I don't think so, but I doubt it. Even if I did, they wear helmets with shields, so it's impossible to recognize them," I said. "That, and I don't really know any of my neighbors."

"How many snowmobiles did you see tonight?"

"When we were ice skating, I saw three or four across the lake. But when the machine hit Max, I think it was just one."

"Did you notice the particular make of the machine?"

I thought back then shook my head. "No. I hadn't been paying attention until I saw Max get hit. And then it was too late. Whoever it was took off."

He frowned. "Unfortunately, hit and runs happen with snowmobiles the same as they do with vehicles. Which way did the snowmobile take off?"

I pointed in the direction it had gone. "East along the shoreline."

"Do you know anyone who lives that way?"

"No. But as I said, I don't know anyone who lives out here except Claire. I kinda keep to myself."

"Have you seen this particular snowmobile around before?"

"Again, as I said, I didn't get a good look at it."

"You don't know if it has been on your property?"

I struggled to swallow my irritation. How many times and ways was he going to ask the same question? "No."

"Can you remember anything else that might help me out?"

I thought for a moment. "No."

"Alrighty then." He stood and pushed in his chair. "I'm going to head down there and see what I can find."

I nodded and stood, closing the door behind him. Claire left the girls watching what I've come to know as *The Baby-Sitters Club*—Syd's favorite—and came back into the kitchen.

"Claire," I said quietly, wrapping my arms around my middle, "what if this wasn't an accident? What if it wasn't a hit and run at all but a murder attempt?"

She gasped, and her eyes opened wide. "Did you mention that to the police?"

"No."

"Why not?"

"Because then I'd have to go through the whole story from the beginning. Starting with Lenny's murder."

"What's wrong with that? Especially if it's all connected and they can catch the person?" I stared blankly at her, not saying anything. "Did you at least tell Levi? I'm assuming that was him who called."

"Yes. I mean, yes, it was him who called, but no, I didn't tell him. Yet."

"Why not?"

"Deputy Olsen was right here. And when I walked into the living room, the girls were within earshot. I haven't exactly had the opportunity."

"Call him back."

"I will later. I need to call Daisy's gramma first." I reached for my phone, at the same time watching the deputy through the big picture window as he slowly made his way to the lake. The beam of his flashlight weaved back and forth in front of him and on all sides. Before I dialed Sharon's number, I turned back to Claire. "I was just thinking—I may have spoken prematurely. Will the school even allow Daisy to go to school with Syd if she's not enrolled?"

"We'll need to provide proof of immunizations at the very least. But I'm the president of the PTO in a small town. I think I can pull some strings." She winked at me. "When you talk to Sharon, see if she can pull up Daisy's immunization record and print a copy. Everything's electronic now so it shouldn't be an issue."

I nodded and punched in the number. Fifteen minutes later, ten of those explaining Max's accident, my request to keep Daisy overnight, and the immunization record request, and the other five dodging questions about Violet, I hung up from Sharon. Claire and the girls were instantly at my side.

"Well?" Sydney asked, her brown eyes looking up at me expectantly. "Does Daisy get to go to school with me tomorrow?"

I managed a smile, not quite feeling it. "She does. You guys owe me, though. It took some work convincing her. She wanted Daisy with her."

"What'd you say that changed her mind?" Daisy asked.

"I told her this would allow her an opportunity to go to the hospital to be with your dad."

"Can I go be with my dad now?"

I tilted my head. "No, sweetie. Not tonight."

"When then?" she whined.

"Your gramma will pick you up at the school tomorrow afternoon and take you from there," I said.

"Mom, can Daisy stay overnight at our house tonight?" Sydney asked, pulling on Claire's hand.

"It would make things easier," Claire said, watching me.

I shook my head. "Uh-uh. Sorry, guys. I told Sharon that she'd be with me tonight. I can't let her stay somewhere else."

"I get that. I wouldn't want Syd going somewhere other than where I knew she was, either. What about the immunization record?"

"She's going to text it to me. I'll forward it to you."

Claire nodded. "Come on, kiddo," she said to Syd, draping an arm around her neck. "We need to get going. This is far too late for you to be up on a school night."

Sydney grabbed her coat and hat and gave Daisy a big grin. "See you tomorrow morning. Mom, what time are we picking her up?"

"I'll be here at seven," Claire said to me as she grabbed her coat and gloves. Then, before she closed the door behind her, she turned back toward me. "Actually, can you bring her over to my house? If you're feeling up to it, that is. That way, she can try on some of Syd's clothes and find something she likes."

"It's a plan. The earlier, the better. That way, I can get to the hospital to see Max before I head to the salon."

We watched Claire and Syd get into their car, pull out of the driveway, and into their own just a block down the road. When Claire blinked the outside light, the sign we'd made for each other to let the other know we were tucked inside safely, I turned to Daisy. "You, my friend, need to get to bed if you're going to school in the morning."

"I'm not your friend," she said, rolling her eyes. "I'm your niece. Remember?"

I looked at her as though she'd told me the biggest news of the century. "Well, then, *niece*, it's bedtime!"

"Melanie?"

"Yeah?" I cocked my head, expecting some profound question about her mom or her dad.

"Sydney isn't your niece, and she calls you Aunt Melanie. You're my aunt for real, so..." she trailed off, and bit her lower lip, dipping her chin slightly.

I smiled at her, bent over, and hugged her. "There's nothing I'd like better than if you called me Aunt Melanie."

She grinned. "Awesome! Aunt Melanie," she added, trying it on for size.

I stood and touched the back of my hand to her cheek. "Come on, kiddo. We need to get you ready for bed. I'll show you to your room and where everything is." I began walking toward the spare room on the main level and turned to see her rooted in place. "What's wrong?"

"Can't I sleep in your room?" I studied her. "I promise I won't take up much room. I'm kinda small."

Kinda? She was tiny and looked so alone. I smiled and held my hand out to her. "Come on."

Half an hour later, she was showered, dressed in one of my t-shirts, and snuggled under the covers in my bed. I sat with her until she fell asleep, then did my routine of getting ready for bed, including a hot bath. The last thing I did was check my phone to see if I had any missed calls from Levi. Nothing. "What did you do, Melanie?" I whispered into the darkened room. The more I sought answers, the more questions arose.

26

I slept fitfully. When I finally fell into a decent sleep, it seemed only minutes before my alarm went off. I hit the snooze button and fell back to sleep, hitting it again two more times. The fourth time I groaned and threw my arm over my face before I bolted upright. *Oh, no!* I looked over at Daisy, still sound asleep. My first day of being responsible for another human being, a child, and I'd forgotten she was even there!

I glanced at the clock. The six and two zeros taunted me in big red numbers. I touched Daisy's arm. "Daisy?" I shook her gently. "Sweetie, we need to get you up and over to Claire's."

She sat up sleepily. "Where am I?" I turned on my bedside lamp. "Aunt Melanie?"

She remembered, and my heart smiled. Her hair, still wet when she went to bed, stuck up in front, the cowlick more pronounced. She was cute as a button. "Come on, kiddo. I overslept."

"Do you do that a lot?" she said through a yawn.

I shook my head. "Never ever. Come on, bug. We need to get moving. There's a new toothbrush in the bathroom cabinet. Just throw on your pants from yesterday and leave on my t-shirt. You can change into something else when you get to Claire's and see what of

Syd's fits you." I worried just a little. Daisy was tiny for her age. I didn't want her wearing something ill-fitting and have kids tease her. Hopefully, and most likely, knowing Claire as I did, she'd already have gone through Sydney's too-small clothes and picked out some pieces Daisy might like.

***

By the time I fixed her hair exactly the way she wanted it, we were fifteen minutes late getting to Claire's. Just as I'd thought, she had five different adorable outfits laid out. Daisy picked one of the pairs of jeans and a black turtleneck. Simple and so much like—well, like me. The only difference between what I was wearing and what she picked out for today is my top was a black blouse instead of a turtleneck. And my hoop earrings. I had them in every shape, color, and size. Oftentimes, I didn't wear any at all. Daisy wore the tiniest little ladybug earrings. Claire packed up the rest of the outfits and promised Daisy she would leave them at the school for her grandmother when she picked her up.

"Do you pick up Sydney at the same time?" she asked Claire.

"No. Sydney stays in after-school care until the teaching assistant finishes up. Then she brings Sydney home and stays with her until I get home from work."

Daisy appeared to take this in, then said, "Can she come with me and Gramma?"

Claire jumped on it before Sydney began to beg. "Not this time, okay?" She knelt so she was on Daisy's level and took her hands in her own. "I have a feeling you two girls will get to spend plenty of time together."

That seemed to mollify her, and she nodded.

I hugged her, then Sydney, then Claire. "You girls have a fabulous day. And behave, okay? We don't want to get a call from the school."

"Sydney," Claire said as stern as Claire gets—which isn't very— "remember that having a friend with you at school is a privilege. Don't blow it."

"Momm," she said, rolling her eyes. "Trust me."

"Trust me?" I said, biting back laughter. "Gee, Claire, where would she ever get that from?"

Claire glared at me. "I wonder."

"I gotta go," I said. "Daisy, you have my number in your pocket, right?" She nodded. "If you need to call me or your gramma, go to the office and call, okay? Claire, can you be sure the office has my number and Sharon's?"

"Yes. Now go!" She pecked me on the cheek and gave me a gentle shove from the back.

"Boy! This girl can sure tell she's not wanted."

"See you at the salon. And don't forget to cover your face with a scarf. And wear your mittens."

"Yes, Mother," I said, rolling my eyes and feeling like Syd.

***

I arrived at the hospital at seven-fifteen, making darn good time, thanks to Claire. I was the more organized of the two, but when it came to being a mom, Claire had it down pat. I was envious. But for the first time in — well, ever — I didn't feel that familiar empty pang of not being able to have children. I took baby steps through the years working through that issue, but this was one giant step forward. Hopefully, I didn't take an even bigger step back, as was my tendency in my relationship with Levi. I closed my eyes momentarily and sent up a whisper of a prayer. My grandmother had always said God could work miracles.

When I got to the front desk, the woman looked up from the computer. "Can I help you?"

"I'm looking for Max Winters' room. He came in last night."

She looked back down at her computer and frowned. "Hmm, I'm sorry, but only family is allowed in his room."

"I am family," I said.

She frowned again. "Unless you're immediate family, you're not allowed to visit him. And visiting hours aren't for another forty-five minutes."

"I am immediate family," I said. "And can't you make an exception to the hours? It's just forty-five minutes. And I have to get to work." I had a flashback to last Christmas when I stopped to see someone before work and had to weasel my way in to see him too. They may as well just give me a badge.

"His mother and his wife have already been in to see him last night, so unless —"

My eyes popped open. "His wife?"

She tilted her head and gave me a pathetic look. "Oh, honey, I'm sorry. Some men are just like that. Scoundrels."

I was confused for a split second before I exclaimed, "No, no. It's not like that. I'm Max's sister."

"Oh!" she said with apparent relief. "I'm not supposed to let anyone in outside of visiting hours, but since it's so close, well..." She glanced at the computer again. "Room 405."

I set my hand on the counter and tapped once. "Thank you so much."

Riding the elevator up then winding my way through the quiet hallways, I finally reached his room — the last door on the left. I shivered and hoped that didn't mean anything here. I poked my head around the corner. Max was awake, staring out the window at the cloud-covered sky.

"Hi," I said from the doorway. "Mind if I come in?"

He glanced at me. "Knock yourself out."

"How'd you sleep?" I said, then waved my hand in dismissal. "Forget I asked that; dumb question." I gently pulled the only chair in the room beside his bed. "I, uh, heard Pam was here."

His thick brows knit. "Word travels fast in this town."

I made an abrupt sound. "You have no idea."

"I have to have surgery."

"When?"

"Today," he said. "I'm lucky to have my mom here to take care of Daisy."

"How did Pam find out you were in here?"

"Probably the same way you found out *she* was here." He winced as he tried to shift his good leg. "No, she said my mom told her. A little shocking, but whatever."

"Why?"

"Nothin'."

"I can help with Daisy," I said, surprised after I'd said it.

"That'd be great." His attention went back to the sunless sky.

A wave of panic welled up in me. I didn't know how to parent. I mean, I did okay last night, but that was only one night. No one had to know I'd forgotten she was in my house when I woke up, did they? A thousand thoughts scrambled my brain.

"—school?"

I refocused on Max, his gaze studying me. "What?"

"Could you maybe help get her enrolled in school?"

Relief put out the fire of panic. Now that was something I could do. "Which one? There are two elementary schools."

"My mom said she was going to go with Sydney today. Can you try that one? It would be the least amount of change for her since she's already there today. And she would have Sydney with her."

"Sure, I could—"

"Wait, will they take her if she's not in their district?" he asked. "They're pretty strict about district borders where we come from." His brows knit together again. "I don't know yet where we'll end up living. We might be living out of a hotel for a while."

I shook my head. "No, you won't. It's a buyer's market so you'll find something quickly. And you guys can stay with me until you find something." He raised an eyebrow and scowled. "You think you'll have a problem staying out of my stuff, or what?"

"No. I've just come to know that you're a little controlling."

I waved my hand in dismissal and grinned. "That just means you'll be on the ball looking for a place of your own." Getting a smile out of him was satisfying. "I'll see what I can do on the school thing. I'll get a hold of your mom and go from there."

He let the weight of his head rest against his pillow again. "Daisy has had so much change in her life recently. She'll end up in therapy for years when she's older, blaming her old man for everything wrong in her life."

I shrugged. "I do that with Violet, but not in therapy." Getting another half-smile, I said, "How did it go when Pam was here?"

He exhaled for several seconds. "As well as can be expected. Same old, same old. She blames me for not letting her see Daisy. I told her that's in her control. All she has to do is stop the drugs."

"Have you thought about treatment?"

"I suggested that. More than once. Told her I would happily pay for it. She got mad and said she doesn't need treatment, that I was only trying to get her locked up somewhere to keep her away from Daisy."

"Can't help her if she doesn't want to help herself." Silence fell between us. "Hey, Max?" I finally said. "Did you see the snowmobile coming at you?"

He shook his head. "Nope. I literally didn't see what hit me. And by the time I heard it, it was too late. Thank God you saw it happen, though. Or I'd be dead for sure."

"What if it wasn't an accident?" I said quietly, watching him closely.

He narrowed his eyes. "What are you implying?"

"What if it was intentional?" He still didn't appear to understand. "Remember when we talked that very first time, and I made a crack about my criminal history? Well, this is what I meant. I don't even do anything, and somehow I'm involved in a crime. I'm a magnet. Maybe whoever was behind this is the same person who threatened us on the phone about staying away from

Lenny's money. Maybe he's worried we won't heed his warning and has decided to eliminate each of us permanently."

He inhaled deep, tilted his head back, and rubbed his hand over his hair and then over his face. "Geez. You sure know how to send me into surgery in a fit. I hadn't even thought of that." He looked at me. "But who knew I was out at your house?"

"Someone who's watching us very closely. Have you noticed anyone weird hanging around?"

"No. Just the guy that chased me on the road the other day," he said.

"I talked to the hair and makeup person at the funeral home yesterday." I shuddered. "I honestly don't know why anyone would want to do that."

"You're so dramatic." He rubbed his forehead as if to ward off a headache.

"I'm going to do us both a favor and pretend you didn't say that. Anyway, Andie—that's her name, the one who does hair and makeup at the funeral home—said Lenny's daughter-in-law was in talking with the funeral director."

He scrunched up his face, an expression more pronounced than I'd ever seen. "Pam?"

"Nope." I gave him the description Andie had given me. "Does that sound like anyone you know?"

"No. But I smell a rat."

"Could it be related to the person who hit you on the snowmobile? Maybe the man who hit you is posing as Lenny's family." He appeared to think this through. "The funeral director—"

"Mr. Morgan. Stanley Morgan."

"Yeah. I left my number, hoping he'd call me back. It might have even been him last evening when I didn't answer my phone."

"I've talked with him in planning Lenny's funeral. I'll see what I can find out."

I waved my arm around the room. "You're a little tied up. Why don't you let me do it?"

"Okay, yeah. Sure." He nodded, then winced.

"Do you need more pain meds?"

"No, thank you. That's what got Pam started on her downward spiral."

"You're not Pam."

"What I need is to get this surgery over with, so I can get back on the road to doing what I need to do. Thank God my insurance is still active through the end of the month."

"I can help your mom if there's anything else to do for the funeral."

He raised an eyebrow. "Really?"

"Yeah. I guess." I tried to play it cool despite feeling some hope. It would be the perfect opportunity to find out whatever I could from Mr. Morgan and the rest of the staff.

"It's pretty much done. Maybe a loose end or two. But thanks."

"As long as that loose end isn't payment, I'm good with it," I half-teased. "What do they need to do for surgery?"

"Just an internal repair. I got off lucky. It could have been a lot worse."

"Internal repair?" I asked.

"They'll put some screws into the bone to hold it together while it heals."

I shuddered. "Sounds painful."

"As I said, it could be worse."

"Okay, tough guy," I said. "I have to get to work." I stood up. "Need anything before I go?"

"No. Just get with my mom and help her enroll Daisy in school. I'll get to house hunting as soon as I'm able."

With a nod and a wave, I was out the door and back down the empty, quiet hallway in which I came just half an hour ago. But this time, something felt different. It was as though someone was watching me. I reached the empty nurse's station, stopped, and looked around me, first down one hall, then another, and then the third. I turned to carry on my way when the back of someone turning the corner caught my attention. A blue suit. My imagination? I didn't think so. But right now, just about anyone looked suspicious to me. A different nurse came out of a room adjacent to the desk.

"Can I help you?" she asked, eyes bloodshot and rimmed with dark circles. It looked like she was at the end of a long shift.

"Did you happen to see anyone out of the ordinary in here last night?"

"Depends on what you mean by out of the ordinary, honey," she said, her voice weary. "We see all kinds in here."

"I can only imagine," I said, striving to make some sort of connection. "I don't know how you do it."

"Sometimes I don't either. But it's worth it. Knowing I'm helping someone either make it or help them cross to the other side — either way, it can be rewarding."

"So nothing struck you as odd last night or this morning?"

She appeared to think through the previous night. "Nah. Not that I can think of. It was a pretty average night. Mostly quiet." Then she squinted and set her jaw in suspicion. "Why are you asking?"

I shifted my weight from one foot to the other and back again when my knee ached. Between Max and me, we had one good leg. What a pair. And all because of Lenny. Even from the grave, he was dangerous. "Just curious. Thank you. Have a good day."

She relaxed again. "You betcha. You too."

With one last look toward Max's room, seeing nothing but an empty hallway, I began my descent. As I passed the main lobby, that same eerie feeling washed over me that someone, somewhere, was watching me. I shivered, looked around, and made a beeline for my car.

27

As soon as I got in my Jeep, I yanked the door shut and hit the lock. I sat still for a few moments, catching my breath in the safety of my secured vehicle. Fog began to descend and settle in, adding yet another layer of anxiety to what was already there from the presence I couldn't seem to see.

Finally, after one last glance around the parking lot, I started the engine and headed for the salon. What I needed was a good, ordinary day. Ordinary as in what my life used to be a couple of years ago before all this craziness started. Not to mention before Max came into my life. A sliver of resentment weaseled its way in, but I pushed it out before it could get a chance to fester. It served no purpose other than to poison.

Claire pulled into the parking lot right behind me. I was relieved I didn't have to be alone. With all the weird stuff happening, being alone freaked me out. And I was more than a little disappointed and worried that Levi hadn't called this morning. I had thought about calling him a couple of times but put my phone away before pushing the button. He would call me when he was ready. I'm the one who drove him away and wouldn't let him help me when he wanted to. Again. Worry and regret wormed their way into my head. I forced it to the back of my mind and got out of my Jeep.

"Hey there, girlfriend," I called to Claire. "How did Daisy do when you dropped the girls off? Did the school give you any grief?"

"Nope, none at all," she said, grinning. "It was so cute, Mel. You should have seen them. Sydney was so proud to show off her new friend, and Daisy seemed to fit right in."

She caught up to me, and we walked side by side. "Max asked me this morning if I can help his mom get Daisy enrolled in school."

"Which one?" she asked.

"The same one Syd goes to. Do you think they'll take her if they don't live in that district? Because he doesn't know where they're going to end up yet."

"I think enrollment is open. Besides, aren't they staying at the Birch Haven Inn?"

"Yeah."

"That's in the boundaries of Syd's school. When they move, they'll already have a leg in the school, so to speak."

"Speaking of legs, Max has to have surgery today." I explained the procedure as Max had described it to me.

She clenched her teeth together. "Ouch."

"Right?" I unlocked the salon door, and we stepped inside, locking the door again behind us. "I swear someone was watching me at the hospital this morning, Claire."

She looked at me and frowned. "Did you see anyone?"

"No. Just intuition. A gut feeling I couldn't shake. It was so stinkin' strong. It's got me on edge."

"Well, I hate to say it, but your gut has been right too many times." We both scanned the parking lot through the window. "Do you think Max is in any danger?" she asked.

My stomach sank as I connected the dots. "Oh criminy! If what happened was intentional, a move to try and kill him, who's to say they won't try to finish it off in the hospital?" I thought of his room being the last one on the left and hoped with all my might that it wasn't an omen. "At least he'll be in surgery today. No one can get to him there."

"But after surgery he'll be on so many drugs he won't know who comes in and out of his room."

I thought about it a moment. "This isn't like TV where the bad guys can magically get in anywhere they want." But even as I said it, I wasn't convinced.

"You'd better call Levi and see if the police department can send someone to stand outside his room." I didn't say anything, and she looked at me, one eye narrowing. "What aren't you telling me?"

I licked my lips and looked away from her prying eyes. "I might have upset him a little." I searched the parking lot again, still avoiding eye contact with her.

"Again?" she asked incredulously, then sighed. "Melanie, why do you insist on sabotaging your—forget it. What did you do?" she asked, with an odd combination of gentle accusation, something only Claire could pull off.

"I just stink at relationships."

"Sometimes you do, yes. Don't we all. But with you it's only because your walls are as high as the Sears Tower."

"It's the Willis Tower now. Has been since 2009."

"You're missing the point."

"No, I'm not. But I can't disagree with you, either. And just when I think I've made progress, I take a step backward. I have too many freakin' issues to work on in my life. Thank God he knows me well enough to know that."

"Well, losing Levi isn't going to help you with any of those issues. It just adds one more to the list."

She was right, and I knew it full well. And yet—well, sometimes what I want to do and what I do are two very different things. "I like your hair scarf. That royal blue looks perfect with your dark skin tone."

"Nice attempt at changing the subject."

"Did it work?" I asked.

"Only because Babs and Connie just pulled up. But this conversation isn't over."

I saluted her and started back toward the office. "I need to call Sharon and then Mr. Morgan from the funeral home before my first client comes in."

Sharon answered on the first ring.

"Hi, Mrs. Winters. This is Melanie Hogan."

"Melanie," she said warmly. "I want to thank you for saving my Max. From what he told me, if you hadn't seen what happened and ran down to the lake, it could have been a much different outcome. You didn't tell me that part when you called last evening."

"We would have noticed that he didn't come back up to the house."

"It may have been too late by then," she said. "We both owe you."

Uncomfortable with accolades and eager to change the subject, I said, "I'm sure Max already told you, but he asked if I could help enroll Daisy in Lincoln Elementary. When is a good time for you?"

"I can go any time. I'm not doing anything important here in Birch Haven except taking care of Daisy. When she's not at your house, that is. I'd like a chance to talk to you again anyway. This time about Lenny."

My skin crawled at the sound of his name. "I told Max I could help you with the remaining funeral plans since he's laid up. If there's even anything left to do."

"Just a thing or two. But that would be wonderful," she said. "I know Max wasn't happy about helping me."

"He wasn't?"

She laughed bitterly. "No. After the fight he had with Lenny right before the murder—well, that soured him on wanting anything to do with his father."

My breath caught in my throat. "He hasn't said anything about that to me. I thought—"

"He didn't kill him if that's what you're wondering," she said with a chill in her voice.

"No, I wasn't—"

"Max wouldn't hurt anyone. I mean *no* one."

"What was the fight about?" I asked.

"I don't know details. Even if I did, they aren't mine to tell. Max will tell you when he's ready."

You're right, Sharon. Max will tell me, and he'll tell me whether he's ready or not. He and I were going to talk the minute his anesthesia wore off. The fact that he kept such a big piece of information from me was unsettling. If the police find out, that could make Max the prime suspect. Do I say something?

" —today?"

"I'm sorry, what?" I asked.

"Do you have time to enroll Daisy today? I think the sooner she's enrolled and gets back into a routine, the better."

I glanced over my appointment book. "Today should work, but I'll let you know for sure in a little while. I'll need to change some appointments around first."

"You have my number. Just give me a ring."

One down, one to go. I dialed the number for the Birch Haven Funeral Home, and the receptionist answered on the second ring.

"I'm calling for Mr. Morgan, please. This is Melanie Hogan."

"Ms. Hogan, didn't he call you? I thought he'd said —"

It was *him who called last evening.* "We haven't spoken yet. Is he in?"

"He sure is. Just a moment, please."

Music piped through the phone line as I waited for what seemed an eternity. I tapped my pencil on the desk, my usual nervous habit, and bit my lower lip. I glanced at my watch and was just about to hang up when the music stopped.

"This is Stan Morgan."

His voice sounded somewhat stiff, his words clipped, lacking bedside manner. I guess that's not important with the dead, though.

"Hello, Mr. Morgan. This is Melanie Hogan."

"Yes, I got a voicemail from Max Winters a while ago. He said you would be finishing up Mr. Martin's funeral arrangements, along with Sharon Winters. Only one thing more to do — the music."

Easy enough. We could orchestrate some musical mix of devil music. "I was wondering if you could tell me something."

"I can try. What is it?"

"I understand a woman was talking with you the other day claiming to be Lenny — Mr. Martin's daughter-in-law."

"That would be correct," he said pensively. "How did you know that?"

"Someone overheard the introduction."

"Oh."

"Could you tell me her name? As far as we know, Lenny—Mr. Martin doesn't have any family other than Sharon, Max, and myself."

"Hm. Well, she told me she was his daughter-in-law, and I don't ask for ID. She seemed to know an awful lot about him. And she said she was going to foot the entire bill."

"What was her name?"

"Alicia Hollingsworth."

"Alicia Hollingsworth," I repeated to myself. I struggled to find any meaning in the name. Nothing came to mind. "Did you happen to mention this to Max?"

"Not yet. He had this unfortunate accident before I saw him again. When he left the voicemail, he was getting ready to go into surgery. You must know her if she's family."

"Nope. But she's going to foot the entire bill?" Something felt off. "Why would she tell you about Mr. Martin? And *what* did she tell you?" I crossed my fingers and held my breath, hoping he would volunteer some information I could use.

"People tell me about their loved ones more often than you'd think. Ms. Hollingsworth was no different."

"What did she tell you about him?" I asked again.

"Nothing you don't already know, I'm sure."

"Try me," I pressed.

"He was born to Italian immigrants who died fairly young. His father was in business, and his mother was a homemaker."

"Did he say what kind of business?" *Like I had to ask.*

"It was a family business."

I'll bet it was. "Anything else?"

"He loved life and lived it to the full. He regretted never having known his children, that he felt cheated because he didn't get the chance to be a father. That should bring you some comfort in this difficult time, Ms. Hogan."

Except it didn't. Because Max's mother said he didn't want a child. One of them was lying, and I'd be willing to bet which one. This woman who claimed to be Lenny's daughter-in-law was a fraud. "Did Ms. Hollingsworth give you an address?"

"No, just a phone number. I didn't ask for an address because she said she would be back. Later this afternoon, as a matter of fact."

"Maybe I could get that phone number from you," I said. "To be sure everything is financially settled up," I added when he paused.

"How about if I take your phone number and give it to her when she comes back in?"

"Mr. Morgan," I said, starting to think I was out of luck, "I'm Mr. Martin's daughter." I nearly choked on the words. "She's simply his daughter-in-law." *Or so she claims.* "I have a right to know who else is involved in this. Especially if they're paying for it." I could almost see him rocking back and forth on his heels to toes and back, hands clasped behind him, as he talked into a Bluetooth headset. "Mr. Morgan?"

"Just a moment, please. Tonya?" he called to someone on his end. "Look up Alicia Hollingsworth's phone number for me, will you please?"

Seconds ticked by before he relayed the number to me. "Thank you, sir. I'm going to sneak away from work for a bit this afternoon and pop on over there with Sharon. To get the music squared away."

"What time?" he asked.

"Depends on how I can rearrange my clients. I can call you when I get it figured out."

"That will work. Thank you, Ms. Hogan. And, again, I'm sorry about your father."

I shuddered. The fact that Lenny was my father still felt like a terrible nightmare. One I desperately wanted to wake from and couldn't no matter how hard I tried.

I held the slip of paper in my hand with Alicia Hollingsworth's phone number. No time like the present. I used the landline phone so as not to give away my cell phone number. I punched in the numbers and held my breath.

"The number you have called is not a working number. Please hang up and try again. If you feel you have reached this recording in error..."

My pulse quickened. I pulled the phone away from my ear and absently set it back in the cradle. I knew it! Alicia Hollingsworth was a fraud.

28

Hearing the ladies out in the salon laughing and carrying on, I decided to join them. I could get my mind in a better place, if nothing else. It was on a slippery slope and going down fast.

"How's your knee there, chickalina?" Babs asked as soon as I entered the room.

"Better," I said.

"Better than what?" she asked.

"Than it was, smart alec." I grinned at her. Yes, indeed, this was what I needed. At least for now. Until I could get out and do something about my situation, it did absolutely no good to sit and stew in it.

"Claire Bear," I said, "I'm going to try scoot out of here for a bit this afternoon. What does your schedule look like?"

"To go with you or to squeeze in some of your appointments?" she asked.

"The latter, if you're able."

She went behind the front desk and looked at the combined calendar. "I can probably fit your three o'clock cut and color if that will help you."

Connie looked at the books as well. "I'm able to take your four-thirty cut."

"You girls rock it," I said, giving them each a high-five.

"You'll rock it, too," Babs said to me, "if you can figure this mess out."

"That's the goal, kiddo."

***

The morning zipped by. The air was pungent with the smell of hair color, hair spray, and artificial nails. Given the turn of events over the past few days and the necessity of having to rearrange my appointments, I was incredibly grateful that Rubie rescheduled the majority of her appointments for when she returned from her cruise. I looked at the calendar—her vacation was more than half over. And I couldn't be more thrilled. I missed her energy around here. We all did.

I'd slipped into the office to grab my water bottle when Claire was in there mixing a hair color concoction.

"Did you call Levi about putting extra security by Max's room?"

"Crap!" I exclaimed. "I got on the phone with Mr. Morgan from the funeral home and forgot all about it. Ya know that woman who showed up claiming to be Lenny's daughter-in-law? Well," I continued without waiting for her to answer, "she's a fake. I knew it!" I took a swig of water then briefly filled her in on the highlights of the conversation with Stan Morgan.

"This just keeps getting weirder. You better take a minute and call Levi to get extra security on Max. Now."

I looked at my watch. "Max is probably in surgery."

"All the more reason to call now," she said, "so it's in place when he's brought back to his room."

I knew delaying the call to Levi for selfish reasons only put Max at risk, yet my small cell phone felt like it weighed a thousand pounds. Nevertheless, I managed to pick it up. "I'll call him now." It rang and rang until finally, I hung up. "It went to voice mail."

"Well, I didn't hear you leave one so call him back. You avoiding this hardly seems like a good reason to put Max's life in jeopardy. This is completely out of character for you, Melanie." I hung my head. "Want me to call Cole?"

"Yes, please." It felt like I should have added the word, *ma'am*. "And I'll call Levi back and leave a voice mail." I took a slow breath and again hit the speed dial number assigned to Levi, leaving the promised message, but not without adding that there was no urgency in calling me back. After all, Claire had already set her color mixture down and was on the phone with Cole.

I listened as she gave him an abbreviated run-down of the situation. After she hung up, she picked up her color bowl again and started for the door. "He's going to talk to the chief right now to see if they can get someone over there immediately."

Claire hurried back to her waiting client, and I greeted my next one, taking her back to my chair, grateful for the diversion. The next thing I knew, it was two o'clock, and my cell phone lit up with an incoming call.

"Ms. Hogan?" the woman said. "This is Stacy from Lincoln Elementary. I'm calling to let you know of an incident we just had at the school. A woman showed up here trying to take Daisy from the playground at afternoon recess just now. I tried calling her grandmother, but there was no answer."

Panic gripped me. "Who was it?"

"Sydney didn't know her, and Daisy isn't talking."

"Any of the other kids—did they see her? You said it was out at recess, right?"

"Yes. But no one else appears to have seen anything. It was on the north side of the school. The playground is on the south side." My heart raced. Something was really strange about this whole thing. Why would the girls be over on that side to begin with? Didn't they have playground monitors?

"Where is she now? Daisy, I mean."

"She's here in the office."

I took a deep breath. "Keep her there. I'll call her grandmother right now and see if I can get a hold of her. What did this woman look like? Did she have longish, blond hair?"

"I didn't see her. Only Sydney and Daisy did. And like I said, Daisy isn't talking. But—"

"It might have been her mother, Pam. She's the non-custodial parent. I'm not sure how much Claire told you when she dropped the girls off this morning, but Daisy's father was in an accident last night. He's asked that his mother, Sharon, and I enroll Daisy in school there. Now I'm not so sure that's a good idea."

"If it's her mother, she'll find her no matter where she is. If you ask me, it's all the more reason to enroll her here because the custody situation is already on our radar. But you said her mother has blond hair?"

"Yes. Just below the shoulder."

"Hm. That doesn't sound like the woman at the school today. Not according to Sydney's description of her," Stacy said. She recited Sydney's description of the woman. I gasped. It was the same woman from the funeral home! I was sure of it! "The police are on their way."

"I'll be right there."

"We'll keep her in the office with us until you get here."

"Is Sydney with her?"

"No. I sent her back to class."

I called Sharon on my way to the school and left a voice mail for her, praying she'd get it as soon as possible. I also called the hotel front desk and asked them to get an urgent message to Sharon's room.

By the time I pulled into the school parking lot, a police car was already parked by the entrance. I ran in through the front door, into the office, and to the front desk. I scanned the room and saw Cole talking with Daisy and Sydney through the window of a small conference room off to the side of Stacy's desk. I didn't see Sharon yet. I looked at my phone to see if I had any missed calls from her. Just as I did, the screen lit up.

"Melanie, what happened? Is Daisy okay? Where is she?" Sharon's panicked voice shot off question after question.

"I'm here at the school now. An officer is talking with both her and Sydney."

"What happened?" Her voice was on the verge of hysteria. I recounted the incident again, this time in more detail as I knew it. "Goodness," she said, "I just laid down for a little nap and must have fallen asleep harder than I thought. And my phone somehow got on silent." Her words tumbled one over the other.

The image of my grandmother flashed through my mind. "She's a smart girl, Sharon. She knew not to go with the woman." I explained how to get to the school.

"I'll be right there," she said, the last word clipped off as the line went dead.

I crossed the room to the front desk, where Stacy watched Cole and the girls through the window. "Daisy's grandmother is on her way. Appears Cole—Officer Mahoney called Sydney to the office after you called me?"

"Yes. Said he needed to talk to both girls. He thought they might talk more if they were together. Looks like Sydney's doing most of the talking."

I smiled. "That sounds about right." I looked at them, Sydney chatting it up with Cole, animatedly at that, while Daisy, other than giving Syd an occasional irritated glance, looked somewhat sullen. I tilted my head to the side. *What happened out there, Daisy? And how did you come to be on that side of the school?* "Did you call Claire yet?" I asked Stacy. I hadn't realized Sydney's potential involvement in the incident when I'd left the salon, so I hadn't taken the time to say anything other than there was an issue with Daisy that I needed to take care of.

"No, I didn't think there was any reason to." The look I gave her apparently concerned her because she rushed on. "I believe Officer Mahoney did. Sydney wasn't with Daisy when it happened. Sydney went to look for her. When the woman saw Sydney, she quickly left. But not before she got a look at the woman."

Cole glanced out the window, saw me, and motioned me into the room. He didn't have to ask me twice. I immediately went over by the girls, an arm around each one's shoulders. "What happened?" I asked.

"Where's my gramma?" Daisy asked.

"She's on her way."

"I'm gonna be in so much trouble," she whispered.

"Why, honey?" I leaned over in front of her, so I was at eye level. "What did you do to make you think you're going to be in trouble?" I held my breath expectantly.

"Nothing," she said in little more than a whisper.

I looked at Cole, and he shrugged.

"That's all I've been able to get out of her," he said.

"Don't they have, like, school resource officers or something here?" I asked. "Someone to watch out for these things?"

"Not at the elementary schools," he said.

"What about playground monitors? They had those when I was in school."

"They depend on volunteers. And to be honest, the kids get to know who's on duty on which day and know who they can bamboozle."

"Daisy's only been here a few hours," I scoffed. "Not long enough to know that."

Cole raised an eyebrow. "You'd be surprised at how fast word gets around."

"Besides, Aunt Mel," Sydney said, "that was a long time ago when you were in school." *Ouch!* She may as well have called me a dinosaur. But under the circumstances, I decided to let that zinger go. "She didn't do anything, anyway. The lady was trying to get her to go with her. That's all."

But why Daisy, why now, and why the same woman from the funeral home? And who is she? Questions just kept piling up like a mound of laundry on top of the ones I already had. "Daisy, who was she? Did you know her?" She shook her head, tucked her hands under her thighs, and avoided eye contact, all signs she wasn't upfront with me. "Your dad wanted your gramma and me to enroll you in school today, but I don't think it's a good idea. We need to let your dad know what happened first and let him decide what he wants to do after that."

"I want to go to school here," she said, looking at the floor. Then, she lifted her face and looked at me. "Everyone is so nice."

"Yeah?" I asked. She nodded. "Given the recent events, I still think we need to talk with your dad first."

"Do I get to go see him?"

"You bet. As soon as your gramma gets here, okay? I have to go somewhere else first, and then I'll meet you at the hospital." I tried to read her expression before I continued. "I should warn you, he had to have surgery this morning to repair his hip, so he might be kinda groggy when you see him." Tears welled up in her eyes, threatening to spill over. I sat next to her and pulled her into a hug. "Oh, sweetie," I said, rocking her gently, "you've been through so much."

I stopped from pushing further about the woman at the school today. She was too fragile right now. And it wasn't my place. If she wasn't going to open up to Cole, then it was a job for Max. But I was going to be sure she stayed safe in the meantime. That was my only job right now.

"Daisy!" Sharon said, running over and sweeping her into a giant hug. Her frazzled hair—flatter on one side— and her wrinkled blouse revealed she hadn't taken time to look in the mirror after her nap before rushing out the door. Her skin looked pasty; her makeup had smudged.

"Are you okay? What happened?" She pulled back and looked at Daisy, a hand on each of her cheeks, cupping her face. She brushed a wisp of hair off Daisy's forehead.

"Do I get to go to school here?" Daisy asked her.

"Absolutely not." Sharon's eyes grew wide, and her mouth drew a tight line. "Honey, what have I told you about talking to strangers? What were you thinking?"

"Told ya I'd be in trouble," Daisy said to me under her breath.

"Could you ladies stay out by Stacy for a few?" Cole asked. "We'll only be another minute or two."

I led Sharon out of the room and into the main office, leaving Cole with the girls. I gestured toward Stacy. "The school secretary made a good point. Daisy must go to school somewhere, and they're aware of this woman. Another school wouldn't be." I took a breath and said just loud enough for her to hear, "And I might have mentioned Pam." I met her gaze, an unhappy one at that.

"What did you mention about Pam?"

"Just that she's the noncustodial parent. At first, I assumed it was her that tried to pick up Daisy. So they're aware of that as well."

Sharon took a moment to mull over what I said. "I need to run this by her father first."

"I would expect nothing less," I said. "Have you talked with him since he's been out of surgery? I assume he's out?"

"The doctor called and said that everything went as well as he hoped it would. He was still in recovery. I was waiting to go back until I picked up Daisy."

I thought it odd that she wouldn't have stayed at the hospital while he was in surgery. I wouldn't care if my child was eighty, nothing could have kept me from the hospital until I knew everything was okay. But then, I had to remember a man like Lenny had swayed this woman.

"Sharon—" I paused, deciding whether to ask, whether it was any of my business. This whole having a family thing could be so complicated. I finally figured I had nothing to lose. "Why did you tell Pam that Max was in the hospital? I thought they didn't get along."

"Oh, it's not that they don't get along," Sharon said. "Pam is just mad because Max won't let her be part of their lives as long as she's using. Drugs," she added as if I didn't know. "But what do you mean why did I tell her about Max?"

"It's certainly not my intent to be nosy, and I'm not judging, I swear, but—"

"I didn't tell Pam anything about Max. And I never would. That woman is poison."

I might not understand how Sharon could have left the hospital while her son was in surgery, but there was no question of how protective of him she was.

"She was at the hospital last night. I guess she told Max that you told her about it."

Anger flashed in her eyes, and it chilled me. "Why, I wouldn't tell that woman where my son is! Ever. She's one you need to watch out for, Melanie. She'll do anything to get my son back. She's toxic to him and my granddaughter. I will do whatever it takes to keep her out of their lives."

"Anything?" I asked.

Her eyes locked on mine. "Anything."

29

When we left the school, Sharon and Daisy went to the hospital to see Max. I headed to the funeral home. I volunteered to go alone so she could focus on Max and Daisy, surprised when she agreed.

Levi would be awake by now, and I knew I needed to call him. And I wanted to. But what would I say? I decided to make the call and pray the words would come once I heard his voice. I pulled over to the side of the road, turned my phone over in my hand a time or two, and then punched in the speed dial number assigned to him. I waited while it rang.

"You've reached Levi," the recording said, "you know what to do."

I waited for the beep, my heart beating too fast. "Hi Levi, it's me. Melanie. Call when you get a minute, okay? Please," I stammered, hating that it sounded like I was begging. "Okay, then, I guess I'll talk to you later." I paused for a minute, then blurted, "I love you." Of that I was absolutely sure.

I pulled back onto the road and wound my way through city streets until I reached the funeral home. With all that had gone on that afternoon, I'd forgotten to call Mr. Morgan and let him know what time I would be there. All I could do was hope he was there and available. Just as I put my hand on the door handle to open my car door, my cell phone played. I inhaled quickly, my pulse quickening with part hope and part fear. I looked at the display, took a deep breath, and answered.

"Hi, Levi. Thanks for calling."

"Did you have any doubt that I would?"

"Earlier when I called —"

"I was trying to give you the space you're requesting."

I grasped onto the gentle warmth beneath the apparent distance in his tone. "Well, I wouldn't blame you if you wouldn't have called me back this time," I said. "But I'm glad you did. I know I haven't been easy. Again." He chuckled. "How was your day?"

"You weren't in it, so it was uneventful."

I laughed quietly. "You miss those days, I bet."

"I miss *you*."

I smiled and murmured, "It's only been a day."

"In the ways that are important, it's been a heckuva lot longer than that."

I choked back emotion I didn't want to feel right now. "Sorry. Really, I am."

"You up for talking before I go into work tonight? I found something you should probably know about."

Curiosity waged war for my attention. "What is it?"

"I drove out to your house today and took a look down by the lake where Max was hit."

My pulse kicked up a notch. "Did you find something?"

"I did."

"Are you there now?"

"Left a few minutes ago. I'm headed back into town," he said.

"I can meet you at your house later if that's okay. Or if you're not going anywhere in particular right now, you could meet me at the funeral home when you get to town." It was only fifteen minutes from my house into town. If he'd just left, he could probably be here in about ten minutes. "I can wait in the parking lot for you. I'm here now."

"The funeral home?"

It occurred to me that he didn't know I'd agreed to help Max with the remaining funeral arrangements. It may have been only a little more than a day, but so much life had happened in that timespan. I missed him as part of it. I filled him in on the bare essentials until we talked later that evening. Silence followed. "Levi?"

"Yeah, I'm here."

"Whatcha thinking?"

"About how much happens in your life in just a few hours. And that a talk is overdue."

Anxiety tied my stomach in knots. I sure didn't like the sound of that. *A talk is overdue.* That could only mean one thing. My stupid insecurities have caused me to lose this man that I've come to love more than life itself. A lump formed in my throat. "Okay. This evening then?"

"Business first. I can meet you at the funeral home. If you still want me to."

"I do," I said. "Yes, I do."

"Alrighty then. I'm about five minutes out."

I sat in my car as I waited for Levi, my mind traveling into my likely future. The one without Levi. And I didn't like it. At all.

I absently stared out my windshield at the entrance to the funeral home, barely noticing the door opening, until a woman appeared, followed by Mr. Morgan. It was *the* woman!

I bolted upright then quickly slid down in my seat, knocking my knee on the steering column. I muttered an expletive likely to make a sailor proud and stayed low, just able to see over the dashboard. The woman looked in my direction, apparently satisfied that she hadn't seen anything, then up at Mr. Morgan.

I watched as she spoke to him—the hair, the makeup, the sunglasses, the fur coat. Alicia Hollingsworth. Neither she nor the name meant anything to me. Why did I fear that it soon would? Another sibling is not what I'd envisioned, nor wanted, in that bleak future I had contemplated a few moments ago.

I watched her movements, her gestures. I debated whether to get out and approach her or continue watching for just a moment longer to see what I could discover. If I got out now, she could run, and I'd have nothing. On the other hand, if I stayed put and out of sight, she would probably still be there when Levi arrived, and he could arrest her for attempting to kidnap Daisy. Just then, he pulled into the parking lot and next to me.

I sat up, acknowledged Levi through my window, and then looked at the front entrance of the funeral home. The woman was gone. "Darn!" Criminals could sense a cop car, on sight or unseen, whether the vehicle was marked or not. She couldn't have gotten far unless she had a car parked in the small employee parking lot in the back.

I quickly opened my door and called to Levi over the top of my car as I pointed to where Alicia had stood only a moment ago. "That's the woman! That's the woman who tried to take Daisy from school today! She was right there talking with Mr. Morgan." Mr. Morgan had opened the door to go back inside but now looked in our direction. "That woman," I called over to him. "Where did she go?" I looked at Levi, already running toward the back of the building as he talked into his handheld police radio.

"I have no idea," Mr. Morgan said, frowning. "Home, I would imagine."

"Where does she live?" I asked. "I need an address. Now!"

"Not around here. She's staying at a hotel on the other side of town."

Oh no! The same as Max and his family? "Where's her car?" I barked, indicating the mostly empty parking lot. "If she's staying on the other side of town, where's her car?"

Levi reappeared from the back of the building. "She got away. The bus stop is back there, and she disappeared with the bus."

I was now two feet in front of Mr. Morgan. "That woman who you're so chummy with, the one you're trying to protect for some unknown reason, tried to kidnap my niece this afternoon." My cheeks grew hot, my heart palpitating.

"I've called the station," Levi said. "They can track where the bus is heading, and they'll get her, Melanie. I promise. *We'll* get her."

"I want the name of the hotel and room number," I said, glaring at Mr. Morgan. "It's time to stop being evasive and protecting her. Who is she to you, anyway? *Why* are you protecting her?"

Mr. Morgan tugged on his jacket sleeves and adjusted his shirt cuffs while clearing his throat. "I'm not sure I like your insinuation, Ms. Hogan. If you're here to finish the arrangements for your father, then let's focus on that, shall we?"

"I'm not doing anything until you hand over the hotel and room number for Ms. Hollingsworth. My brother's family could be in danger!"

Levi's phone rang. "It's the department," he said, stepping off to the side to answer it.

"Mr. Morgan, please. I'm begging you. They'll find her anyway. If the police discover in the process that you're protecting a criminal, it won't look good for you and your business." I swallowed a bitter laugh. His business was pretty much guaranteed. No one can evade death, and there was only one other funeral home in Birch Haven. And from outside appearances, I wouldn't trust that anyone going into that one alive wouldn't become funeral home business rather than walking out. Honestly, I couldn't believe the town hadn't condemned the place. The roof sagged, and the siding was a sore sight.

Levi walked back over to us, his phone still in his hand. "Come on," he said to me. "They've got her. They're bringing her to the station."

"I'll meet you there," I said, trotting to my car, slowing to a fast walk when my knee complained. "Or I could ride with you," I suggested. "And we could come back here afterward to get my car." I wanted to spend time with him, even if it was on the way to the station. What surprised me is it didn't feel like a sacrifice of my independence at all. Instead, it felt like we were a team—this incredible man and me.

He held my gaze for a moment, then gave me a small smile and nodded toward his car. "Come on." He opened the door for me, his hand brushing the small of my back as I got in. Lucky me. But I feared I still wasn't out of the woods yet. And I couldn't blame him.

When Levi got in on his side and started the car, I glanced at him out of the corner of my eye. I gently reached for his hand. He held mine loosely. It was as if he wasn't quite sure what he wanted.

Between finding out who this woman was and what was going on with my man and me, my stomach felt tied in knots, and I feared I was going to vomit.

"What did you find at my house by the lake?" I asked.

"A woman's glove."

"Where? And why wouldn't they have found it when they checked the scene?"

"Good question, Detective Hogan."

"Well, where was it?"

"By the boat shed."

I shrugged. "Not exactly in the middle of the crime scene, then. What did it look like?" I asked, trying to remember which ones each of us was wearing that night.

"Black. I'll bring it in for DNA testing. Will we find DNA from you, Claire, or the girls on it?" He looked across the car at me then back to the street as he waited to turn left onto the main road.

"Black? Uh-uh." I shook my head. "Claire doesn't wear black, Sydney had green mittens, and Daisy had purple." I only remembered because they matched the pom-poms on their skates.

"And you?"

"Black. But not gloves. I wore mittens. They keep my fingers warmer."

He nodded. "I assumed it wasn't any of yours, but I wanted to be sure to eliminate any surprises."

"Do you think the driver of the snowmobile was a woman?" I asked.

"Hard to say. It's unlikely that the driver would lose a glove. Unless he—or she, in this case—wasn't wearing them. Gloves don't just fall off when you're gripping the handlebars of a snowmobile."

"So we're not any closer to finding out who it was."

"Don't get discouraged yet. Let's wait to see what the DNA tells us. For all we know, there could have been two people on the snowmobile. Lots of people ride doubles."

"And I didn't get a good look at the machine. I was too busy worrying about Max," I said. My shoulders slumped slightly in defeat but straightened again when I thought of Alicia Hollingsworth at the station. I would finally find out who she is and why she wanted Daisy. "I should call Max and let him know about Alicia Hollingsworth."

"He just got out of surgery a bit ago, didn't he? Sharon might not have even told him about it yet. I would wait until we find out exactly who she is and how she's involved."

I nodded. "Anything more on Lenny's murder?"

"No. Detective Walker said they don't have any solid leads yet. Have you gotten any more phone calls?" He glanced over at me.

I shook my head. "No."

"Max?"

"Not that I know of. Unless he did today, and we wouldn't know it since he hasn't had his phone in surgery."

"No more threats of any kind?"

I frowned, not sure where he was going with this. Did something happen that I'd forgotten to tell him? No, I was sure of it. I shook my head. "No. I would have told you if there had been."

"Would you? When?"

I flinched at the too-direct question he volleyed at me. I didn't say anything. Usually, silence was my best friend. The only problem was that a quick sarcastic retort usually won. Not this time. "That's fair," I finally murmured.

We were almost at the police department, and a small part of me was disappointed. As much as I wanted to know who this woman was, I didn't want this time with Levi to end, especially when I had no idea what he'd decided about us. He laced his fingers loosely through mine. I tightened my grasp slightly, but his didn't change. I had an uncomfortable feeling about us. But I had no one to blame other than myself. I could try blaming Violet like I'd done in the past with everything terrible that happened. But oddly, I didn't feel anger toward her this time. This was all on me.

When the police department was within sight, I put my pity party to bed. It was time to solve this once and for all so I could figure out who killed Lenny. And hopefully, get my personal life back on track. Although at this point, that part looked unlikely.

30

Cole met us as soon as we walked into the station. "We've got her, Melanie."

"Who is she? And how does she know Daisy?"

"I don't know," he said. "She's demanding to talk to you or Max. Said she'll tell you everything."

"Well, Max is out of the picture right now. So I guess it's me." I looked at Levi. "Did you know about this?"

"I didn't," he said, looking grim. "I'm going in with her," he told Cole.

"She won't talk if you're in there," Cole said.

"The hell she won't," Levi barked.

"You're the detective," Cole said, "and you typically know more than me about these kinds of things. But I'm telling you, I'm right on this one."

Levi looked at me and took a breath, exhaled slowly, and asked, "You okay with this? I'll be standing right here watching through the glass."

I nodded. "Yeah. I'm good."

I turned and walked into the room in which Alicia Hollingsworth was waiting. I stood by the door for a moment, looking her over. She reeked of money with her perfect hair, perfectly manicured nails, cashmere sweater, and leather boots. Looking more closely, however, it was all as Andie had said — fake; faux fur and leather coat on the back of her chair, boots that showed years of wear and tear, and the unraveling cuffs of her sweater revealing it wasn't cashmere at all. At least she didn't have her sunglasses on so I could see her eyes, pale blue and somewhat glossy. The way she looked at me, the way she moved, calculated, gave me a sense of déjà vu.

"I was wondering which of you would come to talk with me. Protecting big brother?"

"What do you have to say?"

"I don't bite. You can come in further and sit down."

"I'm fine right here," I said. But obviously, I wasn't, because before I realized what I was doing, I crossed the room and stood behind the chair across the table from Alicia. "What were you doing at the funeral home, and why did you try to kidnap Daisy?"

She tipped her head back and emitted a small laugh. "Is that what you think I was doing? Kidnapping Daisy?"

"I know you were."

"It's not as dramatic as you're making this out to be."

"No? Why don't you enlighten me, then," I said.

"Daisy is my niece."

I swallowed hard, a lump forming in my throat. "How?"

"Pam is my sister. She has a right to see her daughter. Max has no right to keep her from her mother." *Pam's sister*?

"Max has never mentioned Pam having a sister," I said.

"We shared a foster home when we were in elementary school. We've been best friends since then. You have no idea what we've been through together."

"I can only imagine," I muttered.

"We're closer than any blood siblings could be. You and Max have nothing on me and Pam."

"So, what, you decide you'll just take Daisy from school? By the way, have you seen Pam lately? She's not exactly in any shape to parent a child."

"As a matter of fact, I have seen her," she said. "She's clean."

"And you're delusional. She's living at a homeless shelter. High."

"Not anymore," Alicia said. "She's getting an apartment in town, and she's clean. Has been for three weeks now."

"She's staying in Birch Haven?" I couldn't decide if I was happy for Daisy or troubled by what it meant. Birch Haven was growing far too fast for my taste.

"Why wouldn't she? Her daughter is here." Her voice was too calm, too practiced. Something felt off.

"Taking her from the school was, what, for her good? Kidnapping is a crime here in Birch Haven, just as it is anywhere else."

She tipped her head back and laughed again. "We're her family."

"Technically, you're not family at all. Not that any court would recognize. And Pam is the noncustodial parent. She doesn't have any rights unless the Court orders it." She kept her gaze fixed on me as if sizing me up. "Why have you been at the funeral home? Why would you pay for Lenny's funeral expenses?"

"Because Pam has asked me to. She wants to do right by Max and Daisy. She's trying to reunite her family. Given your, uh, *lack* of family, you can understand that, can't you?" I got the sense she wanted to uncoil and strike at me. I instinctively backed up a couple of steps, my leg giving me a nasty twinge, a reminder standing on it this long wasn't the brightest of ideas.

"Here's a suggestion," I said, "if Pam truly is sober—and I sincerely hope she is, for her sake as well as Daisy's—tell her to go through the Court for visitation instead of sending her tribe to steal her child. A court usually doesn't look kindly on that."

She leaned forward, eyes narrowed to dangerous slits, and whispered, "Daisy is going to be back with her mother, and Max will know what it feels like to have his child ripped from him. Sooner rather than later. Mark my words on that."

The intensity of her words, with which she most likely meant to intimidate me, backfired, and instead renewed my confidence, setting me back on solid ground. "So much for Pam wanting to reunite her so-called family. And was that a threat, Alicia?"

She tilted her head, sat back, and smiled, lips curled in a way that made me shiver. "No, it's a promise. I wouldn't threaten you, Melanie. I'm sure that's a crime in Birch Haven as well."

I stared at her for a moment. The woman reeked of evil and deceit. Finally, I turned and left, closing the door quietly behind me. Levi met me on the other side of the door. "Alicia is delusional," I said. "And she claims to be Pam's foster sister and best friend."

"I heard," he grumbled. "I listened on the other side."

"Max has never mentioned her. But it's not like we've talked about Pam much." My phone played. I fished it out of my purse and looked at the display.

"Hi, Sharon. How's Max?" As I listened to her, I felt the color drain from my face. My legs grew weak. As soon as I hung up, I said to Levi, "Someone tried to kill Max. When the officer stepped away to grab of cup of coffee, one of the staff saw a nurse they didn't recognize come out of his room. Minutes later, the alarm on the machine monitoring his vitals went off. They were able to save him, but he's in ICU."

Levi put his hand on my arm. "Let's get over there."

Cole came running around the corner. "Levi, there's been an incident at the hospital with Max Winters. Johnson and Collins are on their way."

"I heard," Levi said over his shoulder as he rushed me toward the door. "Melanie and I are headed there now."

"The officer was gone for a few moments at most, and Sharon and Daisy stepped out to the cafeteria," I told him as we sped toward the hospital. "Whoever did this had to have waited for them to leave. I knew someone was there watching this morning. I *knew* it." I ran through the day in my head. "Alicia Hollingsworth said Daisy was going to be back with Pam. That Max would know what it was like to have his daughter ripped from him. Is this what she meant?" Suddenly I felt like I might hyperventilate as realization hit me and my hand flew to my chest.

Levi and I looked at each other and said at the same time. "Pam!"

"Alicia demanding to talk with you was a setup to—"

"To place our focus here instead of at the hospital," I finished as the realization dawned on me. We'd all played right into their hands.

He accelerated, and I grabbed onto the dash as we sped toward the hospital. It was Pam all along. But why threaten Daisy in the phone calls and the letter? And how in the world did she manage to get Lenny to my salon? She's a small woman, and a dead body is—well, dead weight. She had to have help. But who? And what motive would she have to kill Lenny?

"She has a helper," Levi said as if reading my mind. "We need to find out who that is."

"Alicia?"

He nodded. "We might be looking at three people. Even with Alicia's help, it's unlikely the two of them would have been able to carry Lenny's body to the salon unnoticed. He's not a small man."

We skidded around the corner into the hospital parking lot. We both jumped out and jogged toward the entrance. I'd forgotten all about my knee until I twisted it slightly when I reached for the door. It buckled, my grip on the door keeping me upright. I sucked in my breath from the pain and could swear stars circled above me.

"You okay?" Levi asked instantly at my side.

"Yeah, I'm fine," I said, gritting my teeth. "I just want to find Pam. Hopefully, she didn't get away. At least we both know what she looks like."

"I don't see how she could have escaped. The hospital has been on lockdown. Unless she immediately split before they had a chance to lock the doors." He showed his badge to the hospital security guards standing at the door. "She's with me," he told them, nodding toward me. They waved us in — just another day on the job.

More police units screamed up Maple Street to the entrance, lights flashing through the large entrance doors.

"I'm gonna take the stairs," I said.

"I'll take the stairs," he countered. "Your knee. You take the elevator."

"True," I said, jogging over to the bank of elevators, my knee throbbing from the recent twist. The doors opened on the last bank, and I hopped on, turned, and pushed the fourth-floor button when I felt something hard at my back. I froze, and my breath caught as I put my hands up, palms forward. "Pam," I muttered.

"We'll stop right here," the female voice said behind me. She reached around me and pushed the elevator hold button before punching the button to the basement. I began to turn my head. "Don't," she warned, jabbing the gun harder into my back. "You already know it's me. How did you figure it out?"

"It was your glove at the lake, wasn't it? You tried to kill Max, the father of your child. That's pathetic."

"Yeah?" I heard her chuckle. "That stupid glove. I took them off to get a better grip on the handlebar things. Guess I won't do that next time."

"Next time?" I wiped my sweating hands on my pants and hoped she didn't notice the slight hitch in my voice. "Do you honestly think you're going to get out of here? There are police everywhere, and the doors are locked. You can't get away, Pam. Just turn yourself in."

She laughed. "Really? That's all you have for me? Just turn yourself in?"

"You can't get away." I struggled to breathe through the panic.

"Yeah? I disagree." She reached around and dangled a key in front of me. "The nurse who happened to *donate* this uniform to me? Well, that just happened to gain me access to a set of keys. The keys, you see, to the back elevator door behind me. The one that leads to the back hallway and to the basement. As a pharmaceutical rep, I've made plenty of visits to hospitals, Melanie. You don't think I scoped this one out first?"

"But why threaten Daisy? She's your daughter!"

"Exactly! She's *my* daughter. I would never hurt her. But it kept you from suspecting me, didn't it?"

"The man's voice on the phone call. The man at the homeless shelter that you were smoking with," I said before she could answer. Now it all made sense. "You weren't homeless at all, were you?"

"Meh," she said matter of fact. "I figured that was the best way to flesh out someone who didn't have anything to lose by helping me. Lucky for him, he'll come out a winner after I pay him from the inheritance Daisy will get after you and Max are dead. All he had to do was help transport a body and make a few calls and he's set for life. He'll never have to spend another night homeless. It was a win-win."

"How did you find out about the inheritance?"

"I'm not stupid. In fact, I'm downright resourceful."

She jabbed the gun into my back again, and I stumbled forward at the same time the elevator jerked, throwing Pam off balance. I held my breath, sure the gun would mistakenly fire from the jolt. When the shot didn't come, I let it out.

The doors to the basement opened, and Levi stood there, gun pointed. But not before Pam grabbed me from behind, arm around my neck and gun to my head. I caught my breath again, afraid to even breathe. *Don't panic, Melanie. Don't panic,* I thought. I watched Levi carefully, my eyes never leaving him. My safe place.

"Let her go, Pam."

"Not a chance," she said. Her hand holding the gun shook, causing me to panic a bit more. A shaking hand holding a gun can't possibly lead to anything good.

"You'll only make things worse for yourself," Levi said. "Let her go."

"Again, no. She's coming with me until I'm in the clear." Her grip around my neck tightened. "If you want to see your little girlfriend alive, Detective, you'll let me out of here. Alicia is—"

"At the police department. Alicia has been arrested, Pam. She's not going to be your getaway car." Levi kept his gaze trained on her. "But then you knew that since it was a setup to keep us tied up there, allowing you to do your criminal work here."

Pam's arm loosened a little, allowing me to take a breath as she processed Levi's words. "Well, your girlfriend here—"

"She's not my girlfriend, Pam. You must not have gotten that news yet. So your threat won't work."

His statement shook me up more than the gun Pam held against my head. So that was it then. I'd really done it. I chased him away with my stubbornness and fear.

From somewhere within me, I found strength I didn't know I had. All I knew was I had nothing to lose, and I had to at least try. I jerked downward, at the same time jabbing my elbow backward into her midsection, and stomped on her foot with my good heel, crushing down with all my might.

Pam yelped and doubled over, and a shot rang out next to my head. I squatted into a ball, covering my head with my arms, an earsplitting ringing in my ears from the gunshot. I slowly opened my eyes, unsure if I'd been hit or where Pam was. I inched my arms from over my head, wanting to look around me but afraid of what I might see—afraid even more of what I might not. The excruciating pain in my knee let me know I was still alive. The ringing in my ears faded slightly, but it was still all I could hear.

I finally looked up and saw someone lying on the floor. Levi! He'd been hit! As if in slow motion, medical personnel in white coats and green scrubs came running down the hallway and two officers from the other way.

I looked at Levi, lying still. "No!" I cried. "No, no, no!" And then I saw his leg move. I sucked in my breath, and my heart stopped. *Please, oh please, let it have been for real.* I scrambled to my feet, wrenching free from a man in scrubs. "Levi!" I cried. I weaseled my way through the people watching as a doctor worked on Levi, and I peered over the doctor's shoulder just as Levi began to sit up. The doctor rocked back on his heels, giving Levi room and allowing me the opportunity to kneel beside him.

"Damn! That hurt!" he said, shaking his head.

"You're okay?" Relief flooded through me at the sound of his voice, and tears flowed openly. I sniffled.

"You're really okay? But how?" I reached down and put my forehead against his, my hands on either side of his face.

"Easy," he groaned.

I smiled, then laughed. "You're alive! How?" I felt his chest. "Your vest. Thank God!"

I turned to look behind me as Officer Johnson led a handcuffed Pam down the hall. I watched her until she got past us. She turned to look at me through tears. "That money belongs to Daisy. I did this for my daughter."

It dumbfounded me that she genuinely believed that what she did was okay. That her daughter would be okay knowing her mother was a killer. That her mother tried to kill her father. How does that even begin to make sense to anyone, no matter how deranged they were? It felt like Pam should have been Lenny's biological child rather than Max and me.

Turning back toward Levi, I kissed him gently. "You scared me to death. But did you mean what you said to Pam? About you and me?" As afraid as I was to hear the answer, I was simply grateful that he was alive.

He touched my cheek, wiping a tear with his thumb. "I would think you'd trust me a little more than that. You couldn't get rid of me if you tried. And you've been trying," he said, shaking his head.

"No. Not anymore. I'm so, so sorry. You're stuck with me, Detective Wescott, for better or worse. I'm not going anywhere."

"What I don't go through for you, Melanie Hogan," he said, wincing as he shifted his position.

I laughed through sniffles and wrapped my arms around his neck. He flinched, and I pulled back. "Oops! I'm sorry." I placed my hands on either side of his face again. "Levi Wescott, I love you, and if you let me, I want to share all of my life with you and Jackson. No more making you scale walls." The tender smile he gave me was all the answer I needed.

Epilogue

Claire, Cole, Sydney, Max, Daisy, Levi, Jackson, and I sat around my grandmother's dining room table, a dinner my grandmother pulled together to celebrate our newfound family. Nana made my new favorite meal, Knoephla hotdish with butternut squash and double chocolate brownies for dessert. This was the first time we'd all been together, and the fact that it was at my grandmother's house made it even more special. Spirits were high, and laughter rose to insane levels; an outpouring of mutual relief that the events of the past week were just that—in the past.

I sat back and watched all my favorite people, unexpected emotions cropping up. The only people missing were Jack, who said he had previously made plans, and Rubie. I listened as Nana told Claire a story from years ago when I tried to save the neighbor's cat and chased the neighbor boy up a tree to get it. Claire laughed so hard that tears streamed down her cheeks. Levi shook his head and snickered.

Sydney and Jackson compared stories about their teachers, and Daisy joined in with stories from her old school as well as from the few days she had attended her new school. Sharon and I had enrolled her at Sydney's school, and both girls were elated. Max was coming along nicely, as was the sale of Harvey's Drugstore, soon to be Winters Drug Store. When we invited Sharon to join us tonight, she gracefully bowed out, saying as much as she'd like to, she was looking forward to spending a quiet evening with a good movie and a hot bath before packing to go back home in the morning to start the relocation process. As legitimate as that sounded, I think she just needed time to get used to this crazy group of ours.

The doorbell startled me. "Nana, are we expecting someone else?" I asked. Maybe Sharon changed her mind after all.

"I'll get it," Levi said, pushing his chair back, his lips brushing the side of my neck before he went to the door.

We all watched the doorway expectantly, and when they came into the dining room, I couldn't believe my eyes. "Jack!" I jumped up and pulled him into a tight hug. I didn't even care about the pain right now.

"Geez, Hogan! You're killing me!" The kids laughed.

"This night couldn't get any better," I said. "I'm so glad you were able to make it."

"I couldn't tell Rose no," he said, hugging my grandmother.

"I ask you to come over, and you give me some flimsy, lame excuse why you can't. But *she* invites you, and you accept?" I narrowed my eyes at him, the smile belying the visual scolding. Nana looked smug as could be.

After Jack said his hellos around the group, he made an extra effort to walk over to Max and Daisy. First, he acknowledged Daisy, then shook Max's hand.

"Nice to finally meet you, man," Jack said. "I'm impressed that you're sticking around after your introduction to a life that includes Melanie Hogan." I made to hit him in the arm, and he swerved away and grinned. "Just kidding," Jack said. "Melanie and Rose—especially Rose—" he looked at me, his eyes sparkling with amusement, "are two of the best people on the planet. Welcome to the family."

I grinned. This family of mine had grown significantly. But the most surprising thing about it was that I was more than okay with it. In fact, I was ready and wide open to it. It started with just Nana, Claire and Syd, Jack, and me, and it was beautiful. But along the way we'd picked up Levi, Jackson, Rubie, Max, Daisy, and even Sharon, and it became perfect. I couldn't imagine my life without any of them.

Any remaining tension evaporated, and I felt as though I was floating. Every emotion under the sun rummaged through me over the past two weeks. The full realization that I had a brother and a niece, Levi was alive, I buried a father I never knew and still wasn't sure I ever wanted to, and although suffering a setback trying to get away from Pam, my knee was healing. And by the grace of God, I was alive to see it all. I rested my hand on Levi's thigh and shivered as I thought of how close we'd come to not being here tonight.

"Cold?" Levi asked, laying an arm around my shoulders.

I shook my head and smiled. I looked at him, my gaze holding his. "Just happy," I whispered. "Just terribly happy."

I saw him exchange a look with Nana, and she gave him a nod and a wink.

"Melanie Hogan," he said as everyone stopped talking and looked on, "I love you, and there's nothing in this world I wouldn't do for you."

My breath caught as he reached into his pocket and pulled out a small box. My heart rate sped to dangerous levels, and I thought I might pass out as I desperately fought to identify what I felt right now. *Panic? Fear?*

"Will you marry me?" He opened the box to reveal a gorgeous solitary teardrop diamond.

I looked at Nana, eyes glistening with tears of joy. She winked at me, sending tears spilling down her cheeks. The little stinker had set this whole night up. She knew how much it would mean to me to be with the people I loved most in the world when this moment happened.

I looked at Jackson. "Jackson?" I said quietly, holding my breath.

"Yeah!" he said, looking so much like his dad. "It'll be cool."

I knew at that moment, the sheer fear that had held me back from being fully available to Levi had shifted to nothing other than sheer gratitude. And for that, itself, I was grateful.

"Well, then," I said, laughing through tears of my own and looking at Levi, "as long as it's *cool*, there's nothing in this world I'd like more than to be your wife."

"Yeah?" he said quietly, with a smile that made me catch my breath. A smile that made me feel like we were the only two in the room.

"Yeah," I said. "And maybe one of Nana's brownies."

Knoephla Hotish

Ingredients:
- 2 ½ - 3 Cups All Purpose Flour
- 1 Tsp Salt
- 2 Eggs
- 2 ½ Cups Heavy Cream (substitutions can also be: milk or half and half)
- 4 Tblsp Butter
- 8 oz German Sausage, Ham, or any Meats/Sausage you prefer (chopped into cubes for ham, slices for sausage)
- 2 ½ - 3 Cups Sauerkraut (drained)
- 1 Medium Red Onion (thinly sliced)
- 1-2 Cups Pretzels (slightly crushed)

Instructions:

For the Knoephla:

In a medium bowl, combine 2 ½ cups flour, ½ cup of heavy cream, salt, and eggs; Mix until dough ball forms. On a lightly floured surface, roll dough into a rope less than 1 inch, then cut dough into bite-size pieces—I usually cut approx. 1-inch pieces and I use my kitchen scissors to cut over an already pot of boiling, salted water to cook/boil until they float—approximately 5-

8minutes. Using a slotted spoon, I pull cooked Knoephla from water and place on a paper towel to rest while I finish the remaining dough.

In a skillet, on medium-high heat, melt butter; add cooked Knoephla until light golden brown, stirring to prevent burning or overbrowning. Once light golden brown, add the onion and sausage until combined and heated through. Now add the 2 cups of remaining heavy cream and drained sauerkraut. Reduce heat, top with the crushed pretzels, and allow to cook for an additional 15 minutes on low. Or it can be placed into a preheated oven at 350 for 15-20 minutes.

➢ Kerry Keprios

Nana's Double Chocolate Brownies

- 1 stick of margarine
- 1 cup sugar
- 4 eggs, beaten
- 1 can (16 oz.) Hershey's chocolate syrup
- 1 cup flour
- 1/2 cup chopped walnuts

Mix well and bake at 350 degrees for 30-35 minutes in a greased 9x13 pan. Remove and cover with miniature marshmallows. Return to the oven for 3 minutes or until marshmallows are soft. Let cool slightly and frost. (Recipe below.)

Frosting:
- 1 cup sugar
- 1/4 cup milk
- 1/4 cup butter

Bring to a boil and add 1/2 cup dark chocolate chips. Remove from heat and beat about 3 minutes. Spread on slightly warm brownies. Frosting will be thin but thickens as it's beaten.

Dear Reader,

Word of mouth is the best promotion for an author. Please consider leaving a review on Amazon and Goodreads. A sentence or two is all that is needed. By doing this, it helps me, as the author, as well as other readers.

I would love for you to connect with me at:
Website: rhondablackhurst.com
Email: rhondablackhurst@gmail.com
Facebook: www.facebook.com/rjblackhurst
Twitter: @rjblackhurst
Instagram: rhonda.blackhurst

You can sign up for my newsletter here or by visiting my website for the latest information on upcoming books, giveaways, call-outs for recipes, and other valuable information.

Also, I would love for you to sign up for my private Facebook group, Salon Talk, to share lighthearted conversation, jokes, or anything you'd likely share with your stylist.

Best,
Rhonda

Acknowledgements

The industry of independent publishing has been filled with twists and turns through the years, as well as tremendous growth in popularity. It has achieved the respect that the early pioneers didn't get. While many refer to it as self-publishing, that is an inaccurate term because it is far from a solo process. It is comprised of a lot of hard work and a team of people, the author being only one person on that team.

I extend my deepest gratitude to the following people in my tribe:

Rachel Olson (No Sweat Graphics & Formatting) — for your creativity in designing my covers and formatting my words. Thank you for taking my vision and making it beautiful.

Jessica Cornwell (Jessica Cornwell Author Services) — for your expertise in taking my story and making it shine.

Sandy Hilger — Your skill as a beta reader goes above and beyond and far exceeds any expectations I could have.

Sisters in Crime and Sisters in Crime Colorado Chapter, Colorado Authors League, Northern Colorado Writers, and Rocky Mountain Fiction Writers — for community, inspiration, and motivation.

Karen Whalen—for our weekly writing get-togethers and so much more. I appreciate you more than you know.

Monce Portillo—my know-all police officer reference. Thank you!

My dad and mom—a special thanks to you for your never-ending support in my writing journey, encouraging me to live my life's dream.

Clint - my biggest supporter and my go-to for police procedure. Even though I veer off track a bit—which I know drives you crazy—you still answer my questions. It's an honor to share life with you.

Ben & Yvette & the littles, Alex, and Jennifer—for being my whole world. You're my sun on cloudy days, and my rainbow in the rain. Thank you for far more than I could ever say.

And, always, my Lord and Savior, for the unending, underserved GRACE you continually bestow upon me.

About the Author

Born in northern Minnesota, Rhonda now resides in Colorado with her husband and her very spoiled Pomeranian, Roscoe.

Her love of writing took flight at the tender age of four when she was caught writing with her crayons on the knotty pine walls of the family home. In her teens, she tested her hand at journalism by writing an article or two for the city newspaper about school events. She completed a Journalism/Short Story Writing course and was a stringer for a local newspaper.

Recently retired from the District Attorney's Office, she can now be found hibernating in coffee shops or her home office creating characters, settings, and stories, emerging occasionally for coffee and dark chocolate.